CW00746707

TOMOS THE PUB

Mike P. Ireland

MINERVA PRESS
MONTREUX LONDON WASHINGTON

TOMOS THE PUB

ISBN 1 85863 535 7

First Published 1995 by
MINERVA PRESS
1 Cromwell Place,
London SW7 2JE

Printed in Great Britain by
Antony Rowe Ltd., Chippenham, Wiltshire.

TOMOS THE PUB

This book is dedicated to my teacher, R. Gerallt Jones.

Richard Tomos and Margaret Laura Tremlett were busy finalising their packing. It was in the middle of a heat wave in June and while Tom and Mag, as they liked to be called, laboured, most of their neighbours were resting in their sunless best rooms. During these environmentally rare periods of the year, the main topic of conversation was always air conditioning but nobody ever got around to installing it. Tom always gave the excuse that it came under the same category as inside plumbing. Mag's next door friend, Dulcie, was braving the heat in her topless bikini. She was a well preserved woman in her early forties and certainly worth a second glance; but from incessant exposure, close inspection revealed her true age. Tom had no objection since he often viewed her far enough away so as not to notice her surface anomalies. Her provoking display was not exclusive to Tom though and did not go unnoticed by several other local residents, including butch Bessy from number seven. The car peppered, cul-de-sac community consisted of nine-to-fivers with a barkless lack of man's best friend. It came alive on Sunday mornings, scented by the odour of shampooed cars and the weekly joint interrupted by the customary lunchtime trip to the pub.

Number ten was neatly packed and parcelled except for an iron-framed upright piano near the window. Tom and Mag had decided, because of Tom's industrial accident, to sell up and buy a little pub in the small Welsh seaside town of Llanrheidol.

In a pensive but confident mood, Tom said, "I wonder what we will be doing this time next year?" Little did he realise the significance of his statement.

"Do you think we will be inundated with all the town drunks and people who Dowie barred from, dare I say it, our pub?" Mag was busily packing away her treasured bric-a-brac in last months newspapers. Leaving her chore she sat down on the rim of a packing case and sipped a cup of cold, stale tea.

"I still reckon we should change the name from Ty Gwyn to something a bit more upmarket."

"No Tom, I think it sounds nice and homely, particularly if you are thinking of opening up the fireplace."

Tom moved over and took a sip from her cup. "What the hell!" he exclaimed and immediately put the cup down with a thump that resounded throughout the empty room. "Mag," wiping his lips with a grey dusty handkerchief, "I think the fire might be a good idea, the hotter the place gets the more the punters will drink."

"All you think of is money." She smiled and blotted the spilt tea from the loose top of the packing case with her apron.

"That's why we're going there, isn't it?"

"Now don't start Tom, we haven't moved in yet." She positioned her index finger in a defiant gesture. "Miserable sod!"

Picking up the tea cup as if it was full of poison Tom said, "Is that everything packed now? The men are coming in the morning and we want to be ready to move." He went into the kitchen, rinsed the cup under the tap and slowly dried it with his handkerchief.

"Tom! You've just wiped your mouth with that." Mag had observed him through the open door. Tom did not reply but took a cursory look out of the window for a final glimpse at the wrinkled sunbather next door.

"How long will it take, Tom?"

He paused for a moment. "About six hours, these Welsh back roads are very winding."

There was a pregnant pause, then Mag said nostalgically, "I loved Llanrheidol for holidays, but do you think we can live there?"

Tom's immediate reaction was heard on the de-carpeted floor. "Damn! Where's the dustpan and brush?" This was followed by, "It's a bit bloody late now to think about that... What brought this on?" Tom limped into the almost empty room, his small thick set frame towering above seated Mag.

"Well, you know, just the thought of leaving Bristol after so many years."

Tom gave a quick nervous smile and said reassuringly, "Rubbish! Think of all that fresh air and bathing in the sea." He then whispered, "Despite the sewage outlet."

Mag was recollecting weekends down the pub and bingo on Friday nights with Dulcie. She then deviated, and said without any signs of expecting a reply, "Is that really true Tom, does the sewage come back onto the beach when the tide comes in?"

Tom could see she was in one of her nostalgic moods but felt he should reply.

"No, have you ever seen any signs of it?"

Much to Tom's surprise she did reply. "Well, no."

"There you are then; end of story..." Tom immediately changed his attitude and from his gestures, Mag understood the next series of moves like a trained Pavlovian dog.

"That's it," he paused, "let's go to bed." Tom approached Mag and blew gently on her left ear. Mag, although stimulated, thought she would play him a waiting game. After all, it would be the last time in Bristol, probably.

She moved her head quickly away from the warm expired air and nonchalantly said, "Doesn't the place look empty with most of the stuff packed and the children at Mother's?"

Tom grasped her head and rotated it towards him in his large but surprisingly gentle hands and said in a tone at least an octave below his normal voice, "I think we should take advantage of the situation. Have you packed that see-through nightie?"

Mag looked into his gentle hazelly eyes and had to submit with a whimper of an excuse. "I thought you said we should have an early night?"

Tom was excited by the close proximity of Mag and the positive reply irradiating from her. "I did, Mag, but not to sleep."

"What a bloody removal firm. One had a bad back and the other one was drunk or just plain stupid."

"Trust you Tom, anything to save a few pounds."

Tom hovered guiltily, "I thought they could do it. Don from the Club recommended them."

"That figures!" Mag nodded knowingly.

The pub was a little town residence in the busy lane of the itinerant drinkers circuit. Welsh seaside towns have an indigenous population of youngsters, who on Fridays and Saturdays pass from pub to pub in an alcoholic ritual. They are usually confined to small groups of boys followed closely by their female counterparts. The segregation is allowed so that the lads go out, 'On Their Own'. The groups usually stick very closely to the same pubs meeting occasionally at the bigger ones, then fractionating without any apparent obvious motivation. Some groups finish up in their local pub while the majority terminate their predestined wanderings at the only disco in town. The bands of

Celtic warriors rarely do in fact make war unless a crowd appears from a neighbouring town or there is conflict over a female Celt. The constabulary usually make their presence felt by standing around on street corners. They are occasionally harassed by very noisy intoxicated Welsh Amazons who the boys have rejected that night or who are out on a Hen party.

Ty Gwyn was located at the top of a small sloping side street and remained erect due to a sequence of houses stepping their way down to the main road. If one of the motley row of premises was removed they would all collapse, spilling the contents of the Off Licence at the bottom, into the main street. As the name implies, it was painted white with the addition of red shutters covering the windows. Inside, the one room was divided naturally by a structural arch into the bar and a small alcove which contained an open fireplace. The bar was small and took up most of one wall. A few stools were scattered along the bar and tables with chairs on the carpeted bar area. The alcove was similarly furnished with the addition of a dartboard next to the fireplace. It was a small, cosy tavern.

Mag was standing in the middle of the deserted bar next to Tom.

"Well, that's it, we're in our own little pub... I thought it was a good idea of Dowie to suggest we close the place so that we could do the necessary exchange without too much bother."

"Personally, I would have liked the place left open so that we could start earning some dough."

Mag looked at Tom and her euphoria faded.

"I hope you are not going to be obsessed with money? We should enjoy being mine hosts as well, you know."

"And that too!" he replied unconvincingly. "Hello Dowie, I didn't expect to see you so soon. How did you get in?"

He thought for a while because his entry was so natural and unobtrusive.

"The front door was open."

Tom quickly turned and snapped at Mag, "Trust you, you can't get the punters in quick enough to practice your Welsh, can you?"

"I didn't do it." Mag's reply was as sharp as Tom's. She turned and quickly left the bar through the side door that led to the living quarters. Apart from her obvious visual dislike of the comment, she emphasised it by making her footsteps clearly audible as she ascended the stairs to the flat. Tom instinctively remembered Bristol and that was one of her ways of making him aware of her dissatisfaction. It was always short lived. She soon recovered, rejoined the bar and occupied herself with irrelevancies.

"The reason I came round, Tom, was to tell you about a few nuisances I've come across over the years."

"What d'you mean, nuisances?"

"There's Dai the Voice for one. He's an old chap who will not stop singing and he gets on everybody's nerves... I think he was entered for an Eisteddfod when he was a young lad and he has been a bloody tone deaf Caruso ever since."

"He sounds a lot of fun?"

"Don't you kid yourself, Tom. He paws the girls. What happens is that the youngsters, and especially the girls, on their walkabouts, sneak him in with the crowd and buy him a pint just to see him thrown out. They do it just for fun, the little bitches."

"I thought you said he touched up the girls?"

"No, sorry Tom, you've got it wrong. Perhaps I didn't explain. It's only the ones he don't know, like some of the College girls..." He paused expecting a comment, but none came so he continued. "You'll soon know he's in from the ear shatterin' renderin' of Bless this House, if he's reasonably sober. Later on, it's hymns. It's really part of the weekend booze up that you throw him out, because he can then cuss you and move on; most pubs let him in. I don't think the kids realise or possibly care, but he's really very clever, he gets free booze all night and a lot of fun with it. He's definitely one of the local characters... I've just thought of a story about him I must tell you." He moved closer to the bar and sat on a stool. "When he was younger he was banned from every pub in Llanrheidol and one summer's evening he decided to walk to Caerus which is about seven miles away. Needless to say he was drunk before he started."

"If he was banned from all the pubs, where did he get the drink?" inquired Tom.

"Ah!" Dowie was momentarily lost for words. "He's only got about a quarter of a stomach so it wouldn't take much." Dowie even impressed himself at his quick-witted but contentious answer.

"Come on, get on with it, Dowie." Mag was interested.

"Ah! I didn't think you were listenin'. He got about a mile from Caerus when somebody in a car stopped and asked him how far it was to Llanrheidol. He turned around, pointed in the direction of

Llanrheidol and said that it was about seventy miles that way. The car left in disgust and Dai proceeded to walk back to Llanrheidol."

"That sounds a bit far fetched to me," said Mag, attempting to remove a piece of beer mat stuck under the brass rim of one of the pumps.

"It's as true as that beer mat."

Mag fingered the snared object and said, "But it's only a little bit, not really worth bothering about."

Dowie realised his tale was not taken seriously and compensated by emitting a sound from the weather beaten, bearded face. It was a sort of hiccoughy up and down laugh which was very infectious and started Mag off; Tom grinned.

"Another one who is a bit more of a nuisance is Mike the Mouth, he's very loud and cusses usin' four letter words."

"That's one thing neither of us will stand, you know, that's strong foul language. That's right, isn't it Tom?"

"I didn't stand filthy language in the factory and I won't stand it here, especially in mixed company."

Dowie elaborated, "Most people accept bad language, if it's quiet, but this is heard all over the pub. He's all right early in the night but when he has had a few, he starts. I used to let him in early for just one or two pints. He then moved uptown where they are a bit more easy goin'. In fact, the landlord of the Griffin swears like a trooper. Incidentally, the Griffin is a Welsh pub, what I mean is that most of the Welsh speakers, including the students from the College, go there. Swearing in English is regarded as a foreign language, so it's OK. Another..."

"Before you go on, could you tell me something about the state of the cellar? When was the Bass soft spiralled, is it ready to put on tomorrow?"

This interjection broke Mag's concentration and her fascination for Dowie's story telling in his characteristic sing-song voice. It reminded her of Tom's father and his 'Tells of the War'.

"Sorry Tom, I know you want to get things ready for tomorrow. The Bass and the draught bitter is ready, the kegs are no problem, as you know, and you've got plenty of gas."

Mag had been on a little tour of the alcove and returned to a stool by the bar, next to Dowie who was about to speak.

"As I was saying, I think? There's a couple of young girls who come in every Friday night. One has beautiful long blonde hair and LEGS." Realising Mag was there he restrained himself. "She always smells nice." Mag moved tantalisingly, allowing her skirt to ride up over her shapely knee sufficiently to be noticed. She valued her legs as one of her more obvious attractive features. No one said anything for a while and then Dowie, somewhat uncomfortably, started to continue his tale.

"The other girl is bigger but very well proportioned, they usually sit in the corner over there." He pointed to the table in the alcove closest to the fireplace. "The leggy, long-haired girl, Mary, is separated from her husband. If he comes in with his mates and they are not too drunk, you can usually reason with him and he will leave after a few drinks."

"And his friends as well?"

"Tom... shut up! Go and check the Bass or something?"

"Other times, he will hover over the girls and tease his wife. This starts the second one off."

"Are they lezzies?" came an uncharacteristically puerile comment from Tom.

"Probably," answered Dowie with no sign of emotion. "The important thing is to keep the two groups apart as soon as this starts because Carol is a bitch. She's got a punch like a boy." Dowie, who was himself not adverse to fisticuffs, qualified the statement by denigrating the fictitious youth by saying he was drunk and not very capable.

"I hope they do not do this regularly," moaned Tom, "or I'll have to ban them."

"Who?" said Mag.

"The girls, of course, they drink less."

"Unbelievable!"

"I don't think it will come to that Tom. I have never had cause to ban any of them... In fact, the girls are a great attraction and pull in some of the less experienced lads. They look quite attractive in the light of the open fire on a winter's night. The big one tried to chat me up once," he boasted.

Mag's face lit up. "Do many people come in just because of the fire?"

Before Dowie could answer, Tom quickly pointed towards the ash-covered fireplace. "Is the fuel coal and does it cost much?"

"No, wood; it's quite cheap here. After all, we are in wooded Wales," exclaimed Dowie with a hint of sarcasm. "That mess in there at the moment is some stuff I burnt up yesterday, normally, at this time of year, it is cleaned out and covered." Dowie was a stickler for tidiness. "If you don't do that, it gets full of rubbish and looks a mess."

"There will be a few villains who will try it on, usually within the first week. If I'm here, I'll give you a nod. The problem is, they are quite pleasant at first but then they bring in their friends and try to take over. This is followed by rival gangs, see my point?"

"I don't know how to put this, Tom." He hesitated and lowered his voice. "But there will be opportunities."

"What d'you mean, Dowie?"

"Chances to get things on the cheap. One fiddle is sellin' beer slightly over the sell-by date; it sort of drops off a lorry."

"What, literally?"

"Don't be stupid, Mag."

"No, she's not far wrong, Tom. It will get into your delivery by accident. Cash in hand, of course!"

"I suppose it is all right," Tom was undecided. "It's not really stealing."

"Of course not, it's simply bendin' the rules a little. Last month there was an accident on the hill by the station, next to the Griffin. A dray smashed into the wall and crates of lager were all over the road. One barrel rolled off and hit the door of the pub, it was never found again. The kids gathered up the bottles and crates and took them away before the coppers got there. Later they went 'round the pubs sellin' 'um."

"It reminds me of that film Whiskey Galore, you know, when the ship full of whiskey was wrecked on the rocks in Scotland. I remember seeing it in Bristol," Mag took hold of Tom's arm affectionately.

"I was offered some bottles, Mag."

"Did you take them?"

"Too right! I had a couple of bottles of spirits as well." Dowie glanced at his watch, immediately straightened up and threw his shoulders back as if preparing for an affray. "It's time, let's go and finalise the deal at the solicitors, Tom."

"I'll be back before opening, Mag." Tom closed the door and she was left alone in the bar.

* * * * *

The time had eventually arrived when Tom and Mag took on their role as publicans. The eldest boy, Richard, who had just left school was to help them out and look after his younger brother, Mark. Dowie was very helpful and he had persuaded Beryl to stay on and help in the bar and Myfanwy to continue cleaning. The Tremletts knew them both from previous holidays in Llanrheidol. Since it was the beginnings of a blistering day in June, the task was to keep everything cool including themselves. Mag decided to wear a heavily printed cotton dress which would ablute quickly in case of accidents. Tom, who was full of zest and ready to go, was busy in the cellar wetting the towels over the firkin of Bass. Dowie had explained that it was better to have small nine gallon casks because of the turnover; Bass has to be fresh. Tom decided to wear a white shirt with a tie after he had finished his role as cellarman in the damp, cool atmosphere where he was in control. He arrived in the bar to find Mag cleaning the pump for dispensing the real beer. Beryl was having her last fag; it was always her last fag. She looked ready for the day with her mini-skirted bare brown legs and her short mousey brown hair. Her top was unusual, it appeared to be made of crinkly paper and disposable like paper panties.

"What's the time?" questioned Tom nervously as he glanced at his watch which had stopped. He shook it and said, "Must get some new batteries."

"It's ten-thirty, we've got half an hour before opening time," puffed Beryl.

"Anyone fancy a cuppa?" shouted a pinafored, plump figure from the top of the stairs.

"Yeah, that would be nice, Myf," Beryl answered for all the barstaff. Within a few minutes she appeared with a tray containing three cups and some Digestives.

Several biscuit crunching minutes passed, then, putting his cup back on the tray, Tom announced that it was eleven o'clock. He had established this by looking at the clock behind the bar. "We have a till to fill."

"That's clever," said Beryl, who was not the brightest of people.

"I wonder who will be the first in, Tom?" Myfanwy disappeared upstairs with the empties.

"Go on then, open the door and find out!" The heat hit her as she pulled the door inwards and exited a few centimetres from the cool, dimly lit, smoke-free atmosphere.

"That's the first customer to breeze in," she muttered to herself. "No money from him!" She warmed there for a while like a butterfly waiting to fly and watched the tourists meandering towards the beach. Tom soon joined her and put his arm gently around her waist and affectionately squeezed.

"Fancy a drink, dear?"

"Yes, why not, why shouldn't I be the first?" There was no immediate rush to retreat into the coolness of the hostelry since everybody was on the beach. Recollecting from her holiday experiences, Mag thought they would make a move at about noon. First the dehydrated dads who would be wanting a top up from the previous night. Later mums would make their excuses and leave the brats to the mercy of the eldest who was suitably sweetened with a substantial emolument. Tom dropped his arm from around her waist and went back into the pub. Mag followed a little later, sat down on a bar stool and imbibed Tom's first pulled drink.

"Avenue gotcher draught beer?" came a deep broad West country accent from the open door.

"That's a marvellous Bristol accent you've got there. Yes, we've got Bass. We originally came from Bristol." Tom gave the impression that they had been in Llanrheidol for years.

"Whirr 'bouts wast in Bristle?"

"Brislington, on Bath road, near the crisp factory."

"Bewful ther innit?"

He was a large, rotund person, sporting a brightly coloured pair of braces which were themselves supporting a kneed pair of trousers that had seen better days. His coat was thrown over his shoulder.

"Seamy braces?" he said, thumbing them as he sat down on a bar stool next to Tom. "Bough'um down totherend, in street by station." He was sweating profusely, wiping his forehead on the sleeve of his buttoned shirt, he said, "Bleed knot knit."

"Yes, it is a bit warm today." Tom was the only one who could understand his peculiar accent but consciously suppressed his own.

"Scool near though."

"I like to keep it reasonably cool so that the Bass keeps fresh."

"Scot a pint, an' make'un scool, Bass."

His masterful, indecipherable delivery was considered offensive to soft speaking Beryl and annoyed her. Before she could retort, Tom translated his demand.

"Yeah, OK," Beryl snatched a glass, paused and then said abrasively, "we always serve our beer cool in the summer, SIR!"

Tom couldn't help but admire her loyalty but he could sense that she was getting annoyed and he didn't want her to start on her bloody English routine, although he did think that he was a bit rude.

"We always keep the beer cool, it goes through flash coolers under the bar. But the real beer, Bass, is cooled naturally in the cellar. In fact Bass used to be supplied to the British troops in India during the 1800s."

The roly-poly gentleman responded to this meaningless piece of information by uttering, "Be it good nas Newquay?"

Tom turned to Beryl and said patronisingly, "He means Newcastle Brown, on the shelf over there." He pointed to a neat row of highly polished brown bottles.

"Course it's as good as Newquay, it's ten forty-four."

"Was mean?"

Tom was in his element. "It's the specific gravity and is related to the alcoholic content. Newquay is about the same or slightly less but a different flavour, of course."

Here he goes again, thought Mag to herself. Beryl was at the other end of the bar and she joined her.

"D'you understand what he's saying, Mag?"

"Some of it," she whispered, "but even in Bristol, I've never heard an accent quite so strong as his, you know. I think he's doing it for effect. Well, I don't blame him, it's nice." She knowingly grinned at Beryl. "You're proud of your Welsh accent, aren't you?"

"*Duw, Duw*!"

"I know so."

Before the Tremletts took over the pub, they went on a course entitled, 'How to Run a Public House Successfully'. While on the course Tom opted to visit the Bass Brewery at Burton-on-Trent. He was now the self-appointed expert on Bass in Llanrheidol and was always ready to expound his knowledge. He had gained a lot of knowledge on a little subject and misguidedly felt he could compete on the same level as the staff of the local university. Mag could feel THE dissertation on 'The Wonders of Bass' brewing. That's why she kept her distance and remained in conversation with her barmaid. Tom moved his stool a little closer to the visitor and settled himself as if preparing to give a lengthy talk to a learned society.

"To begin with, it was the monks of Burton Abbey who first realised the special quality of the well water at Burton-on-Trent. Later, in 1777 someone called William Bass decided to start a brewery there."

Although not listening, Mag yawned in anticipation of what was to come. "Sorry Beryl. Tom has that effect when he starts on about Bass."

"Well, she had this operation last year, you know, and..."

Mag's conversation faded away as Tom vociferously dominated the bar. "Bass is found the world over, it's even found in famous paintings like Coca-Cola is in that modern painting by..." He thought but could not remember. "Somebody or other... Andy Warhol, that's it! See that painting up there, over the bar, it's a copy of a Manet and can you see the two bottles of Bass?"

"Jew asbestos bleev that?"

Tom got off his stool, moved to behind the bar and pointed, "There and there, look!"

"Bled knell, strewth!" said the fat man, screwing up his eyes to get a better view and concurrently finishing the last drop of ale. "Nother pint, landlady."

"I'm not the landlady, I'm Beryl. This is the landlady."

"Scuse I, B-e-r-y-l," he uttered cautiously, not being sure how she would react to his intimate use of her first name. "Doss yer want drink?"

Beryl could interpret the offer from his sign language. "Yeah, thanks," she was beginning to warm to the man's generous nature.

Aware that Tom was the only one who could understand him, he said, "Gonny thin teat?"

"Only sandwiches and crisps, the bar meals are not ready yet."

"Ussle wait then."

Tom went on, quoting dates and barrelage throughout the centuries. The fat man listened with the concentration of an undergraduate at a nine o'clock lecture. Tom's monotonous loquacity was mellowed by the pleasant tasting liquid. To the surprise of everyone, he broke off his lecture, gave a slight nod indicating to what he was referring and inquired, "Do you like the flavour?"

"Deaf knit lea, Maiden Evan."

"No, made at Burton, matured at Llanrheidol." The fat man laughed. "It's because they brew it the Burton Union way. The beer is stored in the Union Room in very large oak casks known as Unions for the last part of the fermentation. The yeast is over..." He immediately stopped talking at the appearance in the doorway of a beautiful, elegant young girl who was wearing a dress through which the sun filtered and silhouetted her curvaceous limbs. "My God, what a beautiful girl," he thought.

"Ello darlin'," said the solitary Bass drinker. "Come in an' park yer arse. Wanna pint? You should try the Bass, wreck knits great." Tom or the Bass had obviously made an impression. "Give us a good excuse to rest after," he said with a naughty twinkle in his eye. "Meet the wife, 'elen."

Tom immediately jumped off his stool and offered her his seat. She was outstandingly attractive and the thin material of her dress embraced her engorged nipples which had arisen briefly in response to the cool air. Tom felt an electrifying surge through his body, a response which had eluded him since his early days of sexual discovery. He walked away muttering to himself, "Control Tom, control," and disappeared into the Gents to defuse himself with splashes of cold water.

Mag spotted Tom's unusual behaviour and wondered. He was used to seeing more exposed flesh in an English garden but it didn't seem to have the same impact. It might be right what Dulcie said on the eve of their departure from Bristol, that publicans have a greater temptation to stray from the nuptial bond than many.

Beryl dispensed the beer and gave it to Helen. Tom stood out of earshot.

"Haven't had any of this for sometime, it's a bit too strong for..."

"Shut up, 'elen. He thinks we've never heard of the stuff, I might get a free pint."

"You don't really mean that?" She scoured at the fat man and gave Tom a synthetic smile.

"He's getting on my bloody nerves talking about Bass all the time." His ethnic accent had taken a backseat. He was more astute than Tom realised.

Mag came close and acknowledged the beautiful creature. "Are you on holidays?"

"Blige, Oll-daze," interrupted the fat man.

"No, we are down here to give a concert at the Branwyn Hall." She smoldered in a soft, cultured but slightly foreign accent. "Jack's my pianist."

"Yeah! I recognise you now," came a muffled voice from behind the bar. Beryl had temporarily disappeared to retrieve a handkerchief she had dropped. She surfaced, "You're on that poster by the station, the one with the glasses and beard scribbled on it."

"Knit strew," the pianist pushed his glass forward for replenishment. "Boys will be boyos." His joke was as tasteless as the abused poster.

Inquisitive, but only to the extent of being polite, Tom asked them where they were staying. He was informed, by Helen, that they had to travel to Cardiff that evening because of other commitments. He wondered who would drive and hoped to himself that nothing unforeseen would happen to them.

The afternoon moved on slowly with a couple of foreign tourists coming in for refreshments. The musicians had left by now, probably to rehearse.

Opening hours were eleven to eleven, but landlords often closed in the afternoons. It was about two o'clock and the atmosphere was sleepy and quiet and through the window, near the bar, the streets appeared dry, dusty and devoid of a living soul except for a bedraggled, erratically pacing dog. It was attempting to trot one minute, then it stopped, smelt the ground and moved sideways, panting. The impression Tom got was that this rabid-like creature was probably overheated and its attempts to cool down were hampered by the hot pavement. "Throw a bucket of water over the damned thing, that will cool him down." Although as an after thought, Tom recalled that this procedure was usually used on dogs for quite a different reason.

Beryl was due off at two and it was mutually decided that they would close for a few hours and venture out. Monday lunchtime, on such a glorious summer's day, was traditionally quiet in the pubs. A natural event much maligned by the LVA. The Licensed Victuallers have often tried to think up ingenious ways of getting tourists into the pubs during this slack time including pool and darts competitions and even Happy Hours; topless barmaids would not get past the Council. The locals were either working or conning tourists. One of the best was a trip to see the famous dolphins in the Bay which were about as rare as a Union Jack at a Llanrheidol Rugby Club match.

The door was closed followed by the sliding of a heavy bolt to keep out peripatetic customers and the dazzling, burning sun and all was quiet within. Tom went down into the cellar to cool the Bass with one thing on his mind and Mag proceeded upstairs for a cuppa occupied with a second thought. They never did make the beach and secondly they had to pick up the children from her parents' place where they had spent two exhilarating weeks of skin soaring sun, sand and sea.

"I'll go and fetch the boys." Tom was anxious to see their younger son who had been away from them for the first time. Although it was walking distance, he decided to take the car because of the heat.

Mag's parents moved from Bristol just after the war. They had seen enough death and destruction from air raids, to last a lifetime. Their council house was located on a corner which meant that it had an extra bit of garden. Unfortunately, it was the depository for many a discarded commodity. In fact, one day Nana found a skirt, tights and panties neatly folded behind the garden wall. She left them there for several days but no bottomless claimant ever materialised and they finished up in OXFAM.

The inside of the house was typically Welsh in character. A steaming kettle always occupied a predominant position on the Rayburn in the kitchen ready for callers. Nana insisted on proclaiming that her related, more friendly, Welsh from the South invite you in and give you a cup of tea, while the North Walians invite you in and ask you if you want a cup of tea and then make one. The lounge was littered with exquisitely delicate embroidery draped over lavender scented lumps of furniture. The aroma was imprinted on Tom's mind from his courting days. Silver framed, sepia toned photographs which were anonymous to Tom, filled every corner. The Monarch of the Glen dominated one wall and a large mirror on the wall opposite the window.

Tom stopped the car outside and Nana gave him a wave from the window. She was blissfully unaware that her constant vigilance from behind the lace curtains was revealed by the reflections of her back in the mirror. Grandad found it a useful measure for predicting her response to belated homecomings after sessions at the Legion.

She opened the door to Tom's immediate request concerning the whereabouts of his children.

"There's Mark," she pointed to a little boy sitting on the floor playing with a model soldier. He looked up and rushed over to Tom for a large grizzly hug. Tom's beard had grown into the beginnings of stubble and it was customary to rub it against the boy's cheek. He reacted by wriggling, squirming and showing outward signs of disapproval, but when it stopped, the cry was always for more.

With Mark still in his arms Nana said, "Richard's still asleep upstairs, he came in late last night. I think he went out with the boys he met last year at the Rugby Club. Grandad is out in the garden picking up the rubbish."

"It's getting worse than ever, look at this, a bloody condom and it's coloured." Grandad walked in with a weathered piece of elongated rubber dangling from the end of a discarded lollypop stick.

"Grandad! Take that filthy thing out of here and put it in the bin."

Tom's instant reaction was, how did she know what it was?

Grandad made a quick exit and Mark returned to play with his toy and, fortunately, made no inquiry about the perished rubber object.

"How did your first morning go?"

"Very quiet, I think about four people, none of the locals."

"Well, they would be working, Tom."

"Yes, of course. I'm looking forward to tonight though and seeing some of the old characters we've known from years... Can you wake up Richard, Mark? Then we can go and see Mummy in the pub."

"How is Mag?"

"She's fine, she didn't come, she's making tea for us."

Mark responded by grasping his toy and rushing upstairs. It was obvious Richard was awakened from the noise that descended through the lounge ceiling.

"That's not a trampoline," shouted Nana who was used to being obeyed. The noise stopped.

When the Tremletts arrived at Ty Gwyn, tea was ready. After the hugging had stopped, Mark was first to speak and insisted on telling Tom and Mag about his first strokes in the briny. Richard sat there in a heap, displaying no signs of any emotion. Whether it was tiredness or just plain apathy was difficult to ascertain. Tom regarded this indifference as normal. When on the shop floor at work, he constantly reprimanded the trainees for listlessness.

He did eventually move his lips but only to ask whether the shelves in the bar needed stocking. Tom stopped reading his paper and said that it had been done until tomorrow but he could go down and splash the Bass. "Are you staying in tonight with Mark?"

"No," replied the laconic youth.

"Bloody out again, I suppose with those boys from the village?"

Time drifted on towards the second opening of the day. Monday evenings were usually a busy time for pubs in Wales because of the time honoured tradition of Club drinking on Sundays.

"I'll open up," said Mag, eagerly moving towards the door, "if you'll wash up?"

Tom shrugged his shoulders submissively and proceeded to collect up the bread-cleaned plates; Mag was a very good cook. Richard slowly dragged himself from the table, moved across the room and descended to the cellar and subsequently left. Mark found his toy and played contentedly on the empty table. Tom was in the kitchen clashing plates and stacking cups and saucers in places which Mag had designated for them. He could never understand why the knives, forks and spoons went from right to left in the drawer. He was left-handed and his tendency was to place them into the drawer the opposite way around. Tom's sinistral affliction gave him unconventional table manners and he was often found drinking the wine of the person sitting next to him. A life-time habit which he never tried to rectify. Tom sat down in his beloved chair and read the paper. Mark, by now, was engrossed in his favourite television programmes. He was capable of such intense concentration that any amount of distraction went unnoticed. Tom momentarily glanced over his paper and looked lovingly at Mark and could not help but wonder at the beautifully shaped little hands clutching his toy soldier with such passion and the angelic face pulsating with the ever changing colours of the television.

His thoughts wandered to the time some five years ago, when Richard was thirteen and Mag confronted him with a passionate plea for help because she was pregnant. They had become resigned in their ways and after the miscarriage it was generally assumed that their child rearing days were over. Tom's immediate reaction was to get rid of it. This upset Mag immensely and he could not forget the desperation and anguish they both experienced for those few days all those years ago. Tom shook his head quickly, as though he was physically trying to remove the unhappy thoughts, and went back to his paper. He could hear a low murmur of voices and the occasional ting of a small bell in the bar. He smiled to himself. Mag's characteristic laugh bubbled up through the floor of the flat and he knew some of the locals must be in. He was in a dilemma; should he leave Mark and go down and help out, or should he stay upstairs? He pondered over the problem for a while and then his curiosity got the better of him and he decided to venture into his domain of the Welsh landlord. After plying Mark with sweets and pop, he left him to his own devices. As he entered the bar he could see a few familiar faces.

"*Shawd mae*, Tom, you old bugger," shouted Frank from his seat near the unlit fire. He liked it there because he could ogle at the girls when they played darts.

Frank was short and dark and had an eye for the young girls. From what Tom could gather from his holiday visits, Frank was a farmer's son. The family had a large farm near Tregon now run by his two brothers. They also looked after their mother after their father died. Frank now lived in town with his unmarried sister.

"Hello," gesticulated Tom who then faced the bar where Ieuan was balanced on a bar stool.

"All right! Have you done anything that the papers talked about?"

"It's funny you should mention the papers because..." Ieuan started to dig into the inside pocket of his leather jacket. "I did do something last summer, just after you left, that even got mentioned in the Western Mail." He carefully unfolded a piece of well thumbed, slightly yellow paper, "That's not it!" He replaced the cutting in his pocket and proceeded, "I tried to walk across Cardigan Bay from Llanrheidol to Portmeirion in one of those large plastic spheres. It was all to do with a festival at Portmeirion. They were celebrating something to do with the TV series they made in the late sixties called The Prisoner with Patrick McGoohan."

"Oh! I remember, they all wore blazers. They had this huge balloon that stopped anyone escaping."

"Yep! That's right Tom, that's right!... Well, what happened was that the bloody thing hit a log near Cormorant Head and split open."

Mag, who was well-versed in the geography of the area said mockingly, "You didn't get very far, then?"

"No," he replied quickly so as not to temper the moment. "You can imagine the confusion. Luckily there was the inshore rescue inflatable with me so they picked me up straight away... God! It was cold."

Tom was acquainted with Ieuan's status complex and felt compelled to ask him where he got the sphere.

"I went down to Lampeter in my new Jaguar (flagrantly exaggerating the make of his transport) to visit a friend of mine who is the Director of this firm that makes plastic sheeting and he asked me to try it out for a stunt. He knew I was good at that sort of thing because we were in the Marines together; he was my sergeant." Tom had developed this technique of being able to switch off but still give the impression that he was listening by making gestures in the right places. It had been perfected in Bristol to keep him sane when Mag was on the warpath about some poor undeserving victim who happened to be in fashion at the time. "And that's what it's all about."

"Very interesting, another pint?"

"Yep, and one for yourself?"

Tom politely refused and pushed the glass over to Beryl who immediately dispensed Ieuan's favourite tipple. Tom made a rule not to drink until after ten o'clock in the evening.

Mag had migrated to the other end of the bar and was talking to her gin loving holiday friend Lally. She was known to drink four or five large gins before lunch, go off to the library, do some shopping and return in the evenings for another session. This intemperance was only once a week because she lived in an old isolated cottage in the hills about fifteen miles from Llanrheidol where she cared for stray cats. She nearly always missed the last bus home and had to go by taxi. Nobody had ever seen her drunk but she always made her presence known by a distinctive smoker's cough.

"What do you think about us having a holiday together?" whispered Lally to Mag.

"Give me a chance to settle in first, then I might be able to persuade Tom to look after the pub for a week."

"Put another gin in there and don't forget that I only like Schweppes tonic and not that other muck you sell."

"Well really! I know what you like, you know." Mag thought to herself that she was a bit offhandish, normally she was much more affable. Probably that cough was beginning to get her down.

The evening crowd was steady; some came for curiosity and others intending to stay. The men playing darts were a strange combination of locals and people the Tremletts didn't know.

"Who are those three men playing darts, Dowie? They aren't some of your nuisances, are they?"

"Ah! Not really... They're what we call trophy hunters. Usually they don't stay in a pub for more than one season. Most of them are very good players but they want to win all the time so they keep moving down to the lower divisions. The one with the flat cap on is Dai Cot."

"Oh! We don't want people like that; we want a friendly team... Dai Cot did you say?"

"Yeah! He was born and brought up in a small cottage near Llanrheidol."

"Oh!" Tom was beginning to understand.

"Do you fancy a game of darts, Mag?" said Lally unexpectedly putting down her gin and rummaging in her dishevelled shopping basket for her arrows. She had been playing darts since the war and was a good player. In wartime, groups of girls got together and formed teams to pass the time away while their menfolk were at war somewhere in Europe. A lot of them still played, usually in a unisex team.

"Yes, why not... Tom can help in the bar for a while." She moved towards the dartboard, taking it for granted that Tom would confirm her request. There was nobody playing, but Frank was strategically seated.

"D'you like my new dress, Frank?" Mag lifted a part of the skirt with the closed fingers of her hand and submitted it to the old boy for inspection. He grabbed at the material with his well worked hands and felt it with a gentleness reserved for a small child lovingly stroking a kitten. Mag pulled away, feeling flirtishly ashamed at what she had done. Lally gave a single nervous laugh.

"It's too long," grumbled Frank returning his large ungainly hands to the table.

"Short skirts are for young girls." Mag quickly redeeming her impudence, leaned over and said quietly in his ear, "besides, I still wear stockings, Tom likes it." Frank looked away for a moment then picked up his pint glass, took a mouthful and swallowed it with a throaty loud gulp. "That will keep him happy for a while, it's his bloody hormones."

"Mag! I never heard you swear before," exclaimed Lally.

"It's conducive to the public house ambience," said Mag in her intellectual-type voice. Lally smiled and threw her first dart at the board. The girls played while Frank sat quietly drinking at his table. Tom dispensed as little beer as possible, he thought that was Beryl's job. After some time Tom shouted to Mag, that she had better go and put Mark to bed. Mag, in the company of additional female darters, finished off one of her well worn standard jokes, received the usual outcry of girlish laughter and signalled to him that she was going. The rest of the darters moved to an empty table.

Upstairs the response was not a happy one.

"I'm frightened Mummy. What's all that noise downstairs? Are people fighting?"

"No, darling, it's just people enjoying themselves and getting excited, you know, like when you have fun with Daddy. D'you want a drink or something before you go to bed?"

"No thank you, Mummy," he said very politely and almost in a whisper. If Mag had not been so engrossed with the pub she would have noticed the fear and anguish on his face. She took him to bed and quickly returned to the pleasantries downstairs.

"How's Mark?" asked Tom.

"He's fine. I've put him to bed with his soldier." She went and joined the girls.

"Got any of that Aussie beer?" came a loud request from the open doorway.

"No," said Tom apologetically.

"Right!" and the swaying youth disappeared.

The gap was filled quickly by Dowie who watched over his shoulder as the disorientated youth made his way to another hostelry.

"It's a bit cooler now," he said, moving his shirt top in and out in a fanning motion and emitting a faint smell of stale sweat.

"Now here is a genuine Bass drinker, he'll tell you if it's off." Tom turned away from the doubting stranger and poured Dowie a drop of the beer in a wine glass. Using the gestures and mannerisms of a wine connoisseur, Dowie, after due deliberation, declared it to be of the best vintage. The silent stranger stared at Dowie, then at Tom in bewilderment and wrinkles appeared on the shiny black skin of his forehead.

"Don't look so worried," exclaimed Tom, touching the stranger's arm briefly. "Dowie was only joking... It's a strong beer but that's all." The stranger gave a huge toothy smile, had a second pint and left.

"He's probably one of those African students from the College?"

"Can you cope for a little while Beryl, I think there is someone moving about upstairs? If you want help call Mag, I won't be long."

Mag was too busy entertaining the girls to notice Tom leave. He cautiously opened the door of the flat to find Mark huddled up in Tom's favourite chair gently sobbing to himself.

"What's the matter, dear?" To Tom any term of endearment greater than that would be regarded as over sentimental. Mark said nothing but held out his arms. Tom rushed over, picked him up and cuddled him tightly to his chest. He felt the little hands cling to his arm in a vice-like grip.

"I'm frightened, Daddy, I don't like all the noise." His pathetic little voice made Tom's eyes well up.

Tom was distraught. He didn't realise what effect buying the pub would have on family life. It had hit him so suddenly that he felt sick in the stomach. "I won't leave you," he almost sobbed out, "I'll stay with you. Mummy and Beryl can look after the pub." Tom sat down in his chair with the child clinging to him like an octopus around its prey. He could feel his wet eyes against his cheek and gave him an extra hug. Mark responded to this by momentarily relaxing his grip on Tom's arm. "Just calm down now and go to sleep, Daddy will stay with you all night."

Tom must have dozed off since he was awakened by someone shaking his shoulder. It was Mag.

"Don't do that, the baby is asleep, you'll wake him up." Tom was angry but quiet.

"What happened, Tom? You've been up here for hours."

"You might well ask... Mark is very unhappy, he doesn't like being left alone and he is worried about the noise. I'll stay up here tonight and we will talk later. You go down to your cronies," he said indignantly. He had to blame someone and Mag was close at hand.

"That's a bit unfair, Tom. I'm only trying to entertain the customers and make YOU some money," she said defensively. "I'll go down then." She disappeared from sight but not sound as she returned to the bar.

Tom eventually coaxed Mark to bed while he returned to his chair deeply concerned about the future.

Tom was cat-napping when he heard the muffled sound of, 'Time, Gentlemen, Please,' followed by a bell far away in the distance. He was reminded of happier times snoozing on a sunny beach with the sound of children playing, filtering through as soothing whispers. It only lasted a few seconds, then Tom rose to his feet, inspected the sleeping child, heard farewell pleasantries, the door being secured and Mag ascending the stairs.

* * * * *

Tom awoke the following morning after a restless night. They had obviously not thought through the changes in their lifestyle and something had to be done.

He was often neglected as a child and left to cope for himself. The legacy of those impressionable traumatic times lingered on in his mind so much so that as a family man he vowed never to deprive his children of love and affection.

Tom was always up first in the mornings and while preparing breakfast, Mark wandered into the kitchen.

"Hello young lad, want some breakfast?" Tom said trying to show no emotion.

"Yes please." The trauma of the past evening appeared to have disappeared although he did keep close to Tom most of the time. Mark was always very respectful, not like the other one who transmitted information in a series of primeval grunts and groans which were communicable only to his fellow Neanderthals.

"I'll just take this to Mummy first..."

"I'll come with you, Daddy."

After breakfast, Tom and Mag decided to approach Mark about the possibility of his staying with Nana and Grandad. To their surprise he agreed, reluctantly at first, but after Tom explained that he could visit daily and weekends, he accepted the move. Mag's parents were delighted but Tom was a little apprehensive about the ease of the transfer.

That evening, Tom could not settle and kept thinking about Mark and the apparently unconcerned way in which Mag had adjusted to his absence. Tuesday night was quiet which gave the owners time to relax and chat to the customers both old and new. Dowie entered the pub with a strange looking man neither of the Tremletts had ever seen before. He was in his late thirties with a dull white face decorated with a pair of glasses that gave the impression that he had economised and used the bottoms of glass bottles for lenses. His clothes were of good quality but needed cleaning and ironing.

"This is Selwyn, he's in the College. He's usually away on some foreign trip when you've been here on holidays, he stays in a flat in my place." (My place was a house left to Dowie by his parents. While in the pub he let it out to students and holiday makers.) Selwyn leaned across the bar and shook Tom's hand with a loose limp grip and formally greeted him. He drank his half pint and left without saying a thing.

"What an odd character," said Tom cautiously.

"He's OK, but he can be a bit of a nuisance sometimes because he's always forgettin' things and gettin' into trouble. He's a bachelor, like me." Dowie seemed to think that was something to brag about. "I've just remembered, I must tell you this story about his latest balls-up, it's so comical." Mag was instantly magnetised to the area.

"About two weeks ago he was ridin' his bike past the rugby pitch, which is a short cut to our place, and alongside the path is a ditch. He had been to my leaving party, here." Dowie pointed to the dispensing side where Beryl was moving around bottles on the cold tray. "Because he's got bad eyesight and he was drunk and he had no lights on his bike, he went into the ditch, bike and all, didn't he? According to Selwyn, the first thing to go was his glasses, he then started to panic because as he tried to climb up the bank of the ditch he kept slidin' back down again..."

"I can imagine it vividly, his hands digging into the muddy bank as he sank slowly back into the ditch," intercepted Mag, whose laughter appeared excessive for the occasion. Although most of the listeners had heard this story before it was always good entertainment when Dowie was the narrator.

"To continue," he said, "having thought seriously about his problem, Selwyn decided that the best thing to do was to use his bike to help him climb out. In the end he found it by touch and laid it on the bottom of the ditch as a platform. Naturally, when he stood on it, the bike disappeared slowly into the mud producin' a terrible stink. He called it sulphur something; like bad eggs."

"Oh, I know," said Tom, feeling he should say something at this juncture, "Bass can do that, if you're not used to it."

"You can imagine the state he was in by now, plastered in stinkin' mud, cold, wet and tired." Mag was almost hysterical with laughter. "Eventually a couple of lads found him in the early hours of the mornin' and pulled him out. When he got to my place he had sobered up a bit and had the sense to go 'round the back of the house and hose himself down before goin' into his flat. I got home later after closin' up the pub to find a pile of wet, crumpled clothes in the backyard."

"It looked like he was still wearing them tonight," said Mag between periods of laughing.

"Did he find his glasses?" said Tom, feeling uneasy at Mag's liberal reaction to the tale.

"We went back next day with a large fishnet he got from his department in College, he's a biologist. We recovered the bike but never found the glasses."

Dowie left early and the evening dragged on with a low hum of customers and the occasional thump of a dart hitting its target. Tom phoned to find out how Mark was settling in and Richard stayed upstairs watching television.

Wednesday was relatively uneventful. The weather remained deliciously hot and Richard entertained Mark on the beach. The pub was visited by many holiday makers but still only a few of the locals since it was their busy time.

A bit early for darts although it is Thursday, thought Tom. But it'll give Mag a chance to exercise her conviviality. He carried on reading but was uneasy about the voices, they were too deep for girls. He had to satisfy his inquisitiveness by visiting the bar.

Mag was leaning on the counter watching the game. There were four men playing very skilled darts. Occasionally they would cease playing and go into a huddle, then start again.

"What are they doing, Tom?

"I don't know, perhaps they are playing a special game?" Tom was not familiar with this kind of behaviour.

"Who are they?"

"I don't know them, I've never seen them before."

Apart from the Tremletts, they were the sole inhabitants of Ty Gwyn. A fifth member walked in. He was much more amiable than the rest and stopped to pick up a glass of ale and some passing conversation.

"Where's Dowie?"

Mag was a little flustered at the presence of this handsome, smiling, well-dressed stranger and stumbled out, "He sold it to us, we took over last week."

"I didn't know the pub was for sale? Dowie doesn't own the pub anymore, lads."

"Yeah, I know, someone told me last night," came the reply from one of the less presentable of the crowd. The handsome stranger joined the scrum before the start of another game.

"Down on holiday, are you?" Tom felt uneasy.

The recent darter lifted his head and said, "You could say that." There was a touch of incredulity in his answer.

The scene was beginning to become more volatile with disputes breaking out between the players, the stranger inciting the less intelligent ones. Tom was feeling decisively uneasy and was contemplating his next move when Megan walked in.

"Usual please, Mag."

Megan's first act was always to scan the clientele. Her second was completely out of character, "Leave it a minute, Mag, I've left my bag..." She left in a hurry.

"I don't fuckin' care," came a voice from the scrum.

"Language gentlemen! I don't like it in my pub."

Mag was surprised at the response from Tom. He usually liked to be seen and not heard. A subversive mumble came from the darters. It was then that he realised the reason for the huddles, they were gambling on the outcome of each match.

He explained to Mag, "I'll have to break it up, we could lose our license."

"Do be careful, Tom. There's five of them."

With Herculean fortitude he got to the group when the money was changing hands. Tens and fifties was all he could see. Bloody hell! he thought, I wish I could afford to lose money like that.

"Come on boys, break this up... I could lose my license."

"That's yer fuckin' problem."

"Right, come on, out! Or I'll call the police."

The smallest one in the crowd approached Tom, pushed his face threateningly close to Tom's and reached into his pocket. The handsome one immediately interrupted.

"Don't be stupid, Bush, you'll be back inside if you do that."

Tom's adrenaline started to flow, "Get out!" he screamed. Mag was petrified.

They turned and slowly walked towards the door. The smart one looked at Mag as he passed the bar and the pleasant smile she so much admired diversified into a grotesque grin; she shuddered. In the entrance appeared Dowie with Megan close behind. The gamblers' pace quickened as they brushed past them and left silently.

Tom then realised what he had done and began to shake. He remembered occasions of misunderstanding at work but they never got this intimidating.

"Give him one of his specials, on me Mag. It will steady his nerves." Mag was still in shock but responded to Megan's request.

"Thank you... I wondered why you left so fast," said Tom.

"I've patched them up enough times to..." she stopped since she could not see the relevance of any more information.

"Do you know who they are?" Dowie said rhetorically. "They're the Scudmore brothers, really nasty types. They've all been inside. The small one called Bush only came out last week after a three-year stretch for GBH. The talkative one..."

"You mean the one in the smart suit." Mag had a weakness for slick dressers.

"Yeah, he's a con man, lives in London. Cons the foreign tourists. Did some time for passing funny money."

"He certainly had me fooled." Tom was surprised Mag had noticed.

"You won't see them again," said Dowie. "They were tryin' it on. They'll probably go to the Workin' Men's Club near the station, anybody can get in there."

"When I asked them if they were on holiday, they more or less said yes."

"Well, they're right aren't they? They're out of prison," said Mag.

They all laughed; Tom had stopped shaking and grinned. "Incidentally, they knew I'd sold. It was general knowledge weeks ago."

Tom spent the rest of the night basking in his own glory and making sure the incident was the topic of the night's conversation. After hearing the story, Beryl made a big fuss of Tom, he liked that. Mag watched him closely.

Friday lunchtime Megan called in after changing her library books opposite the pub. She didn't appear to be her usual perky self.

"What's wrong, Megan?" said Mag who always did the bar lunchtimes while Tom served bar meals. "It looks like you've seen a ghost. The usual?"

"Yes, please... Can you remember a couple of entertainers who were in Llanrheidol on Monday? I went to their concert, there were posters all over town. They gave a concert at the..."

"Yes," Mag remembered Tom's intense reaction to the girl.

"They have both been involved in a serious accident. They were both dead before they got them to the hospital here." Megan swallowed, she could not get used to death even after so many years in her profession. "The car turned over on that treacherous part of the road going into Llany'... The problem is they think the driver was over the limit."

"Oh, my God! They were drinking here before the concert, you know..."

"Really? I didn't know that, Mag."

"I must tell Tom, he was quite impressed with them." She immediately put down the glass for Megan's drink, pressed the button on the wall and lifted the phone. Tom answered almost immediately thinking it was a request for a meal. "Tom, come down straight away, Megan has some bad news to tell you."

"What is it?" requested Tom. He did not like surprises and particularly not bad ones. Since Megan was in the Casualty Department of the hospital he immediately thought of Mark.

"It's to do with that couple who were here on Monday lunchtime, remember? The pretty girl and her pianist from Bristol." Tom felt relieved, put the phone down and entered the bar. In the meantime, Mag had apologised to Megan and given her a drink. Megan gave a wry smile, since she was used to being the purveyor of bad news and acknowledged the drink physically.

Megan repeated the story to Tom. Mag made a particular point of observing Tom during the deliberations and noticed an appreciable change in his complexion to an ashened white. His reaction was genuine and from the heart. It made Mag realise how easy it was for an intense relationship to develop from just a chance meeting. Could Tom react to the local girls in the same way?

Tom silently left the bar and went upstairs, on the pretence of carrying on with his catering duties. A brief encounter was virtually all that existed between them and they would probably have never met again but his unrequited attraction for the beauty made the disaster so final.

Mark came crashing into the flat from the outside door. Nana was with him but Mag's father had peeled off and gone into the premises below.

"Hello, young lad." Tom soon lost his melancholy, "want a fight?" He immediately put his hands up to defend himself against the forthcoming onslaught. After a while Tom was feeling the strain of his pugnacious son, so he was pleased to receive a message from the bar requesting, in no uncertain terms, that they stop the noise. The affray had awoken Richard who crawled into the kitchen for his breakfast.

"Good afternoon," said Nana sarcastically. "Are you taking Mark to the beach today?" He mumbled something into a bowl of cornflakes which Nana presumed was positive. "Don't forget to take old towels, just in case there's some tar on the beach."

"Yeah, yeah! I've heard it all before," bellowed Richard. Mark left his father sweating profusely on the floor in the lounge and went to join Richard in the kitchen.

"I suppose you want some as well?"

"Yes please, Nana."

The buzzer went and Tom took down the first cottage pie of the day. The pub closed at two, Nana and Tom were joined by Mag and her father. All four talked about coping with Mark and the problems of a new school.

"I'll open up," Tom eagerly wanted to disengage himself from the uncertainty of Mark and the pub; he was still not happy about the situation... Tom was staring at the open door thinking about the silhouetted body of the departed beautiful singer when in walked Dowie and Selwyn.

"Two pints, Tom, we're both out tonight." Dowie volunteered the information. "I'm goin' out mackerel fishing with my cousin from Abermard. If I catch any do you want some?"

"You bet," said Tom eagerly. "I'm partial to a fresh mackerel once or twice a year."

"I'm the same," said Selwyn. "Once or twice a year and that's my lot, nothing like it."

Tom could sense the hidden sexual implication but suppressed his laughter with tightened lips. "Are you going fishing with Dowie?"

"No, I'm going to Cwmareon. I've heard that there are glow worms out there. If it's right, this will be the first record of these animals in this area for fifty years... what I would like landlord, is..."

"The name's Tom, Tom."

Selwyn continued, "a couple of pints of Bass in this vacuum flask, Tom." He produced an expensive, chromium-plated vacuum flask which was a mass of dents and scratches and impregnated with what appeared to be mud.

Tom took the flask and started to fill it. "You're going to look for slow worms? We had plenty of them in the churchyard near us in Bristol."

"No, glow worms!" Selwyn responded as though he was talking to a particularly inept undergraduate. "Slow worms are legless lizards; they look like snakes... Glow worms are insects and the females have their bums on fire so you can see them in the dark. That's what the Bass is for."

"To attract the glow worms?" Tom said sarcastically since he wasn't used to being treated like a child. Dowie could feel the tension building up in Tom and interrupted the conversation by ordering crisps to supplement Selwyn's libation.

Just before they left together, Frank entered with his usual greeting, "*Shawd mae*!" He occupied his usual location near the dartboard ready for the Friday night girls.

Mark waved goodbye from the open door of the pub and was whisked away to the comparative safety of the council estate. In through the vacated space poured about ten youths who were obviously out to have a good time. It was a Stag Night so the usual subsidiary band of girls was absent. They spent a noisy round and left, leaving the pub empty and messy but relatively quiet.

Tom lacked the confidence to serve so many people all at once and was glad that it was over quickly and without any problems. The boys were in good spirits and relatively sober at this stage since Ty Gwyn was about the fourth pub on their list. It's when they start on the shorts and double the number of pubs visited that trouble can break out.

"Stag Night, Frank," said Tom, making the words with his mouth more than his voice since Frank was a little deaf. "The girls won't be coming through just yet." He looked disappointed but resigned to the fact that they would eventually turn up. Mag joined Tom in the bar with an armful of clean wiping up towels which she folded individually over once and put them in a neat pile under the counter.

Tom tapped Mag excitedly on the shoulder, "This is our first weekend, I wonder what will happen? Oh, Dowie will not be coming in tonight, he's gone fishing with his cousin." Mag felt a little disappointed but did not show it and adjusted her thin, silky blouse nervously.

"I suppose Rolff and the gang will be in soon?"

"Tom, why is he called Rolff when his real name is Bernard, according to Beryl?"

"I asked Dowie exactly the same question. Apparently when he was on a school visit to Northern Spain they started drinking cider..."

"Cider in Spain?" Mag was confused.

"Yes," Tom had taken up his usual supercilious air when he thought he knew a little bit more than someone else. "In the Basque Country, they grow mainly apples and not grapes, therefore they make cider and not wine... Can I get on with the story, now?"

"I don't know where you get all this information from, you know, I really don't... Yes, carry on."

"He was the first of the crowd of boys to be sick and when you are sick you go, ROLFF. The name has stuck ever since and, by the way, it's Rolff with two Fs instead of a PH.

"I don't believe you," said Mag adjusting the front of her blouse to reveal a little bit more of her cleavage and glancing briefly around the pub to see if anyone was looking. Not even Frank bothered.

"If you don't believe me ask him yourself. Talk of the devil, here they are now." In walked Rolff, he was only just over one and a half metres high but obviously solid and fit. He was clean shaven and his mousey brown hair was beginning to thin at the crown and the temples despite his age of only twenty-three. This made him look a little older than his contemporaries. He was dressed conventionally with jeans and an open neck shirt except for one outstanding feature. He wore bright blue boots which he had obviously dyed for the occasion.

Rolff sidled up to the bar and in a delivery expected from a comedian giving a one liner said, "A pint of lager, barkeep, sorry, barkeepess." His five friends, who towered above this diminutive joker, were waiting for Rolff's silly comment as an excuse to burst into raucous laughter. Mag had not seen Rolff and the gang before but Tom had from his holiday walkabouts with Dowie. She started to pull the drink thinking to herself that if this was the standard of his jokes at this stage of the evening, what were they going to be like later?

"You'd better give these reprobates a pint as well and one for yourself, Mag." He laboured the point. "Cheers!" She poured herself a G&T and thanked him.

Rolff turned from the bar and noticed Frank near the dartboard, "*Shawd mae*! Waiting for the birds are you?" Frank just grinned.

They all moved over to an empty table opposite the open door with Rolff having the best view. He was in a silly mood and made inane comments about everyone who came in through the door. This delighted his friends immeasurably in their semi-drunken state. Tom was not too happy about this juvenile behaviour, but since it was relatively innocent and most of the victims were aware of this crowd's stupid antics, he didn't make a fuss. And, they were good spenders. They soon got fed up and decided to move on.

The pub was getting busy, so Mag did not have time to ask Rolff about his nickname or the reason for his bright blue boots before they left. Perhaps next time, she thought to herself. Shortly after their departure, in came the female contingent headed by Big Brenda. Brenda Mawr, as she was affectionately called, immediately went over to old Frank and gave him a big wet kiss. He was obviously delighted, perked up and went to the bar for another half. Brenda Mawr reminded Mag of last year's holiday and the grossly overweight, pretty, young, married American women overpopulating Disneyland. She had been chasing Rolff since their stormy affair the previous year. But it was obvious that they were not suited. For some reason the girls were not particularly boisterous on this Friday night. Since some of the girls were in the darts team, Mag thought it would be a friendly gesture to find out the reason for their gloom.

"I won't be a second, Tom," she shouted above the noise of the crowd.

"Hurry up, will you!" Tom did not want a repeat of an earlier episode and Beryl was not there to help him. Mag squeezed her way through the crowd, had a quick chat to the girls and returned to the bar as quickly as possible. Tom was panicking during that brief period. His leg gave him restricted movement and he got into trouble with the change if he had to work quickly. Mag soon calmed him down with a few conciliatory words and a peck on the cheek. During a slight let up in the crowd's demand for alcohol, Mag told Tom what was wrong. It appeared that one of the boys, not Rolff, had been seeing another girl who was not in the gang. This meant open war between the females but for some unknown reason, the boy involved was not in any way implicated. To Rolff's gang it was hilarious and the boy in question a hero. Judging from their mood it was apparent that they were hoping the girls might meet later further up town.

The girls stayed a little longer than usual and they began to relax and liven up. From their vicinity came, Rock of Ages Pledge With Me, in the deep tones of a male voice. The pub was so crowded that neither Tom nor Mag could actually see the purveyor.

They looked at each other and simultaneously uttered, "Dai the Voice is in." Mag laughed and Tom grinned.

"He's drunk, but seriously, I must get rid of him before he starts swearing and touching up the girls." Tom left the bar and like his wife before him, squeezed through the crowd to be confronted by the girls. They were now in a mischievous mood and standing in a circle, enclosing a voice in full throttle.

"Excuse me ladies..."

"Ooh! Bloody ladies, is it?" came a voice from the centre of the circle. "They're just old bags."

This started the girls laughing and stamping their feet. "Throw him out landlord, he's drunk," came a voice from among the circumferenced females.

Tom pushed through the circle and caught hold of Dai, firstly relieving him of his now empty glass. This was not for any protective reasons but just to prevent it getting smashed by accident. Dai's attitude was quite different from the last eviction, he was not malicious, just noisy. Tom marched him to the door under a sea of Welsh abuse. This caused the crowd to applaud, whistle, and the more refined ones to clap.

He firmly but gently pushed Dai out the door to be confronted with, "I hope your bloody mangy old dog dies," in English.

This started another quick burst of applause from the pub as if a winning try had been converted at a Wales vs England match. Tom smiled to himself and said to the crowd as he moved back to the bar, "I haven't got a bloody dog." This brought the house down. He felt a little guilty about throwing Dai out but in reality the entertainment value of this venture was well worth it. Since Tom was new to Ty Gwyn nobody knew how to approach him, so the excitement quickly quietened to a pleasant, busy, warm summer's evening.

Eventually it was time to close up and relax. Tom took down his special bottle of calvados and Mag had another one of her many G&Ts.

"That was a very busy but pleasant evening Mag. I think we should try and get Beryl in to help out, don't you? If they are all like that we'll be quids in. I'll till up, then go and get a take away, the usual?"

"Well, yes," said Mag. "You have certainly learned a lot tonight about handling drunks and wasters, Tom."

"Like everything else in life, it comes down to experience. You go and make a cuppa and if Richard's home ask him if he wants anything from the Chinese and buzz it down to me."

* * * * *

Tom was first up, he liked the privacy before the activities of the day and to cook himself a heart stopping English breakfast. He had tried the traditional Welsh repast of laverbread and cockles fried in bacon fat but dismissed it as too greasy! In his more philosophical moments, he consistently queried the validity of this meal since fewer people in Wales eat breakfast than anywhere else in Britain. He suggested that it might be cooked up solely for the tourists as part of their initiation to Wales.

Mag was aware of Tom's indulgence. Basically she was averse to an unhealthy diet because of her obsession with keeping her fine, trim figure. In her younger days she was a very stunning looker and won several small local beauty competitions including Miss Elegance at the factory where she worked with Tom. In those days Tom was eligible, handsome and the manager.

After taking Mag her morning cuppa, he made his daily excursion to the cellar via the bar. The unpleasant smell of stale cigarette smoke and beer which lingered in the air from the previous night was nauseating. Myfanwy had let herself in and she was beginning to detoxify the place. Tom had his doubts about whether the smell of the deodorant was an improvement or not.

"Shall I polish the tables today, Tom?"

"No, it's Saturday, leave them until Monday now, they're sure to be covered in drinks by closing time."

"OK." She finished clearing the bar, wiped the ash-trays and then applied polish to the tables.

By then Tom had passed through the bar into the cellar. He checked the Bass and the other beers and moved a few empty casks to the cellar door for the delivery men on Monday.

The day was beginning to warm up and Tom felt unusually elated since the holiday spirit seemed to be everywhere. He cautiously bounced back upstairs to the flat and found Mag sipping tea at the breakfast table. She looked very desirable in her almost transparent black nightdress which was last seen on the final night in Bristol. It was loosely covered with an equally diaphanous dressing gown. To Tom, one outstanding feature of Mag's anatomy was her full breasts with the large erect nipples which were prevalent even in the warm weather.

He glanced briefly, but before Mag's signals could enliven the situation, it was discouraged by a characteristic comment that Richard may be down soon so she would be well advised to cover up.

"I thought you like me like this, Tom."

To reinforce his evasive action, he said, "Of course I do, but Myfanwy is downstairs and she might come up. Besides, I thought last night was enough for a while." He gently kissed the nape of her neck.

Mag, who was a little disappointed at Tom's reaction, stood up, lifted up her nightdress exposing her naked body for a second in a provocative pose, then turned, flashed her rear and went upstairs to dress.

Tom shouted to her in his best Bristol accent, "Good on yer gal."

"It must be all this money you're makin', you know, it's going to yer bleedin' head," she shouted back. The coarseness of her dialogue perturbed Tom.

Saturday morning was relatively uneventful. Dowie came in with half a dozen mackerel. Tom was behind the bar but he was quickly relieved by Mag who must have heard Dowie's voice. Tom took the fish upstairs where he remained throughout the lunchtime. Mag was dressed in a thin cotton blouse and a long divided skirt with wide legs. While she quietly talked to Dowie, in the isolation of the bar, she had a fixed silly grin and swayed back and forth with her legs crossed in a provocative way. Dowie was slightly uncomfortable at her stance and made an excuse that he had to distribute the rest of the fish around town.

Dowie did not serve bar meals when he was in Ty Gwyn, only sandwiches which were made by Myfanwy out of the kindness of her heart. She was one of many who thought Dowie a good catch. But she was not under any misapprehension about her chances since she was a single parent. The Tremletts had discussed catering in the pub and they were intending to build up this side of the business. Tom, in his inevitable way, had worked out that there was a lot of money to be made. He was a qualified cook, having done his National Service in the Catering Corps, followed by a course in a Catering College. It was intended that he should concentrate on the cooking side. The menu was to increase from the existing cottage pie to the unimaginative but home-made lasagne, chilli con carne and chicken curry. When he cleaned the beer pipes, the extraneous Guinness would be used for beef in Guinness. This was Tom's prize-winning speciality; he used to serve it in the Officers' Mess. He was already negotiating with several local butchers for good bargains when buying in bulk. Basically, Tom was the business part of the duo and Mag provided the attractive public relations side. Mag, together with Beryl, proved to be very popular with the local males of all ages. Initially, it was really Beryl, when in the employ of Dowie, who started attracting the young element to the pub. Mag pulled in the older ones.

Tom could hear Mark coming up the stairs two at a time which was quite a feat for a child of his stature. He puffed his way into the kitchen where Tom was working.

"Let's have a fight, Dad."

"Oh, not at the moment, Dad's got a pain in his leg," he rubbed his knee. Actually the pain was really intense but he was a proud man and didn't want people to know the extent of his disability. 'If only that bloody crate had not fallen on my leg in the factory, I would be up and about now but not, of course, in Ty Gwyn,' he grumbled to himself.

Mark greeted Nana who had just arrived at the door of the flat with a bag full of groceries. "I've got the veg and meat that you ordered." Mark took it from her but the bag was too heavy for him and he dropped it on the ground.

"Mind the bloody eggs," snarled Tom. He immediately regretted his outburst and took Mark up in his arms apologising profusely.

"Phew! I should think so. He was only trying to help me."

"I know Nana, it's one of those days." They smiled at each other. All three sat together sipping tea and eating some of the sandwiches that were prepared for the bar.

"I suppose Grandad is in the bar?" asked Tom.

"That's right," said Mark. "He's having a pinta beer... Is Richard taking me to the beach today?"

"Go up and ask him, he's in bed."

Mark returned looking very disappointed. "He's going to a party with some of his friends."

"I'll take you later on," said Tom rubbing his leg at the thought of it.

"You're very good to him, Tom..."

"Great! I'll show you my new swimming strokes," Mark proceeded to wave his arms in the air while he walked around the room.

"Leg bad, Tom?"

"No, just a bit of cramp."

Nana knew better.

The day was now very hot, even with all the windows open, and Mark looked bored. The usual mixture of holiday makers and locals were in the bar but it was not busy. Some sandwiches and three cottage pies were sold. The occasional outburst of laughter could be heard in the bar. Lally popped her head in through the door of the bar and told Mag that she would be coming in that night after her shopping spree. That's strange, thought Mag, her day in town is usually Monday.

"It seems very quiet, shall I ring down and ask Mummy if I can take you to the beach?" Mark skipped with excitement.

Nana pottered about in the flat putting things away where no one could find them and the whole atmosphere was quiet and sleepy. The pub closed for the afternoon, Mag and her mother were having a good natter in the flat so Grandad decided to look for Tom and 'The Boy', as he affectionately called Mark.

When Grandad did eventually find the bathers, he was startled to see Tom talking to a scantily clad, sylph-like girl of about twenty. Tom appeared a little flustered when he saw his father-in-law.

"This is one of Mag's darters, you've probably seen her in the pub."

To ease Tom's discomfort he falsely admitted that he had seen her near the dart board.

Mark was splashing away near the waters edge. "Hello, Grandad... watch me swim." He thrashed his arms around in an abortive attempt to do the crawl stroke but his head moved so quickly from one side to side that he lost his co-ordination.

"That's great," said Grandad, "you'll be a good swimmer one day. Are you coming back now? Nana wants to go home..." They finally left just before Mag opened up the pub for the evening session.

To Mag's delight, the first one to enter the bar was Dowie. "Give us a pint, I'm dyin' of thirst. I've been buildin' a small wall in the garden to separate the veg from the flowers." He drank the pint down in one go and requested another.

"My, that's some thirst you've got there, you know," said Mag giving the desiccated brickie another pint.

"Where's Selwyn?"

"You won't see him tonight. He always goes to the University Club on Saturdays, they do very good evening meals with plenty of choice... Have you got a cottage pie? I feel like having a good session tonight so I had better line my stomach." Mag buzzed Tom.

While Tom was still in the bar, Mag said unprompted, "Do you think I could go for a walkabout tonight with Dowie? After all, Beryl is coming in to help." Dowie was overwhelmed at this spontaneous comment from Mag and from past experience in the pub, predicted the answer from Tom.

"You must be bloody joking, it's the busiest day of the week and we need everybody involved. Isn't that right, Dowie?"

"It was when I had Ty Gwyn."

"It was just a thought."

"And a bloody silly one at that." Tom disappeared up the stairs. Mag nervously wiped the counter and quickly glanced at Dowie; he made no comment. The silence was broken by Lally stumbling through the open door. She had a large green plastic Harrods bag bulging with library books. Reading was her preoccupation when not gardening or looking after cats.

"I didn't call in lunchtime because I had to see the solicitor and I didn't want to smell of drink."

"After some more money from that rich husband of yours?"

"No, Dowie, he's dying," Lally's reply was so matter-of-fact and blatantly lacking emotion. They had been divorced for a number of years and there was no love lost between them. He was a business man in the city, had plenty of money and gave her a generous allowance to keep away from the children. Whether this was the reason for her isolated, alcoholic way of life, no one knew. Dowie felt uncomfortable since he could not cope with dying and death.

"I'm sorry Lally, I suppose you want a gin and Schweppes?"

"Make it a double... no treble. There's no need to be sorry, Mag. I simply find it a bother."

The usual itinerants wandered through, Mag forgetting again to ask Rolff about his boots. It was nice to see some extra crowds of lively young people who were obviously on holiday, according to their accents. A number of middle aged couples stayed for a while because they liked Bass or the company or both. Lally dropped down to single G&Ts.

"These are interesting." Dowie moved his bead slightly to the left without obviously turning, indicating they were just entering the door. "Gethin and Christin, Gethin's the hairdresser at the top of town, near the Welsh pub, the other one is his friend, you know?"

Gethin was obviously the male guy and did the ordering. "Can I have a large G&T and a Tia Maria with a drop of soda in it, dearie." Mag smiled and took his order, while Beryl approached them.

"Hello fellas, I haven't seen you for a while. Been on your holidays, have you?" Gethin was always tanned, he had a sunbed in the shop but this was a deeper colour.

"Yes, we've been to Lesbos."

Dowie burst out laughing, Mag smiled but Beryl did not move a muscle in her face and kept it as deadpan as Buster Keaton in one of his silent films.

"I believe it can also be called Mytilene," said Beryl.

"Yes, that's right, dearie... How did you know?"

"Mavis the Travel told me. They also have a lot of nude beaches there, don't they?"

"You're very well informed for a barmaid," bitched Christin, who disapproved of the attraction between Beryl and Gethin.

"Yes, there are. You should have seen some of those lovely bronzed bums, weren't they nice Christin?" He just shook his head as though flicking his hair back and sipped his Tia Maria.

"Did you show off that gorgeous figure of yours in the buff, Geth?" Beryl was teasing him.

"Don't tell her, she's only playing you up. I think we should go now, they're serving cocktails in the Royal Hotel."

"Fellas," Beryl declared to the pub, "C-O-C-K-tails."

Christin put down his drink and walked out, followed reluctantly by Gethin. "See you again, dearies."

"Bye Geth, Christ," Beryl replied with a little forward flick of the wrist.

Mag was astonished, she had never seen Beryl in such a badgering mood before. Beryl apologised to Mag but also explained that they have always teased each other since they were in the infants' school, but they had always been the best of pals. Dowie was aware of this and Lally was too far gone to realise what was happening. Tom was in the cellar messing with the Bass so he missed the whole episode. Mag narrated the sequence to him later when they were upstairs. Their first Saturday night was pleasant and friendly and Tom was well pleased with the takings. There were no incidents and Dai did not appear. A handful of locals, including Dowie, who decided not to go on walkabout after all, stayed after time. Lally was ostensibly waiting for a taxi which she had not even ordered. "They're very busy now. It'll be easier later." She had been saying that on and off since about ten o'clock. Megan came off duty late and Ieuan had been somewhere refereeing a football match. Tom did not like this overtime drinking. He thought that eleven to eleven was quite long enough to be on your feet and pleasant to customers. Mag on the other hand loved this time of day when she could relax and chat.

"What do you think of our local characters, Mag?" Dowie said with the resemblance of a smile on his face.

"You mean Gethin and Christin?"

"The ones! Gethin is a local lad and well known, but the other one is a nasty bit of goods. Gethin picked him up in London during a Hairdressin' Conference... Me, Beryl and Geth were great pals when we were younger. We used to go around together a lot, in fact, some people thought we were related. That's right, isn't it, Beryl? Where is she...?" Dowie located her sitting in the corner by the dartboard, smoking.

"Yeah! But he wasn't like that then..." Beryl paused, took another puff on her cigarette and cautiously said, "in fact, now I come to think of it, I may be wrong... I remember one evening we were all at a beach party and it got a little cold so I cuddled up to Geth. I was only wearing a bikini bottom and he didn't take advantage at all. At the time I just wanted to get warm and didn't think anymore about it, until now."

"That was the time when you danced around the fire to get warm. You had lovely boobs in those days." Dowie focused on Mag to record her reaction since he knew what Beryl was about to do from previous experience.

"What's wrong with them now, Dowie?" She lifted her blouse very briefly exposing a pair of beautifully formed, firm, white breasts.

Mag blushed and wondered if she would ever have the nerve to do it. Hers were bigger and better shaped than Beryl's, she assured herself. Lally dozed on her bar stool. This exhibition was momentarily followed by a silence which was quickly broken by Ieuan who also knew Beryl's reaction to Dowie's comments.

"You need some sun on them, this son!"

They all laughed except for Tom who nervously moved from one foot to the other. He had admired her clothed, but never expected to view one of her main features so soon.

"We used to get up to all sorts of things when we were younger," Ieuan was addressing Mag. He turned to Dowie, "Remember Doug Bungalow? Remember? He was in our class at school."

Dowie explained the origin of the nickname to the Tremletts, "Bungalow, he didn't have much up top."

"That's clever," said Mag, "I must remember that. What would you call Tom, then?"

"I thought it would be obvious, Tomos the Pub."

Dowie remembered, "Ah! Doug, he had a big'un, didn't..."

"Yep, he used to go around showing everybody."

"Christ! I was going to say that, Ieuan," said Dowie indignantly. He wanted to see the expression on Mag's face.

"I think every school had one of those," Tom casually remarked. "I know we did."

"Was it you?"

"Do you mind, Beryl?" Tom flushed.

"It could have been," said Mag.

They all laughed.

"It's not really a laughing matter." Megan was in a serious mood. "During my training in London I came across this poor unfortunate chap who had a permanent erection."

Lally livened up, "A what?"

"A hard on," said Beryl and Ieuan simultaneously.

"It was not funny for him, it's a condition of one of the cancers. I can't remember which one at the moment." Megan paused, "Pancreas, I think? No matter. It's called Priapism after the Greek god of procreation." It was the silly stage for the late drinkers who gaped at each other and burst out laughing again.

The laughter was perpetuated by a comment from Ieuan. "I believe there is a tribe in Africa where all the men go around stiff. They are beginning to die out apparently, which is not surprising, I suppose."

Not realising the implications, Tom said, "These tit-bits of information..." Even Lally laughed but she didn't know why. He started again, "This is all very interesting but I'm off to bed, I'll call a taxi for you Lally." She had dozed off again. In reality, Tom could not wait to get upstairs and put a cold compress on his intensely painful leg.

Just as he was leaving the bar, he heard Mag say to the others, "What are we going to do at the Llanrheidol Carnival, we must have a float. Did you have one last year, Dowie?"

Before he could answer, Lally perked up and slurred, "Yes, I made most of the costumes... It was Robin Hood and his hooligans, a mixture of medieval knights, gangsters and their molls. We didn't win but we had a prize for originality." She then slunk back into her semi-drunken state.

"Why don't we modify the costumes and make it a sort of 1920's Speakeasy or something. We have plenty of girls willing to show off their legs and things." Mag beamed at Beryl.

Beryl smiled back and said provocatively, "It's your turn next."

"What now?" Dowie and Ieuan immediately straightened themselves up on their bar stools. Mag touched the top button of her blouse and then realised her bra was comfortable but not fashionable. "Perhaps another time," she said.

Tom heard the taxi arrive and Mag shut and bolted the outside door. A few glasses clinked on the bar and she came upstairs. Mag immediately unbuttoned her blouse and took off her unattractive flesh coloured bra. She took the wet cool towel from Tom's knee and rubbed it under, over and between her breasts.

"That's lovely, I've been wanting to do that all night, you know." Fortunately for Tom, the shower was temporarily out of action and his knee seemed to stop aching. This prompted him to fetch a sponge and bowl of water from the bathroom to help cool her all over. She put up no resistance and Richard had gone to bed.

The night was hot and sticky, Mag went flat out but Tom could not sleep. He got out of bed and sat in a chair near an open window in the lounge. A few late night drinkers wandered past the pub but most of Llanrheidol was now quiet. Tom thought of Mark in another house and wondered what the future would bring, and then he must have fallen asleep himself.

Tom was awakened by the hot sun shining on his face. It was the beginning of another bright sunny day. He was stiff from sitting in the chair for so long, so he decided to relax in the bath. 'I'm glad Mag didn't decide to do the same last night,' he thought to himself. Tom had been out and bought the Sundays and had had his usual fat swilling breakfast before the rest of the family considered Sunday. It was previously decided that Mag would run the bar at lunchtime and in the evening, since it was usually quiet, while Tom prepared a meal for later Sunday night. They might pick up a few holiday makers and one or two of the locals might pop in. Once the bar meals had become established, Tom hoped they would attract more Sunday customers. According to Dowie, it was a good time to generally clean and stock up in preparation for the week.

Since she was expecting to be sitting around and not doing much, Mag decided to wear her latest purchase from Leda's. It was revealing and cool, but out of place in a bar. Such attire would be more in keeping at the Mayor's Ball or the LVA Dinner. The silk, patterned blouse and heavily pleated white skirt were intended to cover a deficiency in undergarments.

Mag was beginning to change from the dreary, drab housewife that Tom married, to a modern woman. Within the last week she had discarded frocks for separates. Her skirts were shorter and her shoes higher. She was about to replace her thick-banded, incarnadine upper garment which was such a deterrent Saturday night in the bar with more delicate underwear. Mag had to do little with her shoulder length, naturally thick blonde hair but makeup was still confined to lipstick. A hint of eyeshadow was beginning to creep into her repertoire. This metamorphosis manifested itself during the transition from Bristol to Llanrheidol. It was as though the break from English conventional conservatism had rejuvenated her.

Tom, on the other hand, was still wearing a Harris tweed coat and cavalry twills for best. He sometimes wore a cap to cover his balding head but it was not an obsession like some of the more sensitive victims. "Bald is sexy," he would occasionally say if in the right frame of mind. His working clothes consisted of an old pair of corduroys, threadbare at the knees and baggy at the crotch. The pockets were holed beyond redemption, so any useful accessories were carried in shirt pockets or in his elbow-shredded cardigan. It was a present from Mag one Christmas in the years when he did not walk with a limp.

Sunday lunchtime crept slowly by - they sold two cottage pies to a couple of tourists. Mag closed sharply at two o'clock and arrived at the flat just in time to help Tom serve out the roast and two veg. Richard had surfaced but Mark would not be coming, something to do with a sore throat.

"We'll go up to your parents this afternoon, Mag."

"Yes, it would be a pleasant break. Are you coming up to Nana's this afternoon, Richard?"

"No, I'm going swimming with the boys."

Tom decided to go in their car; Sunday driving was a rarity for them even during the later years in Bristol. "It's like old times, Mag. Remember our trips to Cheddar or Weston on Sundays and a drink in the Chester Arms on the way home?"

"Lemonade and crisps for the boys," recollected Mag.

"Yes, but we never left them alone." Tom could not help thinking with sadness of his early days and the times he had to spend outside pubs with just those benefits for company.

"What brought that on?"

"Nothing Mag, I just thought of Mark and the pub."

"Don't be silly, he's fine with my parents... Look at the dust on this car." Mag rubbed her finger along the roof.

"That's mainly sand blown from the beach. It contains a lot of salt from the sea and it will corrode the bodywork. We'll call in at the car-wash." They spent a very pleasant afternoon with Mag's parents sitting around in the sun and talking the usual nonsense that people do when just sitting, with the exception of a few censorious remarks about Mag's flimsy apparel from Nana. They were a little disappointed at not seeing very much of the invalid who had miraculously recovered from his demise and was playing with a new friend. But on the whole, all was at peace with the world.

"I wonder when this weather is going to break?" moaned Tom who had been told by someone he had forgotten, that fine weather keeps the punters away from the pubs.

"Trust you to make that sort of comment," said Mag who had been told the same. Taking heed of her mother's caustic comments, Mag nervously pulled at the hem of her skirt. Grandad moved in his chair to look up at the sky, paused for a while and then rejected the idea of any rain for quite a long time, at least, until after the Carnival in two weeks time. Mag and Tom reluctantly excused themselves from the pleasant company, waved to Mark in the garden opposite and returned to the dusty heat of the town.

Richard had returned and was stocking up in the bar. "We're home!" Mag shouted reassuringly as she passed the bar. She often used this comment when she returned home. Tom could not understand why, because how could she be home if she was not there? To Tom it was one of those British idiosyncrasies that he liked to try and explain to foreigners when his discourse on Bass was depleted.

Sunday evening was a little cooler than the previous two days but it was still extremely warm in the bar. Dowie called in with Selwyn on their way to the Labour Club. He complimented her on the outfit she was wearing. Mag acknowledged with a nod of the head. Like most women, she loved to be noticed.

"I forgot to tell you that Clem comes in on Sundays, Sundays only," Dowie repeated. "That's because he works in the kitchens of the Royal all week and it's his only day off... He's short and pudgy. By the way, he cannot say his L's, he says them as W's. Clem wears a blue blazer covered with badges. Most of them are trains or something to do with steam engines, he's also a train spotter. He sits in Frank's place. Did I tell you that Frank goes to chapel with his sister on Sundays so he doesn't come in?" Mag replied that she did know. "Clem does one peculiar thing, usually just before closing, he will ask for a bwaster. This consists of a double whisky, vodka, gin and a single black rum in a pint glass topped up with bitter ale and a dash of soda."

"My God!" exclaimed Mag.

"I'll write it down for you 'cause he gets a little stroppy if he feels you don't know what a Blaster is." Mag passed Dowie a pencil and a piece of paper torn from a notebook kept behind the bar. She leaned over and the front of her blouse opened slightly to inadvertently expose the erect nipples of her firm breasts. Dowie savoured the moment but remained silent and apparently unmoved. Both men finished their drinks without any conversation and bade Mag farewell. On the way out Dowie said something to Selwyn, who was unaware of the display, and he laughed.

Ieuan came into the pub soon after their departure. He was dressed in a smart multi-flowered shirt, which emphasised the gold necklace around his neck and a pair of tailored shorts.

"You're looking extremely smart tonight, Ieuan. Have you got a date?"

"As a matter of fact I have." Mag looked troubled. "With Megan, I think? We decided last night to talk about the float for the Carnival this evening."

"I can't remember that."

"No, you wouldn't, it was when I was walking her home after you closed up." He then noticed the chic outfit Mag was wearing. "Hey! That looks pretty cool, like the design on the blouse." Concentrating on the blouse he became aware of her emancipation, but without the confidence of a crowd, he was too shy to make any comment. "Pint please, make it a shandy. I feel a bit fragile after last night... Hey! you remembered then?" Ieuan was relieved at Megan's presence.

Megan was a stickler for time, being trained according to the old school of nursing, "Of course! We made arrangements last night, didn't we?"

"Yep, you're right, but don't get stroppy with me," he commanded.

"Sorry Ieuan, I've had a row with Mother again. She is always trying to get me married off." Megan was in her forties and except for her training in London, she had spent all her time in Llanrheidol. She was small in stature, rather plump with grey hair and looked a typical nursing sister. She had a very pleasant disposition and was always helping good causes when not saving lives in the Casualty Department. She did have a boyfriend when training in London but he was a doctor, married and ambitious. "I've been thinking Ieuan, we really can't do anything until we have discussed the costumes with Lally."

"Yes it would make more sense," said Mag. "Didn't she say last night that she had made them?"

"Yes, Lally is very good at making clothes, she studied fashion design at Art College. In fact, she met her ex-husband at the Chelsea Art College Ball. It used to be the function of the year, back in the '50s. I went once with Lally, but never again. I was supposed to be the serious minded, devoted nurse and Lally the uninhibited art student, but not that night... I don't think you know, Mag, but we both come from Llanrheidol. Lally was brought up on a farm just outside." Mag acknowledged her ignorance. "We used to talk about people, especially in the company of boys, in Welsh." A pleasant, gentle smile came over Megan's face. "When she got married, she stayed in Surrey somewhere, but I came home to look after my parents." It was decided to leave the question of the float until Monday.

"What d'you want to drink, Megan?"

"I thought you'd never ask! A half of Bass, please."

They carried on talking about some of their ideas for the float, but it was really academic since Lally had to make the stuff or at least design it. A few couples came and went including one couple from the previous night who said they enjoyed themselves so much that they had to come again. It was a proper pub and they particularly liked the choice of music and the real ale. Mag mentioned that they were trying to keep it a local in the tradition established by the previous owner. In the winter they would have an open log fire.

"Here comes Clem," mentioned Ieuan. "Do you know about his Blaster?"

"Yes, thanks, Dowie explained it to me just before you came in, you know. In fact, he wrote it down for me, look!" Megan moved around on her bar stool in preparation to talk to Clem while Mag came forward to show Ieuan. Seeing the reaction on his face, she realised what she had done and quickly stepped back from her displaying posture. On reflection she wondered if she had done the same thing previously and that would explain the departing joviality between Dowie and Selwyn. No, Dowie wouldn't have been that tactless, she hoped to herself.

"Hello Clem, in for your usual? They really work you in that place, don't they, one night off a week... The youngsters of today wouldn't stand for it, they like their weekends free." With a more authoritative voice, which she had to adopt many times a day in the execution of her duties, Megan whispered, "How's the ulcer now? I hope you are taking those tablets and not overtaxing your stomach."

"No probwem," he bellowed out, completely breaking the secrecy with which the question was delivered. "Eating wike a horse," he patted his corporeal frame. "Be havin' me bwaster soon."

"So much for confidentiality," mumbled Megan into her drink. "I'd better be going, I'm on earlies this week but I'll see you tomorrow." She got off her bar stool and said that she liked the outfit Mag was wearing and wished that she could carry it off as well. A response like that from Megan was praise indeed since she did not give away compliments freely. It made Mag feel less of an exhibit. Megan obviously had not noticed the superficiality of her outfit.

Tom was bored upstairs so he came down. He talked to a couple from the previous night about the Good Old Days and when they left, he nattered to Ieuan about football and the art of refereeing. Tom was not really interested but Ieuan was such a good romancer that he enjoyed the conversation for its entertainment value alone.

"They have this football training scheme for the kids every year at the College," said Ieuan, "and a lot of famous footballers come down to help. They usually ask me to referee some of the matches. I know nearly all the English and the Welsh team players. I'd bring them in here but they're in strict training with no alcohol..." Tom smiled to himself because he knew from Selwyn that the players who did in fact come to Llanrheidol went to the University Club.

"Bwaster!" His gruff delivery was acceptable to Mag because it was obvious that he was not blessed with a high IQ - something that Dowie had omitted in his description of Clem. She picked up the list of ingredients and started to dispense them into a pint glass.

"You're starting early on the Blasters," said Ieuan.

"Goin' to have two tonight, then go home 'cause I want to watch the programme on trains of India on the Tewevision..." Clem left just before closing having forgotten all about his programme. Tom had kept him talking about trains, a subject in which he had a genuine interest, a legacy from the time when his father worked on the GWR out of Bristol. He was a driver and often took Tom, as a little boy, along the track when they were shunting.

After the last customer had left, Tom had his usual drink and Mag a double gin. She was still a bit uneasy about her revelation in the bar and decided to put it to the test. "Tom, stay there at the bar and look at me as I give you a piece of paper."

"Paper, what the hell is going on? Have you had too much to drink?"

"Trust me, Tom." She reached back and picked up the blaster recipe and leaned over the bar in the act of showing Tom the paper.

Tom looked aghast. "How often did you bloody well lean over the counter like that? Do you realise that you are revealing all you've got? I can't believe you could be so bloody stupid. What do you think this place is, a bloody strip joint?"

Mag felt sluttish and started to well up. Her eyes began to water over and her vision went cloudy. "I, I only thought I was being presentable for the customers, you know."

"Presentable! You were practically giving it to them."

"I didn't realise that they could see everything." She held back a muffled sigh. "Why didn't you say something at Mum's this afternoon?"

"If you remember, you had a bloody scarf around your neck..." Tom hated to see Mag upset, his voice changed and he became more subservient. "How many people do you think saw you?"

"I gave Dowie the paper to write the blaster recipe and I showed it to Ieuan."

"Don't worry, Mag," he reassuringly touched her, "at least, they're worth looking at..." He pulled the front of her blouse open. Mag moved quickly away from the bar put her hand against her blouse to close the revealing gap, turned and had another gin from the optic.

"I know Ieuan saw because he blushed a little and turned away. He didn't say anything." By now Tom had come around to her side of the bar and he reassuringly swung her gently round and kissed her affectionately.

He tasted of sour apples. 'That's the calvados,' thought Mag. "Careful Tom, you're getting my nice white skirt dirty."

Tom had unwittingly pushed her up against the counter before he started to fondle her plump, dimpled, bottom. "Oh, take it off then."

She did and also the blouse. They disappeared behind the bar and the empty glasses on the counter reverberated in harmony.

* * * * *

"That's a week gone. I do hope this weather keeps up for the Carnival," said Tom to Mag at the breakfast table. Mag got up earlier than usual on Mondays because the draymen came. "How do you feel this morning, Mag?"

"Embarrassed!"

"Just ignore it. I'm sure Dowie and Ieuan will. Obviously, don't wear that blouse today. Keep it for orgies and things," Tom actually laughed but true to form, only briefly.

"Don't be daft, Tom." She flipped her wrist and her hand landed on his shoulder as a gesture of chastisement.

Lally arrived about noon with her pile of books, had a few drinks as though Saturday night never happened and dismissed herself until the evening. The day drifted slowly along with nothing out of the ordinary happening. Customers came and went and the day got hotter and hotter. No one appeared from Nana's place; there was no shopping to do for Mag and Mark's new found friend was the most important person in his life at present. Richard was out, Tom was preparing a meal and Mag was in the bar. Mag closed early and went for a slow, predetermined walk to Leda's with the specific intention of increasing her wardrobe. Tom rested upstairs in the flat basking in his privacy. Mag opened up the pub again at five o'clock and before she could get back behind the bar, Lally was beside her asking for her usual. Between coughing bouts she steadily consumed the best part of a bottle of gin by eight. The novelty of being 'under new management' and that the first drink was 'on the house' had worn off by now, so no scroungers were around reducing the crowd to mostly regulars and some tourists. Since it was so quiet, Mag decided to join the others on the float committee. She called Tom down from upstairs and joined Megan, Lally, Ieuan and Dowie at Frank's table near the dartboard. He normally stayed at home with his sister on Mondays, except for last Monday. Probably to recover from an overdose of chapel. Mag supplied complimentary drinks for everyone, she knew their fancy by now. When she joined them they were about to draw up a proposal.

"Well Mag, firstly, Beryl could not come tonight, I'll go and see her after the meeting. Secondly, this is what we thought we might do," said Megan who had appointed herself spokesperson. The others instinctively approved of the office since she was so professional at running things. "We can get Beryl and you, if you like, plus some of the girl darters to dress in basques and short dresses with of course, plenty of stocking tops, 'spenders, a good cleavage and strings of beads." Mag slyly scrutinised the proximity where Dowie and Ieuan were sitting but there was no obvious response. "The men will have bright coloured shirts, dicky-bows and if possible, boaters, which Ieuan can try and get from the amateur drama group. He agreed - Lally can modify the dresses we used last year and she has about three basques. Myf's boy and yours, Mag, can black up and go on the float as boot-boys or something like that... The theme for the float will be New Orleans Sound 1920 and we could have a cassette player blasting out jazz... According to Dowie, Selwyn is a traditional jazz collector and he will record some music onto tape for us."

Mag felt a little let down since she hadn't been more involved but equally so, she didn't have to face prolonged exposure to her Sunday audience. "Well, you seem to have it all sewn up, good."

"Thanks Mag, we thought we would have another meeting at the end of the week, just to check everything is going to plan." Meeting closed at nine-thirty, documented Megan.

They distributed themselves about the pub except for Megan who, as promised, went to visit Beryl. There were several of the leggy darters practising on the board. Mag went over to them and explained what the meeting was all about and suggested they might help. The response was overwhelming judging from the squeals they produced.

"That's what we want," Ieuan said to Dowie. "Lots of gorgeous girls surrounded by princely young men." Having an audience, he shouted across to the girls, "We'll be there," and made an affected symbol with his arm. The girls giggled, which was the sign for Ieuan to walk over and play darts with them. They knew him of old and just amused themselves at his expense.

"Dirty old sod! He should know better, a married man of his age." Lally was approaching her inebriated stage.

Mag was getting excited at the proposed idea for the Carnival and told Tom all the details.

Slowly drinking his beer which was in fine form despite the hot weather, Dowie wondered whether he had done the right thing by selling.

The daily routine of the pub more-or-less repeated itself with the occasional stranger visiting. Mark was already less interested in the beach and Richard was off with his friends after his daily chores and showed no interest in the Carnival. Myfanwy's response was the opposite. She had been appointed head cook and bottle washer and was highly motivated. She had already decided how to decorate the lorry which Dowie had ordered from the Brewery. It was a brewer's dray so she knew the area of the floor space and this was to be fully occupied. Mag was constantly on the phone to Lally between her bar duties and her frequent excursions to the shops. Tom mentioned to her several times about controlling her spending but it fell on deaf ears. Secretly, he was delighted with Mag's transformation. Her whole attitude to life appeared to be more exciting. She was doing things in bed that Tom did not realise were possible. The source of her information remained a mystery. Perhaps it was there all the time but not exploited. The evolution of Mag was not the only improvement the Tremletts experienced, Mag was also shopping for Tom. She got him to wear expensive shirts with white collars and bold stripes instead of his usual block check. She also bought him a fine leather waistcoat which was to be worn in the winter. His general appearance was progressing from a middle aged countenance to more like the sartorial elegance of Ieuan, without the garnish of gold.

It was decided that Wednesday would be their weekly night off together. According to Beryl, it was usually a quiet night and she could handle the situation on her own. They went to see Mark and Mag's parents for a few hours and then decided to visit some of their rivals in the town culminating in a meal at the Light of Asia. When they arrived back at Ty Gwyn, Beryl was wiping the glasses and the last customers of the night, Dowie and Ieuan were preparing to go.

"Lally rang, she's bringing in the costumes on Friday for a fitting. I've got my own basque, Mag."

"Any black stockings?"

"Of course, fishnets." Ieuan did not reply, he just grinned at Beryl.

"How was tonight, Beryl?"

"OK, Tom. We had a crowd of fellas in who were on a course at the College."

"It was the football crowd," jumped in Ieuan.

Beryl ignored him. "As I was saying, we had a crowd of young fellas in. One of the barrels ran out but luckily Dowie was around and he changed it for me."

"Thanks, Dowie. I thought you could change a barrel, Beryl?"

"Yeah, but we were busy with the crowd when it happened."

"Oh, I see."

"What's wrong with you Tom? Thick or something? It was obvious to me, and you know full well that Beryl can change a barrel," belittled Mag.

Tom was annoyed at Mag's sarcasm and reacted sharply. "All right! Don't harp on it. I made a mistake, all right!" He moved off in the direction of the toilet with a dual purpose in mind. The second was to check that no one had blocked the drains or flooded it out. This was one of his final jobs at night and that included the Women's, which he hated.

"Are you ready Beryl? I'm going your way and I'll drop you off if you like. I've brought the car because I've been to Shrewsbury for an Area Referees' meeting." Making sure everyone heard as he was leaving he said, "Now about these fishnets..." and disappeared through the door.

"He only does it for show," said Dowie apologetically.

"I can see that," said Mag.

"He really is a very nice lad, never runs anyone down and will go out of his way to help. He does a lot of work for charity with Megan. They are very close but there's nothin' in it, they're like brother and sister. You should hear them arguing sometimes, it can get very heated, particularly when it's over politics." Dowie excused himself. Tom closed up and another day was history.

Friday evening was the time for the fitting. Lally dropped the clothes in lunchtime but had to excuse herself from the evening for personal reasons. Beryl, Mag and the three darters previously contacted turned up. Ieuan was there but he was told quite categorically by Mag that he was to stay in the bar. The girls moved upstairs. Mag was a little shy when the girls started to undress. She could only vaguely recall such a previous experience at PE lessons in school. The girls did not hesitate and totally disrobed for they had to decide who was wearing what and the basques were accompanied by scanty briefs. Eventually Mag succumbed and wondered what all the fuss was about.

There was a lot of moving around, laughing and the occasional scream that could be detected in the bar. Ieuan shuffled around on his seat nervously and mentioned to Dowie that he would like to be a fly on the wall up there. His curiosity got the better of him and he stretched across the counter, as if to disclose a secret and said to Tom, "Do you think they want some drinks?"

Tom replied swiftly, "Yes, I'm sure, if you're paying." Reminding himself that the girls were wasting drinking time up there. Ieuan immediately ordered five individual drinks all of which he knew by heart. The euphoria of the expected festivities put Tom in a frivolous mood and he said to Ieuan, "Would you like to take them up yourself?"

"Who me?"

"Yes you!" Tom handed him the tray of drinks.

As Ieuan left through the door leading to the flat, Tom immediately phoned Mag to warn her. Upstairs went quiet except for Ieuan's voice proclaiming that he was coming with drinkypoos. Tom and Dowie were silently anticipating the outcome. The rest of the patrons saw Ieuan go upstairs, but they were not sure what was going on. Tom came around from behind the bar, looked up at the ceiling and said, "Any minute now, Ssh!" He reassured an old couple in the corner by putting a finger to his mouth. The silence was eerie, like waiting for an impending disaster to strike. They heard the flat door open and all hell let loose. The tray of drinks crashed to the ground followed by pandemonium; the ceiling was pulsating. Amid this commotion there were the muffled sound of a man's voice declaring his innocence. A pair of trousers went past the open window of the pub and landed on the pavement. There was then even more noise and commotion followed by a pair of highly coloured underpants flying past the window. The flat door then opened and closed very quickly. Everyone in the bar was now aware of Ieuan's plight and could hear him slowly creaking his way downstairs. The door open a little and Ieuan poked his head in.

"Could you get my trousers from outside Dowie, please."

Tom stepped forward with the garments he had retrieved earlier and gave them to the bedraggled Ieuan. A little while elapsed and then he emerged combing his hair as the final touch. "Bloody hell! That was really something. All those naked girls pushing and prodding. It was really frightening."

"For the girls or you?" teased Dowie.

Having by now regained his confidence and noticing the two young girls by the dartboard, he said, "Hey! For the girls of course."

The girls tittered and the old couple in the corner chuckled quietly to themselves. Dowie was probably laughing but it was difficult to know with all that facial hair, and Tom actually laughed out loud, again. The carefree atmosphere of Llanrheidol was beginning to work on Tom as well as Mag.

The commotion upstairs got even louder and Tom had to buzz Mag. Eventually the fitting was complete and the girls returned to the bar. Ieuan was the centre of attraction, which inflated his ego even more.

Megan walked in straight from her sanative labours which today included a car accident, two broken arms and a heart attack, and ordered a half of Bass. The committee, except for Lally, moved towards her like moths attracted to a flame. They all gathered at an empty table and sat down. Mag explained why everyone was so animated.

Megan looked straight a Ieuan and said, "I'll bet he had his pretty pants on?"

Dumbfounded at the comment from Megan since she was not present at the audacious occasion, Mag questioned, "How did you know that?"

"Ieuan and I go back a long way. In fact, I think he prepares for these events. She looked over at Ieuan and gave a loving smile which would not be unfamiliar on a mother recognising her child at a prize-giving. The meeting carried on and the activities in the pub settled down to a low murmur. All was nearly ready for next Saturday's Carnival.

Over the next few days, Mag eventually managed to catch Rolff and questioned him about his blue boots. "I wear them because I like blue. Normally they should have bright yellow laces but I couldn't find any."

Mag recalled seeing these bright coloured boots for sale in Bristol but thought they were for girls since heavy boots were all the rage with the emancipated young women. It made her think but not comment. Diverting she said, "How about your name, Rolff? Is it with two F's or a PH?"

"It's my second name, after Sir Rolph Coalmining, under whom my mother served during the war."

"Don't believe him, it's because he was sick," said one of his pals who put an arm around his neck and pulled him back from the bar spilling his drink.

"Stop that, you bloody fool, you're wasting good ale." Rolff wriggled free from the grip, said something in his pal's ear and they reverted to their childish antics. None of the others had blue boots.

"Are you performing at the Carnival?" asked Mag realising afterwards that she had opened herself up to some stupid abuse.

"Only on girls and beer. We are going to finish a pub off though." He was implying that his group were going to select a pub at random and drink it dry. It was a common student trick during Rag week. If the publican was tipped off he stocked up but if not it could be irritating to the regulars. The more discerning imbibers usually removed a particular brand of beer from the establishment.

Tom was serving with Mag and overheard Rolff's ramblings. In the hope of planting a germ of an idea in his head he shouted over the bar, "I hope you don't intend to hit us and the Bass?" He had extra in for the Carnival anyway.

Since their residency in Llanrheidol, Fridays and Saturdays had taken on a whole new meaning. It was no longer the time to relax, do a bit in the garden and watch the box in the evening. There was no garden, and television was now a thing of the past, although Tom did record the occasional nature programme or good play, both of which he enjoyed when allowed to relax. Apart from traditional jazz, these were interests Tom and Selwyn had in common although they didn't know it.

The day of the Carnival had arrived, Dowie had booked the dray for ten o'clock and it was already outside the pub. It occupied a large area of road but there was enough space for small cars to pass. Other vehicles had to reverse and go another way. Most townsfolk were aware of this and accepted this inconvenience on Carnival Day. Later the streets would be sealed off to traffic anyway. Myfanwy was the first to ascend the dray. Her job was to get it clean and tidy before the construction of the display. All the committee, except Lally, were in the pub getting the boards and bunting ready.

"I think we should put up a Bass sign, after all, the Brewery has supplied the dray free."

"Tom, for God's sake! It's already been designed and the Bass sign is in there somewhere."

"All right, I'll leave you to it, Mag."

"Yes, clear off!"

Tom hid himself behind the bar where he was to reside for the interval of the Parade. He nervously rubbed a spot on the bar made by a smudge of glue used to fix the bunting. Megan was watching Myfanwy and as soon as she finished her chore she gave the command and all the decorations were moved out onto the pavement. Myfanwy produced a small set of steps which made access to the lorry much easier for the boss who refused to wear jeans.

Myfanwy produced a plan of the distribution of the various articles and construction commenced. They all beavered away in a very orderly fashion, Dowie doing the large signs, Mag helping him, Ieuan with Megan following behind putting up bunting to disguise some of the structural flaws. After some time Myfanwy materialised with a tray containing large mugs of tea and the familiar Digestives. Work immediately stopped and Megan stepped down and back from the vehicle and cast her eye over the partially constructed float. "It's coming on nicely. We should have it done by twelve." Ieuan was at her side and confirmed the statement.

"Let's have a photo!" exclaimed Mag. "A sort of before and after. I'll go and get Tom's." She jumped down from the lorry and quickly returned with an expensive looking camera.

"D'you know how to use that?" inquired Dowie.

"No, Tom's coming out to do the necessary."

"Come on then, all up on the lorry." Tom took several photos of the group mostly posed with Cheshire cat-like grins, except for Ieuan who insisted on doing silly things with his hands and legs.

"That's it, all finished. I like the floral decorations on the wheels, it gives it a professional touch. We'll meet here again at one-thirty for the start at two. I'm going for a wander round to have a look at the competition." Megan left, the others were drawn into the pub for a well deserved drink. Lally came in just after they had settled around a table.

"Where have you been all morning? As you can see, we've finished all the decorating."

"I've got this terrible cough, Mag and I had to go to the doctors. He's given me some antibiotics." She sat down with the gang and immediately lit up a cigarette.

"D'you know that you're the only one of us who smokes?"

"You don't have to tell me that. I have desperately tried to give up but I just can't. I've even tried acupuncture and hypnotism but no good! How was the fitting last night?" Mag then preceded to tell her about the fun they had with Ieuan. She laughed, coughed, laughed, coughed, coughed, laughed until she became almost exhausted and put the cigarette out in the ash tray. "Bloody fags!"

All the participants had gathered by now and were putting on their outfits either in the toilets or the more shy ones, upstairs in the flat. Ieuan was too excited to bother playing around and sipped his ale. "This place smells like a brothel. Why do girls always put on scent when they undress?" No one replied. Ieuan like Dowie, only had to put on a bow tie, waistcoat and boater and some aftershave.

The float looked splendid in all its glory. There was a large disc at the front with *Ty Gwyn New Orleans Sound 1920* written on it in large patriotic red and green letters. Ieuan had a toy trumpet he got from Myfanwy's boy but Dowie was more sophisticated and sat on a decorated beer crate with a guitar. The girls were dotted around, some sitting with their legs dangling over the side of the lorry while others were moving around and dancing to the restricted music from the small recorder.

"We should have got a larger external speaker to amplify the music," came a comment from the planner.

"What the hell! WE can hear it!" said one of the darters in a basque and fishnet stockings, who was dancing around to the music. The decorated dray moved slowly away from the pub. Megan decided to follow on foot; she was not dressed like the rest. Lally excused herself and stayed behind with Tom.

As they approached the starting line and as if prearranged, a jazz band spotted them and immediately adopted them. This was a fantastic coincidence since not only did they look the part but they had now acquired the sound to go with it. The recorded music was instantly turned off and live music blasted its way around the float. The whole display came alive with some of the band joining the float while some of the girls joined the band. The display was the centre of attraction and was mobbed by people in the crowd, some singing and dancing with the scantily clad girls of Ty Gwyn and others among themselves. For physical reasons, Myfanwy remained on the float while Ieuan was going crazy jumping from the float to the ground running around for a while and then rejoining the lorry. With the combined effects of the effervescent atmosphere and the odd drop of tiddly, Dowie had forsaken his guitar, which was being used as a prop by Beryl and was flirting with Mag who was dressed as a Bordello Madam complete with a slit skirt to expose her second best fishnetted feature.

After seeing the band of revellers disappear around the corner, Lally and Tom returned to the empty pub since most of the town was involved with the Carnival in some way or another. Lally ordered her large G&T and Tom broke a hard and fast rule and pulled himself an early half pint. "Tell me Lally, what's wrong? I know you are not well from that cough of yours but it's not like you to refuse to go out with the girls. Something is definitely wrong, isn't it?"

She paused for a while as if trying to make up the words in her mind and then said, "Promise you won't tell a soul." Tom motioned. "Well I went to the doctor yesterday to complain about this persistent cough and he has referred me to a specialist in the hospital for an X-ray... It's on Monday, a bit fast for my liking, I'm worried."

"Don't worry, Lally," said Tom giving her hand a gentle, reassuring squeeze but furtively feeling disturbed. It brought back a similar rapid encounter for his mother who only lived six months after her X-ray. "They probably had a vacancy (bad choice of word, he thought to himself) and your doctor's request form was next on the list."

"Yes," said Lally not really convinced. "Can I have another?" pushing her glass towards Tom. They sat there for a while, both on the customers side of the bar chatting, generally about recent events, when in walked the Blue Bootees mob. Mag had given Rolff's crowd that title because they were so childish at times. Tom moved back behind the bar.

"We've come to relieve you of all your Bass," said the Lilliputian leader.

Tom was delighted but felt he had to show concern as convincingly as possible. "Oh! Why pick on me? You should be watching the Carnival procession?" He was no thespian.

"Sex pints, please."

"Sex?"

"Sorry, a Freudian slip, six pints."

Tom was amazed that Rolff had ever heard of Freud. On due deliberation Tom realised he really didn't know much about the Blue Bootees, only that they were piss-artists on weekends. "Dowie will know about them, I'll ask him," he mumbled.

"Your float is superb," said one of the larger Blue Bootees in a posh English accent. "Where did you get that rather charming jazz band?"

Tom answered with another question. "What jazz band? When they left here they only had recorded music."

"It's great! The musicians are jumping on and off the float and the girls as well. It's causing all sorts of commotion in town: it's the most popular float in the pageant. Everybody is dancing and running around like people possessed, fantastic! We would have stayed but we have a mission in life, well today. Six more pints, please, barkeep." Rolff, who was more concerned about the rapidity and not the strength of the pints consumed, commented, "Slow down you lot, we've got a barrel of drinking to do."

"Did you know anything about this jazz band, Lally?"

"No Tom, it's a complete mystery to me... All will be revealed on their return, I suppose?"

The Blue Bootees drank, Lally drank, but Tom stopped after about four halves despite the fact that he was off duty at five o'clock. The boys were going well, they were on the second firkin. The only problem was that these young, inexperienced, impetuous drinkers normally go for the weaker beers so they can drink more. The beer they were currently drinking was strong and four of them were already showing signs of wavering. The frequency of their visits to the toilet being a tell-tale sign.

Suddenly the street came alive with music. It was the dray returning several decibels louder and with all but one of the performers with which it left. The missing girl met one of her old boyfriends home on leave and that sealed his fate. Tom intended to take some photos on their return but chaos reigned and he decided against it. He took some later in the pub when the festivities were in full swing. The first to appear in the pub door was Mark.

"Daddy, Daddy, we won, look!" He held up a medium sized, battered, well worn chromium plated cup... "We were the best in town."

"Oh fantastic! Let's go and show everyone in the pub." Tom took the cup from Mark's little hand and held it aloft as he walked into the pub. "Look folks, we won the overall prize for the best float, I think."

"Yes, that's right, you know," slurred Mag as she fell into the pub just behind him. Tom gave the cup to Lally to examine and the Blue Bootee's leader, who was the only one of the group mobile enough to reach the bar. Noise and requests for drinks filled the pub. Beryl, who was less incapable than Mag, stepped in and helped Tom satisfy the insatiable cravings of the crowd. Myfanwy, who was even worse than Mag, did a little jig in the corner by the fireplace, then slept. It reminded Tom of a jelly just removed from its mould. He later discovered that the beer crate on the float was not empty and the whisky bottles did not contain cold tea. It was a contribution given by Megan and Ieuan to help things along. Mark was overwhelmed with the occasion and started to cry with excitement. No one noticed as he crept upstairs to the solitude of Nana, who was doing something in the kitchen. Myfanwy's son, who was a little older than Mark, had obviously indulged somewhere along the line, was dozing under Frank's table. Rolff remained with Lally talking gibberish and the posh one who was the only other Blue Bootee vaguely aware of his surroundings had stopped drinking. They never did deplete the pub of Bass. The excitement carried on for several hours but gradually got quieter as the inebriated musicians surrendered to the temptations of Bacchus.

Tom was still behind the bar at six-thirty and Lally still drinking but at a much slower pace. Most of the revellers had left by now and the pub looked like a battle ground. Empty glasses all over the place, discarded crisp packets and crusts from sandwiches which Nana had made and given out to the crowd. It was just an excuse for her to observe the commotion at first hand and check on Grandad. Megan, who was relatively sober, informed Nana that they hadn't seen him since the start of the Parade. Tom called a taxi and Myfanwy left with her sleepy son, reassuring Tom that she would be back again that night. Mag was upstairs with her family preparing for the night's vigil in the pub. After innumerable cups of coffee and a shower, which was now fixed, she buzzed Tom and asked if he could hold on until seven. He agreed, had another Bass and proceeded to tidy up the place since it was completely deserted except for Lally.

"Look at this, Lally," he held up a pair of briefs. "I didn't see them come off, from the colour, they are from one of the basque girls." He put them in his pocket and carried on cleaning up. Unbeknown to Tom it was done on purpose, one of the girls changed upstairs and brought the panties down and put them under the table where some of the musicians and girls were larking about. She then forgot about them and the joke fizzled out. Lally was beginning to wilt by now and she requested that Tom call her a taxi. It came quickly and she left. The pub was now totally deserted and cleaned up as much as possible. Tom had time to contemplate on the day's events. He also had a spell to look at the cup in more detail. Llanrheidol Carnival Best Display, was engraved on the cup and a little chromium plated disc showed previous winners. 'Must get our name put on there,' thought Tom. 'I'll put it up on the top shelf in the centre of the malts.' He could hear Mag coming down the stairs so he poured himself a pint and came around from behind the bar.

She was equipped with a pretty floral dress and a hangover. "That was really something," she said dolefully. "I don't think I've enjoyed myself so much for years." She suddenly livened up and said, "Well! What d'you think of the cup then?" Tom showed her where he had placed it for maximum display. "We must get our name put on it."

"You bet! It will be done tomorrow, Mag, don't worry about it."

Mag proceeded to tell Tom all about the goings on during the Parade, purposefully missing out Dowie's amorous behaviour. "There was one obvious tourist who appeared to be fascinated by our float, every time we turned a corner, he was there taking pictures. The girls got used to him after a while and as soon as they saw him they would start posing and throwing kisses. He must have used miles of film. I wonder if he will come in here tonight?" It was so quiet compared with the afternoon and such an anticlimax that Mag felt bored and hoped that someone would come in just to talk.

Frank was the first to appear, and before he had sat down Selwyn made an appearance. "You must have had one hell of an afternoon? Dowie is out cold and sleeping like a baby. Pint, please." Mag knew his tipple by now. "I saw the last part of the procession with the Army Cadet Band bringing up the rear. I was completely unaware of the jazz band and your float, otherwise I would have been there like a flash."

"It looks tidy now, but you should have been here this afternoon. You would have loved it, you know, the jazz band came back here and played until they drank themselves silly. They were apparently a band from down south who were on their way home. They stopped for a meal and noticed it was Carnival Day. They were going to march with the procession, you know, but as soon as they spotted us, that was it."

"You didn't happen to catch their name, did you, Mag?"

Tom spoke up and said that they were called the Abertawe Troggs.

"They're well known," said Selwyn. "God! I wish I'd been here," he stamped his foot firmly on the floor in anger. "They were on television last week..."

"Yes, I saw them."

"I didn't know you were into jazz, Tom...? There's not much going on here, I think I'll go to the Club." To Tom's surprise he said, "D'you fancy coming Tom? I can see that it's your evening off. You can tell me about the Troggs."

Tom felt it an honour to be asked. "Well... yes... if... Will you be all right on your own, Mag?" She had no objection and he left with Selwyn. The whole pub was now empty, even upstairs visitors had left. Mag walked around and had a quick look to see if anything had been left behind and then went back behind the bar where she felt comfortable with two umbrellas and a finger stall.

"Two halves of lager, please," requested a bespectacled pipe smoking gentleman, who was present during Ieuan's debagging the previous week. "You had a lovely, jolly float at the procession this afternoon. We enjoyed it so much, you certainly know how to enjoy yourselves here."

"We won the cup for the best float," said Mag, excitedly pointing to its resting place among the malts.

"I thought you might because your float was so much better than the rest."

"Thank you. Have those drinks on me." Mag was in a generous mood and Tom wouldn't know anyway.

Frank had overheard the conversation and swiftly approached the bar with an empty glass. "I missed it all this afternoon. I had to go to the farm for my sister."

"Well! You really missed a lot of fun, that's on me," she refilled his glass.

"*Diolch*!" He sat down by the dartboard.

"What do you think of that performance?" Megan rushed through the door holding out her arms to embrace Mag.

"Fantastic!" replied Mag. "How's your mother?"

"Same as usual, she saw the float from her window, she was quite excited... Who would have believed that a band of that calibre was waiting around the corner, I'm glad I followed you around now. Lady luck is on my side sometimes." Since Megan had assumed responsibility for the whole affair it was not unjustified for her to take personally the good bits with the bad. While they were indulging themselves on the marvellous effort Ieuan popped his head around the corner of the door and mentioned that he would see them on Monday. He had to referee a match tomorrow in Builth and he was travelling up tonight. "He's finished but he won't admit it," declared Megan. She stayed for most of the night and talked to Mag. A few boisterous youngsters came through and some holiday makers but on the whole it was a relatively peaceful night, much appreciated by Mag who was still nursing a headache.

* * * * *

Tom's Sunday started like any other future Sunday: big breakfast, clean beer pipes and get Sunday papers. Mag had recovered from Saturday's ordeal and couldn't wait to get in the bar to literally re-enact the great Carnival triumph. Sunday lunchtime was disappointing, only tourists who wanted a meal. The afternoon visit to Nana's house was a little tense. The question in the air was, what happened to Grandad? He did not come back to Ty Gwyn all day and arrived home at about one o'clock Sunday morning. Hungover, Grandad had no recollection of his whereabouts. Nana had no sympathy with his plight and was communicating by way of Mark. The child found this very funny since they were usually so talkative.

He didn't go straight out to play like he usually did, but sat on Tom's lap for a while. "Did you enjoy yesterday on the float?"

"Yes, I thought it was great... Somebody threw an egg at me but it missed."

"I didn't see that," said Mag.

"You were too busy dancing and drinking with Dowie." He snuggled his head into Tom's chest.

"Sorry for living!" She tickled him in the ribs. "You little fibber. He's always had a vivid imagination, you know," she pronounced with a slight sense of guilt in her voice. They left soon afterwards.

The evening reception was much better than Saturday's with some holiday makers, a few locals girls and Clem. The old folk appeared and thanked Mag profusely for her hospitality and regretfully mentioned that they were leaving early Monday morning on the coach. Dowie and Selwyn turned up, the former none the worst for his ordeal. Selwyn specifically asked for Tom. Mag buzzed upstairs and gave him the phone. "I've managed to get tickets for the Dylan Thomas play we were talking about last night in the Club." Obviously the response was positive because Selwyn confirmed, "Friday then." He replaced the phone, finished his beer and left.

Dowie could foresee that Mag was about to question him concerning Selwyn's behaviour, so he diverted the request by quickly turning to the Carnival cup. "I like where Tom's put the cup. It shows it off on the shelf among the malts." It was during this evening session that Dowie realised how attractive Mag had become to him. It all started as the result of the physical contact during the procession. Mag on the other hand, was completely oblivious to Dowie's feelings and regarded Saturday as an impromptu series of enjoyable events.

Dowie was never married although he had several girlfriends including Myfanwy but her only child was not his. When younger he was a very keen sportsman and didn't have time or the inclination for girls. He was still a keen angler but mostly in the lakes, since the salmon no longer ran in any numbers up the local rivers. There was a sudden lull in the conversation while Dowie finished off his drink and Mag seized this opportunity to satisfy her curiosity by saying, "Is Selwyn queer?" Dowie immediately stopped drinking and regurgitated the contents of his mouth down his beard. He put down his glass and embarrassingly wiped his face with a handkerchief.

"Selwyn queer? Christ! No, he's the opposite if anythin'. A few years ago he nearly lost his job at the College for bein' too familiar with some of his female students." Dowie could see the reason for her inquiry. "I think he is a lonely man and fanatical about jazz, live theatre and naturally, animals, but not necessarily in that order. If he likes someone, he makes a very good friend. We've been pals for years ever since he came to Llanrheidol as a student. We played together in the town's rugby team. He was handsome, rich and brainy, that's why he got the girls," he said with a hint of envy.

"Handsome, did you say?"

"Yeah! that was before his eyesight started to fail. Selwyn has mellowed a lot since then but still has a rovin' eye. You watch out! By the way, his surname is Cocappi, his father was Italian and he had a string of restaurants in South Wales. When he died he left them to Selwyn and his mother. Because of his name and reputation he is known to his students as Cockhappy or Cocky." Mag blushed, put her head down and nervously wiped the bar with a cloth. It was strange but after the familiarity on Saturday, Dowie felt he could communicate with Mag at a more intimate level than earlier in their relationship.

"Now there's a couple of real ones, as you know," Dowie voiced softly across the bar.

"Hello, dearies," said Gethin. "Heard you had a marvellous time yesterday. G&T for me and a Tia Maria with soda for Christin. There were a lot of big hairy musicians about, so I hear."

"Well...," Mag hesitated, "the trumpet player was bald and the banjo player a midget. Is that butch enough for you? But they got us the first prize, you know." Mag threw an arm in the air in triumph and pointed to the cup.

Tom came down and joined Dowie and Mag at the bar. "What's this I hear about you at the Uni Club, last night?" teased Dowie. Tom flushed.

Mag reacted, "I haven't heard about this. What did he do?" Mag faced Tom and before he could answer said, "I hope you didn't start on about Bass?"

"No, I didn't say anything about Bass... I couldn't help it, I put the panties..."

"Panties! What panties?"

"Listen Mag and I'll explain," said Tom forcibly. "I picked up a pair under the table by the door..." He pointed, they all moved their heads. "When I was cleaning up yesterday afternoon and put them in my pocket and then forgot about them... Fortunately, only Selwyn realised what I had in my hand. I assume the others just thought I was into black silk handkerchiefs." He produced the garment from his pocket and brazenly wiped his forehead.

Mag quickly grabbed the item of clothing from him and pushed it under the bar, "Really Tom! How embarrassing."

"Touché!" exclaimed Tom. Mag smiled and subconsciously touched the top button of her dress.

"Selwyn's a great character," carried on Tom. "He really made me feel at home in the College Club. There were no airs and graces like I thought..." He proudly announced that Selwyn was going to get him membership to the Mid-Wales Naturalists' Club.

"Isn't that for nudes?" asked Mag.

"Don't be stupid, that's naturists," said Gethin, who had overheard the conversation despite his preoccupation. He had been observing Christin at the dartboard talking to two young girls. Nobody except possibly another woman could understand the logic behind Mag's statement, but she said for anyone's ears, "Talking about nudes, does anyone know what Rolff does, you know, his job, the Blue Bootee boy?"

"You should have asked me, Mag. To start with they're certainly not nudists," said Dowie wryly.

"I know that, silly."

"I know all about that crowd from Selwyn. In fact, Rolff sometimes stays with us when he's had too much to drink. He's a research student in Selwyn's Department at the College. His research has somethin' to do with breedin' pure animals, I think they call it genetic engineering. He's a very bright lad but goes mad at weekends. Some of the others are also in the same Department, while one is a lawyer and another studies history, they're all studying for their Doctorates. That means they have to study something then write a book about it... Selwyn did his about fifteen year ago. He's a real doctor... a Ph.D."

"I thought it would be something like that," said Tom. "I had an inkling that they were educated from some of the words they use."

"Like marmalade?" uttered the ineloquent Clem, who was replenishing his glass at the bar. The ones in earshot smiled sympathetically. Sunday evening went out with a whimper.

Despite her presence on Saturday this was Lally's regular Llanrheidol day. She entered with a bag full of books, had a large G&T, and was about to disappear on her inevitable shopping spree when Mag decided to join her since Beryl was coming in to work. Tom was summoned from preparing meals. He had increased the variety of meals available on the menu because of his successful negotiations with Ifor Cigydd. Tom's business acumen never let him miss a bargain.

Mag came back with another blouse and skirt. She showed it to Beryl and then went upstairs on the pretext of helping Tom. The blouse was suitably displayed in the privacy of the flat.

"Very nice. Another see-through, you're going mad, but I must admit you are looking much younger and smarter than you used to." He unromantically carried on cutting up the meat with his blood stained hands.

"Ta, kind sir," she exclaimed. "I was talking to Lally over coffee this morning and again she brought up the question of her and me going on holiday. It's very difficult for both of us to get away at the moment. What do you think?"

Tom thought of Lally's condition and for the second time in many years recalled his mother's plight and the inevitable outcome. "When d'you intend on going and for how long?"

Her answer was spontaneous. "We thought the last week in August. Beryl said she would do extra nights and one of the girl darters who is not working..."

"Just a minute! When did you work all this out? On the float yesterday?"

She ignored his question and said, "She will work mornings, if you want her."

"Who's the darter?"

"Mary, the pretty one who used to work in Maynards before it closed down. She comes in on Fridays with her friend, Carol... They were wearing basques on the float."

Tom mused and then remembered. "Oh! The tall girl whose legs go right up to her armpits."

"Yeah! That's her." The holiday took preference to possessiveness.

"Can I think about it for a day or two?"

From Tom's intonation, Mag knew instinctively that he would agree. She turned, forgetting why she originally came upstairs, and returned to the bar.

"The postman dropped these letters in, Mag."

"Thanks Beryl. Most of them look like bills. Well, here's one from Bristol." She opened it at the bar where she was sitting without a drink. "It's from my friend Dulcie, she wants to come down for a few days. You'd like her, she's a great laugh, you know, always playing the fool. I'd better phone her because me and Lally are going on holiday in the last week of August."

"You managed to persuade him, then?" said Beryl with a hint of discomposure.

The covert excitement did not register with Mag and she replied, "Well, he said he would think about it but I know he will come round." Mag disappeared upstairs to tell Tom.

"I've missed old wrinkly, she was so uninhibited." Mag humoured him with a joke about house number seven.

"If the hot weather holds, she could sunbathe like in Bristol, on the flat roof of the pub, no one could see her there." Tom appeared quite agitated.

Mag put the phone down laughing all over her face. "Some of her jokes are disgusting. That's that, she's coming down on Friday for a few days but she's not bringing her husband. Dan had to go to London on union business." Tom knew otherwise.

"That's a pity," said Tom who had recently entered with some bar meals. Secretly he was not unduly concerned.

It was all going Mag's way. She felt unsettled so on the excuse of going for some travel brochures, she left Beryl in charge again. 'I wonder if Lally is in the library,' she thought to herself and by chance, she was right. Mag and Lally eventually arrived back at Ty Gwyn just before she was due to open up.

'About time.' Tom heard her opening the door downstairs.

"I'm fine Tom, I'll go straight into the bar." Mag had an armful of brochures and Lally a large bag of unread books. They trundled into the bar, bent almost double with their burdens. Lally dropped the bag on the floor and attempted to straighten her naturally bent spine, climbed up on a stool and started thumbing through brochures. After dispensing a large G&T they both sat flicking over pages until they found the right country. "We did decide on the Greek Islands didn't we?"

"Yes," said Lally without even looking up. "What about that island Gethin and Christin went to?"

"Don't be silly, Lally. Imagine what people would say."

"Yes, I suppose you're right. We are living in Llanrheidol, not Cardiff." They eventually decided on Rhodes.

"I'll go in tomorrow and see what they have on offer."

"Don't forget, it's near the time the kids go back to school Mag, so we should get a better bargain." Mag hesitated. She remembered about Mark and his new school but in the heat of the moment chose to leave it for later, reassuring herself that Tom would settle the problem with her parents.

Monday night was busy. All the occupants of the float plus a few other girls and later Megan gathered in a makeshift group around the bar and discussed Saturday's events. It started off some horseplay from Ieuan and the whole atmosphere was reminiscent of that afternoon. Mag turned the music up from behind the bar and some started to dance. Mag in her usual diplomatic way explained to several holiday makers what it was all about.

After some time of post-carnival entertainment, Lally, who was known for her absent-mindedness said, "I've just remembered something, you must hear this. It's about Saturday night." Mag turned the music down. "When I got home I didn't feel very well, I think it was the bumpy taxi (a jeer came from somewhere in the crowd) and before I could get into the cottage I was sick on the lawn. I didn't move from the spot and I was sick again. The second time I was sick the previous mess appeared to have moved to the left. Eventually I went into the cottage thinking no more of it. When I got up the following morning I went out to hang some clothes on the line and guess what? The bloody tortoise was covered in sick. Sorry about the swearing but it was so funny." Everybody was hysterical.

Ieuan had to interject on principle. "Did it have bits of red in it? All sick's got red in it."

"Ieuan, d'you mind? I'm tryin' to eat a con carne," shouted Dowie. That made the situation even funnier. Tom could hear the laughter upstairs and finally came down to have it explained by Mag.

"Another good night, Mag." Tom was tilling up.

"In more ways than one." The closeness of the holiday was stirring in her mind. She had never been away without Tom before.

"When will it all end?"

"Never, I hope Tom."

Dulcie arrived in her Mini about lunchtime on Friday. Tom could see her from the upstairs window in the kitchen and went to greet her. "You found us all right then."

"Yes, your map was easy to follow. I'm parked on a yellow line."

"Give me the keys, I'll put it in the backyard out the way." Tom couldn't help noticing the dark wrinkled skin on her neck as his eyes focused on her lowcut blouse. "Plenty of sun in Bristol, is there? We've got a place for you on the flat part of the roof, if you like?" Dulcie didn't understand what he was saying and shrugged it off. "If you want to see Mag, she's in the bar." He pointed to the door. "I'll take your case up, I'm in the middle of cooking."

Dulcie had a magnificent reception from Mag and naturally Dulcie reciprocated. They did not stop talking and even carried on after the pub closed. This garrulity was beginning to get on Tom's nerves so he hit on the idea of telling them to go out somewhere. Instantly the solution came to him. "Why don't you two go up on the roof and do some sunbathing before the weather breaks. It's very private up there, no one will see you." Dulcie now realised what Tom was talking about when she first arrived.

Mag said to Dulcie, "What do you think? We can always look around the town tomorrow?"

"That suits me fine, is the weather likely to turn bad?"

"No, Tom only said that to get rid of us. I know how his mind works."

"Do we need costumes?"

"Only if you are worried about Tom. He will be bringing us up some drinks later on."

"What drinks?"

"You don't mind bringing us something later, do you?" He affirmed the request.

The two disappeared. Tom finished his work and sat down essentially to rest his aching leg from too much standing. The other purpose was to look at the transcript of the play he was going to see that evening. When he came across Polly Garter it triggered his memory and he remembered the girls. "Oh! They'll be parched." He collected their refreshments and took them to the roof. When he got there he was pleasantly shocked. Mag was actually sunbathing topless and Dulcie was completely naked but lying on her front.

"Hi! You took your time. I'm getting myself ready for Rhodes." She immediately realised what she had said and modified it by stating that it depended on him.

The scene made him feel at ease. "All right! You can go."

Mag smiled and expressed her gratitude by giving Tom his usual peck on the cheek, Dulcie lifted herself up on her elbows and took a glass of beer with a ribbing grin on her face. She had a soft spot for Tom and knew he used to observe her sunbathing in Bristol. Tom couldn't help admiring her smooth, firm, round, bottom and concluded that the wrinkles must be localised. This was confirmed when she turned over and sat up to drink. Mag uneasily passed her a towel, which she placed in her lap. For the second time as landlord, Tom experienced the electrifying stimulus of sexual awakening but this time Mag did not notice.

Another glorious week. Mag and Lally booked their holiday and Tom was delighted with his trip to the theatre. Dulcie seemed to be enjoying herself more than anyone and getting darker by the day. The bar residents inquisition about the extent of the sunbathers' tans was never revealed. Like any respectable landlord, Tom retained their confidences.

Dowie had taken a shine to this boisterous belle from Bristol. He was at present a man of means from his sale of the pub and had time on his hands. By the end of the week, Dulcie had seen more seaside towns and night spots than Mag knew existed in Mid-Wales. Despite this, Dulcie reserved her afternoons for Mag and Tom; mostly on the roof. Tom knew every wrinkle by now. With time he became quite complaisant and not only served them with drinks but also suntan applications to inaccessible places, when desired.

One night Dulcie did not come back to the pub. She phoned and told Mag that the Mini had broken down and they had to wait for help. Tom was a little uneasy but kept quiet. Messing around with married women was definitely not within his code of ethics. To cap it all, he found a pair of tights ensheathed briefs stuffed down the backseat of the Mini when he was getting it ready for Dulcie's departure. He confronted her with the garments and she made a poor excuse, knowing full well he would not make a fuss or tell Mag. Tom's opinion of Dowie would never be the same again. He felt that Dulcie was in a relaxed yet vulnerable position and he had taken advantage.

On the whole it was an excellent week, socially. All four of them went out on their night off and had an enjoyable evening in town. It was a most peculiar week for Tom, he felt Dulcie had taken him totally into her confidence and that her frivolous displays of disarray were not to tantalise him. They were simply an extension of her topless reaction to the constraints of middle class morality. Her longing to break away had been restricted by living so long with Dan. Perhaps the Tremletts' move to Llanrheidol and their invitation were well timed and essential to keep her rational. Despite her infidelity she was still Tom's favourite vivacious vamp since she always conducted herself with dignity. She was never improperly dressed in the flat when the relatives were around.

The balmy month of August rolled on with the weather remaining surprisingly good for the West coast but the nights were getting shorter. There was plenty of trade and Ty Gwyn was very popular with locals and tourists alike. The bar meals were becoming so popular that Tom spent most of the time preparing them, Mag was about to go on her holiday with Lally and Tom was becoming apprehensive about the change of staff. Mag reassured him that all was well, she had worked out an itinerary so that he would know who was on and when. Tom could not spare the time to drive them to the airport so they caught the train. It was a strange feeling for Tom because he lacked the confidence to run a pub on his own, Mag was the mainstay. They got through the first lunchtime session without any problems; Beryl closed up and brought the keys to Tom upstairs and left. Richard was hanging around in the lounge of the flat as though he wanted to say something but was waiting for the correct moment. Eventually he spoke. "I've decided to join the Army, Dad."

Tom wasn't surprised, he felt that this was where he would eventually end up. He had enjoyed Army Cadets in Bristol for many years. Tom felt he had to say something simply to reassure the lad that he did care about him.

"Do you know what you are doing? As you know, I was in the mob in '55 doing my National Service which was compulsory then..." He paused for a moment and said, "You don't want to learn just to kill, do you?"

"Dad! They give you Army Entrance Tests, to find out what part of the Army you are best suited for."

"Have you taken one?"

"Yes, yesterday. I won't know the results until later on. They will apparently give me a choice of about three jobs."

"It's so different from my day, we had no choice. And they certainly weren't called jobs. Have you anything in mind?"

"I thought catering, like you, and when I come out I could start up a restaurant of my own."

"That's very sensible of you. Obviously you don't want to make the Andy Clyde Commandos your career. All right, you can start next week helping me in the kitchen... I'll pay you."

"OK, you're on, next week..." He looked dumbfounded and said, "What did you say about Andy Clyde?"

"When I was in the mob they used to call us in the Army Catering Corps the Andy Clyde Commandos, all corps had a nickname."

"But who was Andy Clyde, was he made up like Kilroy?"

"Have you heard of Hopalong Cassidy?" Tom drew a blank. "He was one of those old cowboys in B movies. In fact, he was in a film last week on telly, just after the Abertawe Troggs." Tom drew another blank. "His sidekick was a mindless clown called Andy Clyde. A lot of their films were made in the '40s when the war was on and they were very popular... It would be interesting to know what the nickname of the ACC is now. If you get in you must let me know."

Richard became much more relaxed and started to talk to his father about how he felt leaving Bristol and some of the great mates he had found in Llanrheidol. In spite of that, he wanted to see a bit of the world before settling down.

"You're good at figures Dad, aren't you?"

"All right, if it's not too complicated."

"One of the tests we had was number sequences and I just could not figure out one of them. It was: quarter - half - one - three - six - twelve - twenty-four - and... I made it forty-eight."

"Oh, that was quite popular as a party piece just after we changed to decimalisation in '71. To be exact, 15 February which was Grandad Tremlett's birthday. It's the old money: farthing - halfpenny - penny - thru'pence - sixpence - shilling - florin and halfcrown, which was thirty pennies... thirty is the answer."

"How the bloody hell did they expect us to know that. We've only been taught decimal money?"

"Richard!"

"Sorry, but it is stupid, isn't it?"

Tom shrugged his shoulders, cocked his head on one side and used the well worn cliché, "That's the Army."

Richard had reverted to the talkative child Tom had loved so much in his pre-teens when life was an adventure. He took Mark and his pal to the beach again on several afternoons and did his jobs without being told. Since Tom was going to have help with the catering he decided to increase the menu to a choice of about seven different bar meals.

The week without Mag was much less tense than he anticipated. He only employed Mary for one morning because Beryl insisted on working extra hours. Beryl was so helpful, his only objection was that she lingered around and chatted a bit too much after closing at night. But even so, it wasn't the same without Mag and the late night sessions she so carefully staged.

On Tuesday night when Mag phoned from Rhodes, Tom was upstairs and Beryl buzzed him to come to the bar. Dowie talked to her in the meantime but put the phone down before Tom could get there. His excuse was that she had run out of money. Tom was very disappointed, but had no way of ringing back. As expected the pub received the inevitable postcard illustrating the flute playing satyr of Greek mythology with the enormous erect penis. There are currently at least four pubs in Llanrheidol proudly displaying this unnatural phallic exhibitionism, but the number depends on how many of the townsfolk do Greece that year. 'It's the sort of word you don't normally retain,' thought Tom. "What do you call it, Megan?" Tom pointed to the postcard pinned to the shelf below the cup.

"Priapism."

"That's it."

There were a few inane comments from Ieuan and giggles from some of the girls. Tom thought it immature but Dowie was indifferent, having seen it all before. Selwyn seized on it as an ideal opportunity to air his dislike of package holidays.

"Is that all people think of when they go to Greece?" He proceeded to expound to all within earshot the wonders of Greek mythology and how numerous animals were named after gods and goddesses. "Remember the jelly blob which changed shape when you looked at it under the microscope in biology lessons at school. It was called Amoeba..."

"I remember," interrupted Tom, showing some interest.

"I preferred the sex lessons," said someone by the dartboard.

Selwyn carried on. "One species is called *Amoeba proteus*. Proteus was a Greek god who lived in the sea and was capable of changing shape at will."

"Boring! Boring," said one of the more adventurous girls near the dartboard. Selwyn could give a terrifying glance if he felt offended but she caught him in a good mood.

"Sorry, I'm talking shop again." Everyone went back to their own business. Tom suggested that it was time they started thinking about darts teams. Would they have a men's and a women's team or two mixed teams? Tom was not surprised to be told to keep the sexes separate.

Mag was due back at any moment, on the three o'clock train. Tom took Mark to meet it. He was so excited when he saw them he had tears in his eyes and couldn't stop jumping up and down. He ran to Mag as soon as the train stopped. She picked him up and hugged him. Lally was not too well so she called a taxi and went straight home. "She's caught a bug or something that made her cough." Mag left Llanrheidol with one suitcase and came back with two more holdalls. She kissed Tom endearingly and then walked on in front with Mark, leaving Tom to carry the baggage.

Tom decided to open up to give her time with the family. After giving out the presents and seeing them leave for home quite late that night, she decided to come down to the bar. Richard stayed upstairs and watched the television.

She received a wonderful reception, especially from the girls. It was even possible to see signs of Dowie smiling and Ieuan was full of his usual sexual innuendoes about nude beaches and randy Greeks. It was a pleasant evening, busy but not hectic and Mag fell straight back into the routine, although she did spend more time socialising on the wrong side of the bar. Tom gave her all the news but it was not until they were upstairs, after closing, that he mentioned Richard's future career. She was not surprised. During this late night conversation Tom discovered the answer to the mysteriously shortened phone call from Rhodes. She thought the line had been disconnected. He did not pursue the matter.

Tom was concerned about Lally and the way she quickly left for home. "How's Lally been?"

Mag was baffled at his concern but answered, "She was very slow, it took her about an hour to get up and start preparing for breakfast. After a good cough, a ciggy and a small G&T, she was ready."

"That was a bit early for a drink? Did you join her?"

"My God, No! I wanted a cuppa... She got very niggly if we were on the beach after about three, you know. I think she was used to having a nap. And forgetful! I spent a lot of time going back to places to get something she had forgotten, she was always too puffed to go back... But it was not all gloom and doom though, and we did have lots of fun... One particular bar we went to was full of queers and they obviously thought we were a couple of lezzies."

"Why?" inquired Tom, who could not see the connection.

"Because we were together and in a queers' bar."

Tom pulled a face, he was still not convinced, "But you didn't know it was a queer's bar."

"Exactly! Never mind! Well, we got on so well there without any aggravation that we went there every night for drinks. They were not expensive but you know how mean Lally is and at night she always carried with her a small bottle of the duty free. Actually a half bottle she bought on the plane. This was to keep topping up her first drink until the ice ran out. She also carried a disc camera in the same bag. One evening when she was a little tiddly she obviously did not put the top of the bottle on tight enough and it leaked out over the camera. This started the camera flashing. She panicked because she thought it might catch on fire and emptied the contents of her bag on the table including the bottle of gin. Flashing camera and gin bottle caused an uproar and it was the running joke for the rest of the week. It's the first time I have ever seen Lally blush. Needless to say the bottle was not used in that bar again."

"What about the camera?"

"I think it died of alcoholic poisoning." They both laughed and hugged each other. Tom said how good it was to see her home and they went to bed.

Mag put the phone down. "Poor Lally, what with her cold and all, you know, she now tells me that when she got back home there was a letter telling her that her ex-husband has died. She's not going to the funeral because they had been divorced for years and his relatives didn't want her there." Tom disappeared into the cellar and she carried on messing around in the bar and getting in Myfanwy's way. Normally Mag would not be in the bar so early but this morning, she had a compulsion to check for herself that everything was in the right place, and during this inspection Lally rang.

* * * * *

Over the last month, Selwyn had moved out of Dowie's place and was buying a two bedroomed cottage. Rolff had taken Selwyn's old flat.

It was beginning to feel like autumn with the cool evening mist and the smell of burning leaves emanating from shrouded town backgardens. College students were beginning to drift back and the town started to swell to the volume of the summer months. On the advice of Dowie, Tom was going to allow them into Ty Gwyn but they had to behave themselves like anyone else. The main culprits were the first year students recently released from their maternal ties. The worst behaved ones were the compulsory three-times-a-Sunday chapel going girls.

Darts in the winter months was on a Thursday, so Lally made a seasonal change for her day in Llanrheidol. The garden, which was less attractive at this time of year, was also too physically demanding since the onset of her affliction.

Term started in earnest with gangs of youngsters frequenting the pub on their busy way up town. Some were wearing L plates to signify they had not consumed the requisite amount of alcohol to become Members. Mag found it all very amusing while Tom tolerated their innocent activities since it kept them in gainful employment. Most of the tourists had gone, but numerous office workers had cottoned on to the bar meals. Together with the regulars, town gangs and students they were extremely busy on Friday nights in particular. There were even times when the stock of glasses ran out and customers had to find an empty one before they could have a drink. Tom was getting more confident and he would occasionally open up the bar in the evenings.

It was decided that the Thursday before the beginning of the winter darts league should be a Friendly between the two teams. Megan announced her team to include Mary and her friend Carol. They used to come in on Fridays only but since the Carnival and after Mary's brief spell working with Tom, their frequency had increased. Mary and Carol were inseparable which made any carnal inclinations the male regulars may have had, out of the question. They never seemed to be with boys but as usual, Ieuan got on very well with them. A couple of nurses Megan knew were always ready to make up the team if they were short. Dowie's team included half the Blue Bootees, Rolff had been cajoled into playing by his landlord. The posh talking Englishman, David, who thought it was all rather provincial, and the historian, Gareth, who was from Llanelli. Frank was the final player. He was one of the few men of his age who didn't go to war; essential work on the farm, apparently! During his younger years he was therefore subjected to a surfeit of female company which may be the reason why he never married but still likes to observe.

Tom opened up that evening with Lally following him back to the bar, "First again, Lally. How are you by the way, you've been fairly quiet recently?" Tom intuitively passed her tipple.

She took a large gulp, her reddened eyes started to look watery, she gave a nervous cough and said, "I've got the big C."

"What?" said Tom, more in alarm than due to lack of hearing.

"I've got lung cancer."

"Oh, my God! Are you really sure?"

"Well of course I'm bloody sure. They told me this afternoon."

"Oh Lally, poor Lally, who knows about this?"

"Just you and please don't tell anyone, not even Mag... You didn't mention anything before, did you?"

"Of course not. Bloody hell! I can't believe it! Don't you think you should tell Mag, she is your best pal?"

"Not just yet, she's going to see Dulcie in November and she wants me to go with her. I'll find an excuse not to go and tell her when she comes back. If I do it that way, it will not spoil her break."

"Oh, there you two go again, Mag has not mentioned this trip to me. You've blown it now, haven't you?" Tom gave a forced smiled and touched Lally's hand affectionately. Just then in walked Dowie, Tom quickly withdrew his hand. Dowie noticed, but made no mention of the incident.

"Right! You're in for a smashing tonight. Don't forget you are playing the fourth division champions from last year."

"Dowie, you're deluding yourself. Firstly we are girls, well, some of us." She was referring to age not sex. "Secondly we are determined to show you what we can do. Remember the war years?" Megan grinned.

Players started to appear one by one until all the girl's team were present, including the two nurses. Tom recognised them from previous nights because one was Nigerian and the other looked Chinese. Ieuan was the only man not there. "If he doesn't appear before eight we can claim one game," said Lally.

"Christ! You said you were keen but this is a bit much."

Dowie was one of the old school and not amused. The thought of playing against women was bad enough but cantankerous ones was outrageous. Lally was teasing after all, she was not the captain. Ieuan came in within a minute of eight o'clock to the cheers of his team mates. He thought it was because he was the best thrower and much needed.

"We will play two pairs and three singles games. Double to start and finish." Gareth and Frank opened up the match against Mary and Carol. Frank was in his element, he could indulge in his favourite indoor sport at close hand. This was a ploy put on by Megan, who was aware of Frank's sexual fantasies but took a chance with Gareth. It paid off and the girls won the first match easily. Mag was sitting with Dowie at the bar while Tom and Beryl served. No one spoke but the pleasure on Mag's face said it all. Megan clapped and congratulated the winners. "The losers buy the drinks, it's customary," she said.

Frank had already brushed aside Gareth saying, "You can get'um next time." It was a brisk attempt to impress the girls.

After the second doubles game it was one each. The three following singles games were much more stressful because of the intimacy of the relationship and it was not possible to blame a partner for bad play. David beat Myfanwy and Tom lost to Lally. There was a final game between Dowie and Mag to clinch the match.

At this stage, Dowie was tense like a coiled spring and he burst out at Tom. "Christ! Tom. You let her win that, she played a bloody awful game."

"Bloody hell! You're wrong. I was very lucky, you know how good she is on the double." He lied, but felt it justified.

Megan could see the pent up emotion in Dowie's face and lunged forward saying, "Come on chaps, it's only a game and a Friendly at that." Lally and Tom went over to the bar. Megan was aware of the importance of this last game in the competition and quizzed herself about whether Dowie would let Mag win or would his chauvinism get the better of him and play to win? Mary and Carol, who were much more perceptive than the others, predicted Dowie losing. Mag was quite indifferent to the relevance of the game to the match, she played to win but lost on the double. A huge cheer went up from the boys. The anticipated result came as a surprise to the streetwise females. Mag and Beryl went behind the bar while Tom stayed with Lally talking quietly at a table slightly away from the excitement. The customary sandwiches and pickled onions appeared and all the rivalry was soon forgotten.

Dowie was still unsure about the relationship between Lally and Tom and it gave him his first opportunity to start planting seeds of deception in Mag's mind. He requested his usual and surreptitiously mentioned that Lally and Tom seemed to be getting on well and they obviously didn't want them to know what they were talking about. Mag glanced over to the table, but was not baited, she knew Lally too well. She got her kicks out of a bottle, thought Mag. The two in question broke off their conversation with a huge laugh from Tom. Such a display of emotion was a rare event even to Mag, so it must have been something worth following up. On their arrival at the bar Ieuan gave Lally his stool, which was her natural habitat and wandered over to joke with the girls. Tom stood behind Lally. Before Mag could inquire the reason for the outburst from Tom, he spoke to Dowie at his side. "Tell me Dowie," giving the impression that his conversation with Lally included the subject, "who was the group of girls and boys sat at the table near the door?"

Dowie, who was feeling a little guilty about his thoughts, responded with a sharp reply. "Opposition Tom, opposition. Remember a while back I was telling you and Mag," he looked over and acknowledged her, "about various nuisances..."

"Yes," said Mag in response to his acknowledgement.

"The boy wearin' the Llanrheidol Rugby Club shirt was Mike the Mouth. Since I told you about him, he has started goin' out with this girl, nice respectable Welsh family and he has changed a lot. His girl is *Plaid*."

"What's *Plaid*?" inquired Mag.

"The Welsh Nationalist Party, it's political. Their sign is three green triangles."

"I've seen that around a lot, you know. Always reminds me of three pine trees," said Mag.

Ieuan had returned to the bar and Dowie continued, "She goes to the Griffin, so he goes there as well. I saw him in here with her a few weeks ago but he wasn't swearin' so I didn't mention it, Tom. It can't be a political thing with Mike, otherwise he would be swearin' in English. It's more likely that she doesn't like it... Yeah, they came to have a nose. To see what sort of competition they were up against."

"Which of our teams will play the Griffin?"

Megan who had recently joined the bar crowd replied almost instantaneously. She had all the fixtures in her head, "Them Mag. Dowie's team has been promoted, remember?" Using her best sarcastic wit she said, "That's why they beat us tonight," and glared at Ieuan.

"Hey! Don't blame me. I let you win our game."

Dowie's comment about the tête-à-tête between Tom and Lally unsettled Mag and she had to make a remark in her oblique way. "I think that Welsh comedian on the wireless, you know, Ryan something, is very funny. Tell me Tom, what were you and Lally laughing about just now?"

He was used to her roundabout ways of asking questions and replied without any doubts. "Oh, she was telling me briefly about your experience on the beach near Kalithies. It was farcical." He said, as though it was a crime, "I just had to laugh out loud."

"You mean our holiday in Rhodes? I'm surprised at you Lally, you told me not to say anything." Mag was quite sharp.

"Yes, that's right, but it just came out."

Tom could perceive the crowd physically moving slightly towards the bar to get a better reception. "You tell them Lally, you can do it first hand. Besides, I'd like to hear the full story."

"What the hell. You're a long time dead." The comment appeared superfluous but Tom knew better. "We decided to take a bus ride from the hotel to a secluded beach further down the coast."

"I bet it was a nude one?"

"Shut up," said Tom. Ieuan was not offended by the remark, someone shut him up every day but he was a little surprised that it came from Tom.

"After making sure I had my fags..."

"Cancer pills, you mean," said Megan indignantly.

Tom winced but Lally showed no emotion whatsoever and continued, "...and liquid refreshments, we took off. Incidentally, a trip in a Greek village bus is really something of an experience. To start with, the seats are wooden slats. My bum must have looked like a Maltese Cross by the time we got to the..."

"What makes a Maltese cross?"

"Shut UP, Ieuan! You're so irritating with your stupid jokes," remarked Megan. "We want to hear the story."

"Yep, enough said, mum's the word."

"Can I carry on now?" There was a pause... "The beach was about a thousand steps below us. After we had a cool drink in the little taverna at the top, we went down to the beach. Then the ritual started, first it was get into a cossy, put up the umbrella and make sure that your footwear was safe because the sand was so hot. At this point I realised that I had left my sunglasses in the taverna. Mag, bless her soul, offered to go back and fetch them." Mag looked at Tom with slightly lifted eyebrows accentuated by a similar movement of her head, confirming a previous account of Lally.

"It must have been at least fifteen minutes and almost straight up," said Mag. Ieuan made no comment, just smiled.

Lally continued, "I was all nicely greased with my bikini top in my holdall with the essentials and lay back on the hot sand which I could feel through the hotel towel... I had not settled long when people kept passing me in the direction of the steps. It was very much a family beach with no single men as far as I could see."

"Not the place for Beryl then."

"Ieuan!" exclaimed someone nearby.

"The people appeared to get noisier and started walking faster as time went on. The children were particularly excited. My curiosity got the better of me so I sat up to see what all the commotion was about. All I could see was a slight hazy mist in the distance and what appeared to be water on the beach. I assumed it to be the normal mirage seen on hot sunny days. The breeze was freshening and very welcome."

"I was still climbing the steps," inserted Mag, "and children kept rushing past me to be first at the top. I thought they were just playing like, you know, children do (Mag, like Tom, did not like the word kids). The first crowd to pass Lally had caught me up by now. I didn't speak Greek and they had no English but one old lady tapped me on the shoulder and pointed to the far end of the long beach. I took my sunglasses off and in the distance I could see this huge cloud of dust, it was a sand storm! I grabbed Lally's glasses which were still sitting on the table and tried to rush down to warn her. It was difficult because of the families hurrying up the steps."

Lally was getting excited about reliving the incident and started to cough, but insisted on recalling the story. "By this time I had stood up on the now deserted beach. The wind was now becoming fresh and little bits of papers and light objects were rushing around and past me on the sand. I looked towards the steps and saw Mag about halfway down frantically waving her arms about and shouting something I could not hear. I think I must have panicked at this stage..."

"Yes you did! I was trying to tell you to come off the beach but you didn't move." Mag was getting equally excited by now and everyone in their vicinity was spellbound, even Dowie.

"I couldn't move. I was paralysed and then it came. There was this great rush of wind and sand. All I could do was stand there with my eyes closed waiting for it to go. It was stinging my body and seemed to go on forever then it turned and moved out to sea. By this time Mag had arrived. All she could do was laugh. Tell them Mag." Lally started to cough again.

"Well," Mag laughed to herself. "You should have seen her." Lally sipped her drink. "Because she was covered in grease the sand had stuck and she was covered from head to toe in sand," she laughed again, Lally joined in and the rest could see the funny side of it. Trying to hold back the laughter, Mag carried on. "She was absolutely plastered in sand except for her bikini bottom and two spots for her eyes and her nostrils. Her hair, ears and even her eyelids were covered in sand, you know. I couldn't stop laughing but Lally was furious and every time she moved to shout at me she looked even funnier. Eventually she could see the funny side of it as well and we just broke down and laughed and laughed."

"Remember those Greek kids?" Lally coughed.

"Oh yes! The families were returning to the beach by now, some were sympathetic but the majority thought it was so amusing, especially the children. They all gathered around Lally and pulled her down to the sea where they showed her how to use a mixture of sand and water to remove the mess... We eventually got her cleaned up and the rest of the afternoon was relatively uneventful."

Lally had been laughing so much between her coughing bouts that her eyes were quite red and watery, a condition which earlier was for quite a different reason.

"Another delightful money making evening over." Mag was beginning to think like Tom.

When they had retired that evening, Tom said, "You didn't tell me you were intending to go to Bristol?"

"Lally told you I suppose? Trust her!"

"It just slipped out..."

"That's the second slip out today, what's Lally doing to you?"

Tom didn't like the sexual intonation in her remarks and said, "Don't be crude, Mag, it's not like you to slag off Lally."

"Well, you seem to be very concerned about her since we came back from holidays."

He did not reply. "I don't mind you going off but why didn't you tell me?" Tom was not too forthcoming with his displeasure because he had not mentioned his impending weekend trip with Selwyn.

"I'm going Christmas shopping, you know, I do it every year but I thought this year I would take Lally and we could both stay with Dulcie."

'Dan will love that, some hopes,' thought Tom. "If you go to Bristol, I'll go for a bird weekend with Selwyn."

"Bird weekend? What do you mean?" Recollecting what Dowie had said to her about Selwyn's exploits.

"Selwyn is taking some of his students to an island just off the coast, near Pembroke to do some bird ringing. They want a cook and Selwyn suggested I did it. I can learn a bit more about birds as well; the ones with feathers, that is." Mag smiled nervously, from eye contact, she knew what was coming next. "That reminds me, I haven't seen you perform for sometime now. Haven't you bought anything I should see?"

"Clear off!" She stepped back to avoid any advance that Tom might make but it did not materialise. "It's too cold," she hugged herself and affectedly lifted the collar of her blouse.

"What will happen to the darts?" inquired Tom.

"I'm not going until the Friday and I'll be back on the Monday."

Lally excused herself from the trip so Mag reluctantly had to go on her own. Her visible accoutrements were not typical of Mag Llanrheidol. A heavy overcoat, fleece-lined boots, tweed skirt and jumper but underneath was still the unshackled Mag. This attire was not only to keep out the inclement weather but because that was the image she left behind in Bristol. It was a Jekyll and Hyde transmutation which she disliked but felt necessary to keep the peace between Dulcie and Dan. As far as Mag was concerned, the Celtic environment had produced a permanent transfiguration which would be displayed on any future visits.

Tom opened up that Friday to the sonorous buzzing of the telephone. It was Megan from work. "Lally's been admitted to hospital with severe breathing problems but she implored me not to tell anyone except you and certainly not to get in touch with Mag. I'll call round and see you when I get off and give you more details." It was the usual busy night but Mag had arranged for Mary to come in and help. Tom's mind was not on the job and when Megan arrived, he excused himself and they both went upstairs. No one noticed, it was too busy. Megan sat down while Tom stood by the dining table. "She's got lung cancer."

"I know," replied Tom.

"How did you know?"

"Lally told me on the night of the Friendly darts match but swore me to secrecy. I didn't even tell Mag."

"I'll certainly know where to get rid of my frustrating confidences in future," replied Megan reassuringly. "Do you know if she has any relatives around we should contact?"

"I don't know. Perhaps we should get in touch with Mag."

"No! She was most adamant that we did not contact Mag... Don't worry, I'll have a word with her tomorrow morning."

Megan pensively and also apologetically said, "I thought you would like to know the situation."

"Yes, thanks very much, I appreciate it." Tom gratefully acknowledged Megan, "She's a great character and I'm very fond of her."

Megan had experienced such anguish by distraught relatives on numerous similar occasions and thought she should reassure Tom by saying, "Although it's not visiting time and you're not family, come into Casualty tomorrow morning and I'll take you to see her."

"Oh, thanks a lot Megan." Tom was apprehensive about visiting since he had not experienced the trauma of serious illness since his mother died. They both returned to the chaos in the bar. Megan did not stay for her half of Bass.

"What's wrong Tom? You look very worried about something?" came an inquiry from a busy barmaid in between supplying the avaricious crowd with their orders and washing up glasses. "Why has Megan gone?"

"She came to give me a message. I'll take over there, Beryl." He grabbed a glass from her hand and blindly started to wipe it. "I'll tell you later, when it's quieter." She returned to the other job with Mary. Later on that evening, when the top of town was busy, he told them the news in the presence of Dowie and Ieuan.

"We must have a whip round and get her some flowers," suggested Beryl. She started to collect in a mug with a broken handle which harboured an unclaimed pipe still stuffed with tobacco. It was surprising how generous people can be. Old Frank gave a fiver and declared that the contents of the mug was the pipe he lost at the darts match. The Blue Bootees collected about three pounds between them and they only knew her as a passing acquaintance.

"I'll see Myfanwy in the morning," said Tom. "She can go and get some flowers and I'll take them in. Megan is arranging for me to visit."

She was much worse than Tom expected. There was a cylinder of oxygen next to her bed for use whenever it was needed. She could talk but only very slowly and quietly. As soon as she saw Tom she put out a frail small hand for him to grasp.

"D-o-n't t-e-l-l M-a-g," she slowly delivered.

"No, I promised, if you remember." Lally gave a weak but knowing hint of a smile. Megan left them together.

"These are from all at Ty Gwyn. I hope you like them. Someone suggested we brought you something from your garden but there's nothing much around this time of year, only slugs and weeds." She smiled.

"I-'v-e b-e-a-t-e-n t-h-e b-u-g-g-e-r t-o i-t." She was too tired to go on.

It was the first time she had mentioned her ex-husband since his death. It must have been playing on her mind, thought Tom. He stayed for a little while but he could see she was very weak, and excused himself. Tom reported back to his anxiously awaiting employees. Myfanwy had stayed just to hear the result.

"I still think I should ring Mag." Tom was in a quandary. "I think I'll pop up and see Mag's mother, perhaps she can help me out of this mess. Can you hold the fort for about half an hour, Beryl?"

"Anything for you." He did not comprehend the inflection.

He arrived at Mag's parents when Mark, his pal and Grandad were off to the playing fields, ostensibly for the boys to play but in reality for Grandad to study the form for the afternoon meeting. He liked a flutter. Nana had often come across old betting slips in his pocket, when articles of clothing needed cleaning or ironing. Tom had a quick word with Mark, kissed him and squashed a pound coin in his hand, "That's for some ice-cream." Mark acknowledged Tom's generosity, turned to his pal, said something and all three left.

Nana had been informed of Tom's dilemma from a previous phone call, but he wanted to meet her face to face. Since his parents had died Tom adopted his mother-in-law as a matriarchal confessor and confided in her various problems that needed evaluating. Unbeknown to Mag, she was in fact his confidante about going into the pub. After a certain amount of amiable discourse it all condensed to the same old problem, "Don't forget, you promised? And besides, Mag will be back on Monday anyway." Tom went away clearer in his mind and finally convinced that he had done the right thing.

Saturday night was full, busy and noisy. The attitude of the few people who knew Lally was a little subdued but not morose. Ieuan was still darting with the girls and Frank still carried out his favourite ocular pastime. The majority of the itinerant revellers who were out enjoying themselves were completely unaware of the concern the minority had for Lally. Near closing time, most of the jollification had migrated to noisier dwellings and only a few courting couples and regulars were left behind. Tom was down in the cellar doing something to the barrels. While he was away Megan commented on Tom taking Lally's illness very badly, and that he was in a terrible predicament about Mag not knowing.

"D'you think there is more to it than that?" Megan perked up at Dowie's mischievous comment. "I saw him holdin' Lally's hand on the night we had the Friendly match."

Megan leapt off her bar stool and puffed herself up in a fearful rage. "For God's sake, Dowie... Tom told me you saw them; he was consoling her... She had just heard she had the big C. What a terrible thing to say, I'm disgusted with you." She turned away from him in an obvious gesture of rejection.

"You mean, cancer?"

"Yes, Ieuan, lung cancer, that's exactly what I mean."

"Poor girl!" The outcry was not related to her age but gender. "My father had that, he literally rotted away."

"Ieuan! Don't talk like that. We're talking about Lally." Beryl was quite distraught.

Dowie looked dejected and wondered to himself why he had made such an aspersion in the first place. He liked Tom and Mag and why was he getting at Tom all the time? He touched Megan on the shoulder and said, "I'm sorry Meg, it was a bit nasty. I don't know what came into my head, I apologise."

Megan was still riled at Dowie's implication and said, "Tom and Lally are like Ieuan and me, just good friends. There doesn't have to be any more to it than that. Besides, what about you and Myfanwy? You were going out together for a long time before you bust up but you are still good friends. And there's Beryl..."

"Yeah, I get your point. Let's drop it."

Tom returned from the cellar. "What was all that shouting about, Megan?"

"Nothing special."

He did not expect a reply so did not respond to the comment. Tom clicked his fingers and shook his head to express that he had just remembered something. "Did you manage to find out if she had any relatives that should be contacted, Megan?"

"Yes, she has a sister living in Surrey, but again Lally doesn't want her contacted nor her two daughters. That's the one who is living with her sister and the married one living in Liverpool."

Tom was disturbed from his doctors' nightmare breakfast at about ten o'clock on Sunday morning by the ringing of the telephone in the bar. He insisted on not having an extension in the flat simply for the sake of peace. Tom wandered slowly down to the bar thinking it was Mag confirming the arrival of her train, but to his surprise it was Megan. She told him to come quickly to the hospital, Lally was in a serious state. He slipped on an old windcheater and rushed to the hospital. Although he was not next of kin, Megan worked it so that he could see her. He got there at about ten forty-five. She died at eleven o'clock. He knew the moment she died from the relaxation of her hand in his. Her breathing was too shallow to detect any abrupt change. Tom was beside himself, he really took it to heart, he just could not speak without his voice breaking. Megan rang Nana who got on the phone to Mag. She also got in touch with Lally's relatives in Surrey. As a matter of respect, Tom did not open that evening, and posted a notice to that effect on the outside door of the pub. Megan, in her usual efficient manner, thought of Clem and caught him before his weekly visit and took him round to her place with a few cans as consolation.

She died intestate but Lally's relatives thought it might be fitting for her to be cremated in her place of origin. The funeral was the following Wednesday. Lally's sister and her younger daughter came down on Tuesday afternoon and stayed in the Royal. Mag offered them accommodation but they declined. Lally's other married daughter had been so systematically poisoned by her father's family against Lally that she refused to attend the funeral. Dulcie did not come down but sent a bouquet of late summer wild flowers. It was a bleak day with a hint of rain in the air, a condition not unfamiliar in this part of Wales. Megan commented that it was unusual that there were more women than men at the crematorium. It was a sad, but simple service with one hymn in Welsh, Calfari. Tom could not help thinking of the way her own flesh and blood had rejected her throughout the latter part of her life. What had she done so evil as to warrant such deplorable treatment?

Mag invited all back to the pub for a few drinks and the traditional snacks. Both relatives came back. Her sister left early with the excuse of having to pack but Lally's daughter stayed for a while. Tom thought she resembled Lally when she was young but he had no photographic evidence to substantiate his belief. Lally's daughter was getting on well with the Blue Bootie with the posh accent. David was obviously public school and this appealed. Marlborough College was infinitely better than her small, expensive, Daddy-sent-me, North London School for Ladies. She had a bit too much to drink, felt it was not lady-like and excused herself, promising to write and come down again.

"I've heard that all before," said David. "Once back in her natural environment with her expensive friends she'll soon forget the noisy, beer swilling, intellectuals from the principality."

Tom had drunk more than most and he misconstrued David's criticism and felt quite proud to be considered an egghead. 'I do know more about Bass than anyone else in Llanrheidol,' he thought.

It was drifting into evening and everyone was beginning to relax and feel less despondent. Dowie bought Mag a drink, Beryl bought Ieuan a drink and everyone bought Tom a drink. The remains of the refreshments were left for anyone who entered the pub. Selwyn and Tom discussed the weekend trip, then Selwyn disappeared to finalise the excursion. Mag was talking generally about Lally to anyone who was willing to listen.

Tom had reached the candid talkative stage and interrupted her to state that the last person he mentioned to Lally was Selwyn and he proceeded to eulogise on his last words. "When I gave her the flowers from the pub, I said that it would have been nice to have given her some from her own garden but it was the wrong time; it only contained weeds and slugs for Selwyn, ha, ha."

Dowie could sense that the conversation was beginning to get morbid so he counteracted with one of his entertaining anecdotes. "Talkin' about Selwyn and slugs." His introduction was more to the point than the brainless openings to some of Mag's comments. "One evenin' he was out collectin' slugs in the lane that runs behind my house when the batteries of his torch ran out. It was not completely dark so he could see the slugs as long dart objects once his eyes had become used to the dark. For some reason which I cannot remember, I was in the garden too. All of a sudden, I heard Selwyn's swearing in Welsh. This was quickly followed by some well known English ones that are banded here. He then appeared with his right hand slightly cupped and the fingers separated and pointin' upwards. I can hear him now," continued Dowie donning Tom's reading glasses from the bar and assuming a Selwynian pose, 'Bastard dogs! Look at this Dowie.' He then caught hold of my arm, with his other hand, of course and pulled me in through the open door to the lighted kitchen. 'Look!' He showed me the sticky, smelly mess on his fingers."

"What was it, Dowie?" asked Mag innocently.

"Dog's shit and fresh at that. He thought it was a nice big, black slug but when he picked it up it squashed between his fingers..." Everyone laughed; Dowie had achieved his aim.

Before Ieuan could counter attack, Tom sputtered, "I hate bloody dogs. They're smelly, dirty and noisy. I just don't know what people see in them."

"Some are useful," said Dowie. "Sheep dogs are a great help on the farm and there are guard-dogs, but I agree with you Tom, as pets they're a bloody nuisance."

"I've got a little Scotty," said Beryl, "and I wouldn't swap him for anything. He keeps me company at night."

"There's no answer to that," exclaimed Ieuan.

"To tell the truth, I think they are a good excuse to be a peeping Tom," muttered the landlord. "If you're wandering round an estate late at night on your own it looks suspicious but if you've got a dog with you it's a good excuse. I'm sure several people who walk their dogs along the lane at the back of this pub late at night just do it to have a look at the young girls in the students' hostel over there." He pointed at the wall but everyone knew what he meant.

"Hey! How do you know that, Tom?" questioned Ieuan.

"Oh, I've seen them from the back window of the flat. You can come and see for yerself, if you like."

Ieuan was countered again by Mag, "No you damned well can't. You're randy enough as it is." Ieuan was unmoved and shrugged his shoulders in submission.

"Now about this lane. Shit alley I call it." Tom took no heed of Mag's comments, he felt his objections to the nocturnal perambulations of certain folk was more important. "One of the doggy lovers who prowls around at night and lets his dog shit everywhere is a retired copper. Now how can I report a bloody copper to the police?"

"It would be a bit difficult," said Dowie, who was talking from experience.

"Yees, they would get me for something before the week's out, you bet. We stay open later than we should most nights for example."

"You don't like the police, do you Tom?" said Ieuan.

"Let's just say, once a copper always a copper and the retired ones are the worst. Have to keep their hand in, I suppose... And it justifies their large pension."

Tom disappeared into the cellar to change a barrel and Mag felt she should explain his dislike of policemen. "Our next door neighbour on the other side from Dulcie was a retired policeman and he was always watching every move Tom made. It used to make him so mad, you know. Occasionally Tom would bring home boxes of rejected crisps or something from the factory. He would be there watching through the net curtains, you could see them move. The fact that Tom gave most of the goods to the old peoples' home at the bottom of the road was not important. As far as I know, he never reported Tom but you can rest assured, the police knew about his activities."

"What are you going to do about the darts team, Megan?" inquired Dowie who showed a vested interest. "Who is going to replace Lally?"

"One of the nurses said she would join on a regular basis provided she's not on duty, then her friend will step in. She's a Nigerian nurse called Rose and her friend is Ya-Hui, everyone calls her Yah. They were at the Friendly game."

Ieuan had been quiet long enough and seized the opportunity to insert some humour into the conversation, "I'll bet Rose is a good player?"

"Why," inquired Megan.

"Throwing all those spears around at home in the jungle."

Megan threw her head in the air and inaudibly parted her lips in contempt of Ieuan's naïveté and said, "She's from Brixton you dope, born and bred. The only spear she has seen is spearmint chewing gum."

"Hey! That's very droll."

* * * * *

It was a sobering thought, but after a few weeks everything was back to normal. Except for a few who really cared, it was as though Lally never existed. The first year students had settled down and although they still came through on birthdays and any excuse for a party, fewer frequented Ty Gwyn regularly except for the occasional couple and some postgraduates. They had found more convivial watering holes further up town. The Royal had started up a late night disco on Friday nights and a lot of the locals started going there after the pubs closed.

"How did they manage to get an extension to three o'clock in the morning, Dowie?"

"The Taffia, Tom. To you, a mixture of businessmen and bent councillors who had their palms greased. The townsfolk don't care because it's somewhere to go late at night. The students got their own disco on campus and the young kids their disco up town."

Mag still missed Lally and was only just beginning to get back to her vivacious self. Richard had been accepted for the Army and was going just after Christmas. Mark had settled in his new school and with Mag's parents, and only rarely came to the pub. Tom visited him every week when he took Grandad to the Legion in town and Mag and Tom spoilt him on their visits. He was developing into a very talkative youngster with an awesome sense of imagination. He occupied most of the time during their brief reunions on Wednesdays. On the last visit, he was the captain of the school swimming team and the best diver in the class. An outstanding feat since the school swimming pool did not possess a diving board.

The season of good cheer was rapidly approaching. The Town Council had decided to improve on the rows of boring coloured lights, by embellishing the streets with some tatty decorations purchased from Blackpool Council. The weeks up to Christmas were extremely busy with students calling in motley waves before going off to the sombre safety of the parental nest. One particularly cheery party was the College girls' hockey team. Ieuan had reason to resurrect his debagging encounter when he found himself immersed in solid muscular thighs complimented with St. Trinians outfits. Tom and Dowie also considered the event to be the highlight of that particular evening. Not to be left out, Beryl and Mag were not slow in recalling their carnal contributions to the Carnival.

When the students had gone down there was a perceptible hush in the town and some pubs were relatively empty. Relative, because not one public house of the twenty-five in Llanrheidol was ever deplete of customers. Even the so called student pubs contained a hard core of locals. They were the skeleton crew that kept some establishments ticking over between term time and summer visitors.

Christmas parties were a lucrative line of social events, bank staff, office staff, shop staff, and just groups of people with relatives down for the holidays, and they all had their exclusive form of entertainment. The wildest crowds were from the banks. Once they were on the run the wires started to hum sending out warning salvos. On one occasion, Tom and Mag were phoned too late and one particular bank group smashed glasses, took ashtrays and harassed Beryl and Mag. At the beginning, it was all in good nature, but later after the alcohol started to take affect, it began to get spiteful. The females in the group boisterously objected to the fuss the males were making of the girls behind the bar. Old chestnuts such as, 'Get 'um Down' and 'Let's See yer Knockers,' came flowing out. At one stage a bank girl, as a token of resentment, started to do a combination of these demands. That sort of thing was all very well in a private party, thought Tom, but not for all and sundry to see. It was stopped more for the girl's sake than anything else. Later, up town, she apparently got as far as her panties before being bundled off in a taxi.

After an exhausting evening, Tom and Mag collapsed in fireside chairs in the flat when she said, "I think we should have a private party just before Christmas. We can invite all the regulars and I thought some of Richard's friends since he will be going soon. Sunday would be best, that's our quietest day. As a gesture, we could supply the refreshments and they'd have to buy the drinks." Remembering that it was Clem's night, Mag quickly and almost inaudibly said, "Clem can have free drinks all night, poor luv." There was no reply from Tom, he was sound asleep. It was decided and all the relevant people informed. Any gatecrashers would be dealt with by Dowie.

With the business running well and all the excitement of everyone enjoying themselves, Tom and Mag felt compelled to go with the gang to a late-night disco at the Royal. Even Selwyn had been goaded into attending. To Tom's delight the Tremletts were admitted free because of their occupation. It was a clever entrepreneurial move since most publicans would then recommend the Royal after closing time. Tom had not been to a disco for many years and certainly not since taking up residency in Llanrheidol. Mag, unbeknown to Tom, went to one recently in Bristol with Dulcie. They picked up a couple of young lads who scrounged a lift in Dulcie's Mini. It surprised Mag how much room there was in the back of one of those things. Dulcie's night away from the pub with Dowie took on a whole new meaning after that.

The disco was a revelation to Tom with flashing lights and the unyielding noise. The din was so loud that conversation was limited to grunts and groans. Tom could now begin to understand the limited vocabulary and the necessity for visible intonation so frequently used by the youngsters. Much to the amusement of Ty Gwyners, Selwyn appeared befuddled by the combination of unfamiliar stimuli and was prancing around the dance floor with some tart he had picked up in the bar. Tom was stupefied since he did not share the intimate secrets of Selwyn's love-life revealed to Mag. He only knew he was a bit of a boy when he was younger and the nickname given to him by the students. He thought Cocky meant he was a bit stand offish. It was a much needed evening of spontaneous tomfoolery. "This is really great," Tom said to Mag as he was trying to copy the gyrations around him on the floor. "We must do this again."

She replied, "I didn't realise what fun it could be just going off and leaving everything. No wonder they all come here after closing." Apart from themselves, other publicans Tom knew from the LVA meetings were there. One well disposed ally was Babs, from the White Hart. She appreciated Tom's company and he enjoyed hers. Mag was not over-keen, she reminded her of a seasoned Dulcie and to cap it all, she kept pulling Tom on to the dance floor.

Just as they were about to go on one of their jaunts, Mag reminded Tom that he had a bad leg. "It's all right at the moment."

He gave it a quick rub and slithered off with Babs. Dowie stepped in and danced with Mag, so did Ieuan, Rolff and even Selwyn who supposedly came under protest. By now he had lost his lady of easy virtue. The night terminated with Tom coupled to Mag limping home to babbling disapproval about overdoing it. Mag went with the crowd to the disco again the following Friday before Christmas while Tom had taken the day off to go to a meeting with Selwyn. Tom was in bed when he heard Mag arrive home with Dowie who left her at the door.

When Tom was visiting Mark on the busy penultimate week before Christmas, Mag got together with some of the locals and suggested a theme for the Christmas Party. It came to her one night when Tom was doing at the back window of the flat exactly what she had banned Ieuan from doing. Since Tom was almost obsessed with the lane behind the pub and the gathering of dogs and their owners which he called collectively 'A Shit of Walkers', Mag suggested that the theme should be 'Puppy Pubing Tomos Night'.

Selwyn appreciated the pun and agreed. But inadvertently spoilt Mag's scholarly accomplishment by making an alternative suggestion. "What about Voyeurism Night?"

"No, that's too deep," said Mag a little dejected. "And, you know, half the customers wouldn't know what it meant, anyway." In fact, she didn't know herself.

"I think Tom's name should be in there." Ieuan was in one of his rare serious moods but still curious, "If I could see through the upstairs window, perhaps I could get some inspiration, Mag."

To his surprise, she replied, "Yes." She knew he was not really interested in the behaviour of the canine species. "They've all gone home for the vacation." There was a brief break in the conversation, then he declined the offer. "We could use all the Carnival stuff again that Lally left with me." She bowed her head solemnly for a moment as if in worship, "It's in the cellar."

"Yes please!" Rolff was not with his usual crowd, most of whom had departed for other fleshpots. He had adopted the extraordinary characteristic of being seen with a girl, the very pretty nurse, Yah. It was amazing the transformation, he was still humorous in his comments but they were not so stupid. "Can I have a basque?"

Yah saw the funny side of it and laughed out, "You in a basque?" She was not that unfamiliar with such Western undergarments since she was born in Shrewsbury. Only her parents were acquainted with the Eastern dress of young girls in Taiwan.

"Bugger! The gas has gone on the lager, won't be long." Mag disappeared into Tom's domain.

"Before you wear a basque, let's see your legs." Beryl leaned over the bar and looked down at his feet. "Where's your blue boots gone?" she screeched.

"We're into silly T-shirts, now." At that precise moment he was not wearing one to show her.

"You can't do that," Beryl shrieked with a degree of indignation which was not strong enough to be insulting. "You can't. Mag has christened you lot the Blue Bootees, she'll do her nut!"

"Very well, I'll wear them on Friday nights, just to keep the peace." Yah gave him a warm, oriental smile which made Ieuan feel a little envious but he quickly laughed it off by referring to the group as Bootees.

"By the way, why are we called the Blue Bootees?"

"Mag thought Bootees instead of Boots because you acted like children."

"Fair enough!" Rolff shrugged his shoulders and carried on drinking.

Mag reappeared and immediately started talking as though she had to make up for the time wasted in the cellar. "We have plenty of scope, there are the lookers and the looked at, just about anything goes."

"I will be working Friday week until late but I'll come along after duty." Yah was the sort of oriental beauty who no one could envisage flaunting her body to anyone. 'It's on the cards that she will turn up in her nurses uniform,' thought Mag.

Rolff was particularly enthusiastic about this party since it was the first crazy social event with Yah. They had been to a few College dances but not anything wild. He recoiled at the thought of a repeat of the Carnival evening. "Gareth said he will bring along his guitar. He's not going home 'til the New Year..."

"My God!" interrupted Mag, "that's another one." And with a nonchalant gesture of her hand she said, "we'll worry about that later." Megan, Ieuan and Dowie registered the comment but said nothing.

Because the boys had been invited, Richard had made a particular effort and excelled in the display of culinary delights for the evening.

"The Royal could not have done better at ten pounds a head, Richard."

Sunday lunchtime was the usual wearisome shift and Mag was in residence while Tom prepared a made-up lunch. Richard was up early for once to finalise the refreshments. "What are you going to wear at the party tonight?" Tom asked Richard who was remarkably alert for so early in the morning.

"We have all decided to come dressed as gangsters, like the 20s. What will you wear, Dad?"

"Just a leather waistcoat and one of my best striped shirts. Your mother will be going as a gangster's moll or whatever she was supposed to be at the Carnival." The rhetoric between Richard and his dad had become much more cordial since they worked together over the summer.

"I'm looking forward to seeing Mary and Carol and what they will be wearing. They've got amazing figures. Some of the boys still talk about them at the Carnival."

Tom stopped what he was doing and casually stated that Mary would be wearing her basque plus accessories but Carol would be wearing something different because she had let Rolff borrow her basque.

"No!" he swivelled around on the spot. You mean Rolff from the College? He's got a girlfriend. She's gorgeous." Richard was at that adolescent stage in his life when every girl older and even sparingly attractive became the object of his sexual fantasies. "Shall I put the stuffing in these vol-au-vent cases?"

"Leave it until later this afternoon, otherwise they may get stale." Tom took a pride in anything that was cooked in Ty Gwyn. "Don't you underestimate Rolff, according to Selwyn he's very bright..." Shooting off at a tangent more appropriate to Mag, Tom said, "He had a girl before Yah, she was crazy about him but he didn't want to know. They called her Brenda Mawr. She could see no future with Rolff so she went out and got pregnant by a postman," Richard grinned. "She now lives in wedded bliss at Abermadd, where Dowie's cousin lives, the fisherman. So there won't be any fighting among the girls tonight."

Richard was not sure what his father meant but he had seen girls' squabbling further up town on weekends. They carried on chatting about this and that and at times they could hear the low murmur of voices in the bar. Ieuan was there before going off to referee a match. Surprisingly, Myfanwy, who did not clean on Sundays, wanted to make final sleeping arrangements about her little family. She also wanted something to wear. Her figure was not compatible with a basque, she would look more befitting in a dancehall girls' outfit like the ones seen in so many Westerns, all frills and low-cut; she was well blessed in her upper regions. Richard and Myfanwy's boys were going to stay upstairs with Nana. They had plenty to eat and drink and Tom had acquired for them some videos. Nana, not wanting a repeat of the Carnival fiasco, insisted that Grandad came to the party this time and did not go elsewhere.

Tom opened just before six o'clock, half expecting Lally to fall in through the doorway with a bag full of books. Only two old ladies scuttled past on their way to evening service at Capel Als in the next street. Mag waited to settle everyone in the flat before joining the party. Beryl was working that night but only for a while. Richard had set up the trestle table Selwyn borrowed from the College and a smaller three-ply board supported on its ends by four crates of lager. He was hurrying to finish laying out the refreshments so that he could fetch back his shy friends. The reason was not because they were unaccustomed to drinking in pubs, since this was the preoccupation of most of the youth in Llanrheidol. It was the anticipation after the exaggerated tales of the Carnival party.

Dowie, dressed as a Mississippi Gambler was not perceptibly 'on the door' but he was watching who came in. Without Tom's consent he let Mike the Mouth in with another male friend who frequented the Griffin. He had met Mike in the street on the previous day and he almost pleaded with Dowie to get Tom to let him into the party.

Dowie took a chance, since he was a regular at the pub during Dowie's time. By eight o'clock all who had been invited were in residence, so Tom shut the outside door. He had invited Gethin and Christin, who missed the last Carnival do, but they were off to some snowy retreat in Italy for Christmas. Although initially it was quite chilly in the bar, Tom decided not to light a fire. The bar soon filled and warmed up.

Mag who was much more observant than Tom, pointed out that Richard and his pals were obviously slightly embarrassed by all the naked flesh. The double negative girl, as Tom called her because she was the only non-darter that didn't return to Ty Gwyn after the Carnival was in a wanton mood. She had substituted her mini French maid's uniform for a sexy lace see-through catsuit. Although she did not currently have a boyfriend all virile male minds were aflame as to what sensual delights must await the next one. She selected the most timid of the boys and glided up to him. By now all the eyes in the pub were directed her way and the idle banter had subsided. She turned towards him, pushed the table at which they were sitting back with her rear, lifted one leg and straddled across his lap and proceeded to kiss his neck and face. The pub went wild. His pals were initially in shock, but eventually joined in the hilarity. As a final gesture she slowly brought her leg high above his head, climbed off his lap and slinked away ruffling his hair as she left to join the other girls. There was uproar and lewd suggestions which humiliated the red-faced boy even more.

As the noise died down from the corner near the fireplace came a blast of noisy obscenities. "I don't fuckin' care, it's not your fuckin' problem." It was Mike the Mouth back to his original revolting self.

"Mike, language! I told you when you came in to control it," Dowie shouted across the room.

He still carried on, "It's this fuckin' idiot with the girl's clothes on." He was referring to Rolff who was innocently acting silly but in no way offensively. It boiled down to the fact that Mike was resentful of Rolff's popularity in the pub and especially with the girls. He was the centre of attraction when Dowie, who was not so particular about bad language, was landlord.

"I won't tell you again. Next time, you're out!" His friend was slovenly decorating a chair in a drunken stupor. Dowie turned to Tom who was surprised at the outburst since he did not realise Mike was in the party. "Ah! Sorry about Mike. I let him in, he said he would be good and I didn't want to bother you at the time."

Mag was next to Tom and hastily spoke for him, "Don't worry Dowie, I'm sure you did it with Christmas spirit. Have one on me?"

"I felt like laying one on Mike," he said belligerently. "I'll have a wee dram of malt." He was trying unsuccessfully to mimic a Scotsman. The malts were not on optics so Tom dispensed Dowie's drink straight from the bottle. It was a sure sign that he was enjoying himself despite the dispute. It settled as quickly as it had started and the jesting started to rise again. The annoying thing was that Mike was a weedy little runt full of his own importance and needed large males around him for protection. His personality made him the perfect school bully.

Beryl was not in her usual basque, she had substituted it for a tennis outfit which was more practical when serving. Mag had moved from behind the bar to talk to Dowie and Ieuan.

"Shit!" uttered Beryl, only Tom heard. "I've sat in some beer. Somebody must have spilt a pint and some of it has splashed on to this." She pointed to the stool kept behind the bar for fatigued helpers. "There's nothing else I can do," she whispered to Tom as she stepped into the open entrance of the cellar, where only Tom could see her and quickly removed her white tennis pants. Tom could not help but notice and thought that at least the outfit was authentic since she would normally be wearing much briefer undergarments than those. She threw the wet undies down the stairs into the cellar while Tom casually passed her a hand towel to wipe. She re-entered the serving area, no one had noticed the incident. Beryl returned the towel to Tom who proceeded to wipe his face with it.

"Tom!" She teased him with a smirk. "I'll stay behind the bar for the rest of the night. Do you mind?"

"Oh, all right but don't bend over too often."

The brisk use of the towel had not dried her skirt which sporadically touched her skin and tickled. On such events Beryl would furtively lift the hem of her skirt and give a little scratch. To Tom it was like stroking a smouldering fire and rekindled salacious thoughts he had forgotten existed. The physical art of being so close to her made it extremely difficult not to pat her flushed bare bottom.

Fortunately for Tom the demand for drinks had revived and Mary came behind to help. Although she was extremely attractive in her Carnival getup the vibes were not the same despite the overflowing glands. When she became aware of Beryl's plight she audibly chuckled into her hand. Tom nudged her quickly, before anyone noticed and requested her to be quiet. "We'll let the rest know later when the crowd has thinned out and Beryl has had a few drinks." He liked to work with Mary; she was always so feminine and smelt nice. Beryl had made a temporary exit to the cellar to change a barrel. Tom had volunteered, provided Beryl stood at the top of the stairs as he came up from the cellar. She declined his offer; Mary knew their secret.

Grandad had palled up with Frank, they were sat next to the young boys recalling the so called 'good old days' when paradoxically beer was one penny a pint but they forgot to declare that they only earned thirty shillings a week. "Never mind, it's all over now and the young ones have got it made," concluded Frank. The timid philosophical one who had now recovered from his sexual harassment, suggested it was not quite like that but did not pursue the matter. Nana looked in the door and informed Grandad that the taxi was waiting and that the boys were safely tucked up in bed. He reluctantly crept out of the pub to the cheers of the boys. Frank who was feeling out of his depth trying to compete with the youngsters decided to leave at the same time.

Clem was floating on air after his three Blasters but decided enough was enough. He told Mag and Tom how much he had enjoyed himself. "The best party for years," he exclaimed. "The vow-au-vents are just wike the ones Chef makes in the Royal."

Tom noticed Richard, had overheard the conversation and said, "Couldn't have a better reference than that." Tom felt proud that all his teaching was not in vain.

Gareth started to play his guitar. He was good at the oldies and soon started a sing-a-long. Mag was astonished that some of the young boys seemed to know the words. But she then understood; they were the songs on the cult 50's and 60's tapes so much in fashion. Tom was still behind the bar but Mary had returned to Carol and the chatting throng. There was a tapping on the window near the bar which was the clandestine signal that someone wanted to come in. He peeped through the window and saw Yah. The singing was in full swing and everyone was preoccupied, so Tom made his way through the crowd and quietly opened the door. Yah came in wearing an exquisite silk, oriental dress. Gareth stopped playing and everyone turned and gazed. She looked resplendent. In her pinned up hair she had exotic decorations of gold and silver and she was made-up beautifully.

Rolff was muzzled, he had never seen her like this before. In his rush to meet her he went over on one of his high heels and twisted his ankle but still got to her in record time. "You look fantastic," he said, catching hold of her arm to prevent another accident.

"You don't look bad yourself," she said, twanging one of his black suspenders. This shattered the silence with jeers of approval and Gareth played a few bars of the notorious, The Stripper, then stopped for a break. Dowie moved off his stool and made room for her but she insisted on going over to sit with what remained of Rolff's crowd. She sat down very elegantly exposing a long strip of dusky thigh through the slit in the side of her dress. This was immediately but artistically covered.

Mag made straight for Yah. "Where did you get that gorgeous dress from? It's pure silk isn't it?" Mag fingered her folded skirt.

Yah smiled gently at Mag and stated that her mother had sent it to her from Shrewsbury together with the elaborate head dressings. "It is traditional Taiwanese, I told her on the phone that I was going to a special Christmas party."

To relieve her obvious exasperation at being over-dressed Mag caught hold of her arm affectionately and said, "Well, isn't it? We are all friends having a good time." Rolff gave Mag an approving hug. She also twanged his suspender.

"Everybody's doing that tonight. Now I know what the girls have to go through." He only said it as a spontaneous response to Mag's flirtation. He knew, like the rest of the regular males, that it was an unwritten rule not to handle the girls. That was their prerogative. In this way they felt secure and uninhibited. Tom mentioned something to Gareth and he started playing again; the pub purred.

"The attraction between Yah and Rolff appears to be so bizarre." Selwyn was talking glumly to Tom. "She is such a beautiful, elegant lady and Rolff is so outlandishly basqued with holed fishnet stockings. How could Cupid have deciphered the signals?"

Mike the Mouth was bellicosely drunk by now and his voice was booming over the rest. His friend appeared to have revived and they were both sitting alone at a table drinking bottles of lager. "Why don't you play some fuckin' Welsh songs?" Mike's friend yelled out. This was actually on Gareth's programme but he was waiting until later. Then Mike pitched in with, "What's all these fuckin' kids doing in here?" He took a swig from a bottle of lager he had prised open on the side of the makeshift table.

Tom had cottoned on by now and shouted across from behind the bar, "Where did you get those bottles?"

"From the fuckin' crate under the table, what of it?" Gareth was the first to move. He shot over to the loud mouthed yobs and said something in Welsh at them. They immediately cowered down like scolded cats. Gareth grabbed hold of Mike by his shirt collar and trundled him across the floor partly dragging him because his feet did not have time to co-ordinate walking. In the meantime, Dowie got hold of his friend who was using the most abusive language and repeated the move with the exception that he accidentally hit the thug in the mouth with such force that it started to bleed. They were quickly muscled from the pub.

Tom was fuming, "The bastards! Not only did they take advantage of my hospitality and eat my food but they actually pinched my bloody beer as well, fucking bastards!" His face was pallid with rage. To think that some scum could stoop so low. Tom felt betrayed.

"Tom, Tom! Now calm down! Calm down." Mag reassured him. Megan appeared and echoed Mag's concern.

"Bastards!" he repeated. He was shaking so much he couldn't lift his drink. Dowie showed no emotion.

Gareth came up to Tom so unperturbed and said, "Don't let it get to you, Tom. I'm always throwing drunks out of the Rugby Club. It's unfortunately one of those things." He then casually walked over to his spot, took up his guitar and started gently strumming and singing "THE GRAND OLD DUKE OF YORK, HE ONLY HAD TWO MEN, HE MARCHED THEM ACROSS THE ROOM, AND HE THREW THEM OUT AGAIN." The party goers were revitalised.

Selwyn could see that Tom was still upset and thought he might console him with a little science. "Did you notice the different ways those two characters exited the pub?" Mag, Dowie and Megan were also within earshot and Gareth stopped playing out of courtesy, Selwyn continued, "Mike was the lighter of the two and he was catapulted out into the middle of the road while his friend who was heavier was simply dumped on the pavement."

"Is that it?" said Megan. "That's not very scientific, is it? Just nonsense."

"Yes, you're right, but it got Tom's attention, didn't it?" They laughed.

Collectively Richard and his friends decided to call it a night. The mini-gangsters thanked Mag for a pleasantly varied evening. Just as they were leaving, the timid one who had now plucked up enough courage walked over to the crowd in the corner and grabbed the double negative girl, who was leaning against the wall; he threw his arms around her and gave her a kiss, disengaged himself and said, "See you sometime baby." She stood transfixed, not believing that he would retaliate.

"Good, God! Slaughter On Tenth Avenue, Llanrheidol style," said Selwyn, who was beginning to feel less depressed. That finally brought the party spirit back.

"All right, folks. There ain't nobody here but us chickens so let's get down to it." This unpredictable comment came from Tom who had fully recovered by way of excess apple brandy. "I'll start."

"Start what?" asked Mag.

"The cabaret, of course." He caught hold of Beryl's hand and walked her round from behind the bar.

"My God! He's not going to sing, is he?" she declared out loud. Mag didn't appreciate his rough, earthy voice. The whole pub went silent.

"No, I'm just goin' to start the cabaret." He turned Beryl so that her back faced the audience and lifted her skirt very quickly. "That's what you've been missing all night, folks."

"Good God!" The repeated comment did not come from Selwyn this time.

"This is why I have not left the bar all night." Beryl turned provocatively and went back behind the bar.

Mag was taken aback at Tom's public flaunting, which was compounded by Megan's infectious comment, "Good God! He's coming out of his shell isn't he, Mag?" She was pleased that her husband was eventually losing some of his inhibitions, but agitated about the uncertainty of what had been going on behind the bar all evening. Mag's imagination was racing. Appropriately, Gareth started to play The Stripper once again.

This started Tom thinking along the lines that every male in the place was hoping, "Let's have a strip contest... The winner gets a bottle of bubbly." He received no comments that appeared to be opposed to it.

"What the Dickens has got into Tom?" Megan asked Mag. She just shook her head unknowingly.

"I've got the original 45 by David Rose, Gareth. I'll go and fetch it and you can have a rest from playing... It only lasts about two minutes so I'll have to play it twice."

"Just a minute, before you go off half cocked..." This caused an outburst of laughter. "Shit! I didn't mean it like that," said Beryl still retaining her modesty behind the bar. "If... I say, if some of us decide to join in your little game we will do it on two conditions."

"Pray what are those my little serving wench?" Selwyn bowed his body and moved his hand from his head to his waist, as though doffing his cap.

"You daft bugger... Two things," she repented, "firstly we want a fire, it's too cold otherwise..."

"Too right!" answered the negative girl.

"...and secondly, some of you men have to be involved."

"Yeah, that's right Beryl, let's get some men in on the act." It was Myfanwy stressing an interest in the activities.

"That's the booze talking," said Dowie, who had been remarkably quiet throughout the proceedings, to Mag and Tom... "She'll never do it."

"Yes, I agree," said Tom taking it upon himself to answer for the whole male presence. "Fire coming up, you go and fetch the record, Mag," and Tom disappeared into the bowels of the cellar which contained stores of coal and logs for the winter.

"Who do you think will do it, Dowie?" inquired Mag.

He didn't want to commit himself so he passed the question over to Megan and walked away. It seemed appropriate since Tom had uneventfully given her the job of deciding on the best act. "Obviously Beryl, most people here have already seen her topless," she said without any malice. "Certainly Joan," she pointed to the double negative girl who performed with the timid youth earlier.

"Well, that's her name is it?" Mag, like Tom, didn't know her real name.

"Possibly Mary but I doubt it. It depends on what mood Carol's in and..." Megan hesitated to collect her thoughts and said "...possibly you."

"You must be joking?" Mag tingled in anticipation.

"Let's wait and see. Dowie and Ieuan have already seen your boobs, haven't they?"

"How the hell did you know that, Megan?" Thinking she may have been spotted on the roof with Dulcie.

"I didn't notice at the time but Ieuan told me later about the blouse you had on that Sunday evening in the summer. We have no secrets between us but we don't go around broadcasting them. He knows more about Lally and me when we were in London than he cares to admit..." She readdressed the present topic. "In a friendly crowd like this, anything can happen... It reminds me of the nurses and doctors parties I, we used to go to..." She had a twinkle in her eye and a frivolous grin on her face. "Lally would have loved this."

As Tom came up from the cellar he approached Beryl and suggested that they started the proceedings off by demonstrating what really happened behind the bar. "Yeah. OK, Tom, but I'll have to get my others," she teasingly lifted the hem of her skirt, "I left them upstairs when I changed." Beryl quickly nipped out from behind the bar and up the stairs before she was noticed. On the way back, Ieuan made a request, she lifted her shirt. It was followed by the appropriate primitive grunts of disapproval.

Beryl responded with a very atypical saying which was probably a product of the inordinate amount of time she spent watching television. "Just a reconstruction, RECONSTRUCTION," she sang out. "Like they say on the telly."

Back at the bar Tom said to the gathered crowd, "I have asked Selwyn to introduce the acts because he's used to talking la-de-da and

I have asked Megan to do the judging. Before the main acts we have a few other performances. Selwyn! It's all yours."

Selwyn stood up with his back to the lit fire, clapped his hands to get their attention, cleared his throat and proceeded. "You've all seen the end product, no pun intended (Rolff and Gareth laughed) of the sexy goings on behind the bar tonight, but the evidence is only circumstantial. Tom and Beryl have consented to re-enact the unexpurgated version of How Beryl Lost Her Drawers."

"Get 'um off," came a pathetic cry from Ieuan.

A stool was strategically placed in the centre of the makeshift stage in front of the pleasantly glowing fire and sprinkled with beer. Selwyn informed the patrons that this was to give it the correct feel of authenticity. After some wasted time fictitiously pulling pints, Beryl sat on the stool... The finale of Tom wiping his face with the bum drying towel brought the house down. Beryl and Tom returned to behind the bar, one of whom remained enticingly knickerless for the rest of the night.

Selwyn was over-reacting to his elected position as Master of Ceremonies. "I have just had a request from one of your peers to perform on this Bacchanalian Feast of Delights..."

"Cut down on those bloody big words, will you?" Carol had actually made a contribution to the revelry.

He apologised and said, "Myf wants to do the can-can." And sat down on his chair with a clatter. Myfanwy gave an abortive attempt at the can-can to the strains of Gareth's guitar. She soon tired of prancing around and stopped. The only response was from Megan who clapped out of sympathy and for Gareth's dexterity. Dowie continued to occupy a bar stool enjoying the entertainment but having no intention of participating, despite Selwyn's attempts to get him to tell a few oriental stories disrobed to the waist for authenticity.

"It would not have been one of the better sights anyway, with his brewers' goitre hanging over his belt unless it was a Sumo wrestler's demonstration," said Selwyn remorsefully. Some chuckled; Dowie was not pleased. The proceedings were livened up when Gareth and Rolff gave their party-piece rendition of a guitar player and Flamenco dancer. It was somewhat different from their usual routine. Rolff's basque kept falling down exposing his hairy chest, and his twisted ankle did nothing for his foot work. Selwyn pronounced that they did at least try to amuse the crowd and that was more than some. Yah followed with a small demonstration of Taiwanese dancing without music.

The party was beginning to become idle so Selwyn in his newly appointed dictatorial office decided that it needed invigorating.

"Come on. Good God, where are all the strippers? There's still a bottle of bubbly to be won."

"I've done my share," said Beryl, who was standing noticeably close to Tom behind the bar. Selwyn agreed.

Mag, who was less reluctant to perform than on a previous lock-in session, moved off her stool next to Dowie and said, "Tom started the last lot, you know, so I suppose it is my turn to start this lot." Cheers of approval circulated the room. She was clearly not too steady on her feet but managed to get to the sacrificial spot near the fire.

"I knew she would do it," Megan said to Tom. "I felt it in my bones."

Tom was confused. "I'm shocked, I would have bet you anything she would have said no." Dowie said nothing, he looked excited.

"Are you ready, Tom?" she slurred out.

"You've got four minutes." He raised a handful of digits in the air. Someone laughed by the bar.

The music started and she began to take off her dress to the strains of the doublet. All were la, la-ing to the beat. She was slow and shapeless, finishing up at the end of the musical interlude without a bra but all the encumbrances of the lower half. She received the biggest ovation of the night for her ingenuous endeavour. Tom was relieved but Ieuan was actually standing on a chair and whistling through his teeth. "Sush!" said Tom. We'll have the police here complaining." Mag brazenly picked up her clothes and walked over to the bar, sat on her stool between Megan and Dowie and shamelessly dressed.

After some verbal encouragement from Selwyn, Mary, followed by Joan, exhibited their assets. Before their independent acts Tom had the foresight to turn off the lights in the pub except for the spotlight over the dartboard. This was turned to cover the area in front of the fire. They were less drunk and more accomplished than Mag so subsequently at the end of the music they had completed the task. Their lithe, naked bodies glowed in the firelight, it was truly magical. Having only one article of clothing on in the first place, Joan was outstanding, she twirled around and positioned her body in the most controversially contorted ways. The party guests were ecstatic.

While everyone was occupied complimenting the girls on their magnificent natural talent and trying to get an encore, Ieuan moved into the spotlight. Tom observed the situation but did not start the recording since Ieuan was in no state to ensnare the audience. His lower portion was exposed first and despite the inordinate amount of alcohol he had consumed, Megan noticed he was getting over excited. She mentioned it to Tom and he instantly moved the spotlight. Megan told Ieuan that it was time to go on to something new and he believed her. No one else except Mag spotted Ieuan's predicament and his vain attempt to outdo his predecessors.

Megan suggested that the champagne go to Joan. It was a unanimous decision. Selwyn's concluding speech in his honoured position waxed lyrical about Joan as the most outstanding exhibition of lively, raw, bawdy entertainment ever to be demonstrated in Ty Gwyn, nay Llanrheidol, nay Wales... She insisted on Mary being present and they jointly received the bottle. It was immediately opened and left on the counter for anyone to drink while they jointly entertained the pub with a much requested encore.

No one could possibly follow the last act. Rolff strummed on Gareth's guitar for a while and eventually the party folded up at about four-thirty in the morning. Tom, Mag and Myfanwy stayed by the dying embers, contemplating whether to go to bed or not. "Must clean out that fireplace tomorrow, sorry, today. It's not cold enough yet to keep it going." No one made any reference to the party, they were too pleasantly tired.

* * * * *

Megan was banging on the door at ten o'clock. She had come to help clean up. 'A very nice gesture,' thought Mag, who with Myfanwy's help, was already in the process of getting the pub ready for opening; Tom was predictably in the cellar. Monday was hectic with crowds of carousers coming through at lunchtime as well as the evening since the following day was Christmas Eve. There was no time to reflect on the past except briefly. It was an extremely tiring time and tempers frayed between Mag and Tom and by the end of the morning they were only communicating when necessary. Mag never held a grudge for long and they had settled their grievances by the evening. A small group of regulars stayed after closing and subsequently the topic of the party had to be analysed.

"I told you you would perform, didn't I, Mag?"

"Yes, you did... I would have bet a fortune that you would be wrong."

"It was the booze," said Tom sarcastically, not realising that she really wanted to do it but her clumsy technique and in fact, the booze restricted her.

Tom encountered a strange feeling when he saw Mag exposing herself in public, but it was not tested to the full since she never really got to a prohibitive stage. Tom reassured himself that the amount of flesh she revealed was a common incident seen by hundreds on any European beach in the summer. It was the after effects of immodestly walking back to the bar he found somewhat disconcerting.

"I liked that little thing you did with Beryl," said Dowie who was settled on a stool next to Mag. "It started everythin' off nicely without too much T and A."

"T and A?" questioned Mag.

"Tit and arse," replied Dowie.

Quickly moving away from a potentially embarrassing situation, Tom said, "Weren't Mary and Joan amazing? Who would have thought Mary would have done it, she's so quiet?"

"I think Carol has a better figure than Mary but, of course, she wouldn't do it... But what about Joan, then. She really was professional." Ieuan could recall his incident but not the reason why he was stopped. "That's why I packed it up after her. I couldn't see any sense in continuing." Ieuan didn't notice Megan glance at Tom. Arrangements were made for Christmas Day and they all dispersed.

Nana had done most of the Christmas preparation including the customary turkey and veg. They were going to have the meal after closing lunchtime. Tom decided not to open that evening. Apart from family the Tremletts had invited Megan, Beryl, Dowie and Myfanwy and son. All the Blue Bootees had departed from Llanrheidol for their own characteristic festivities. Rolff had taken Yah to see his parents in Cardiff by courtesy of motorised Selwyn and Clem was on duty. Ieuan had to stay within the confines of his home. His wife insisted, at least on this one day of the year when they experienced the sobriety of her parents. Dowie stayed in the bar with

Mag for the morning session. Mag was bored with only one customer but happy to be away from the pandemonium upstairs of breakfast, presents and food.

Mag declared that the Yuletide Feast would be downstairs in the bar because of the numbers. It was, as tradition allows, the time for excess. Mark was sick twice before tea. The children had presents selected for the specific amusement of adults. The remote controlled car was a firm favourite with Dowie while Tom, Mag and the rest were running a competition on a computer game. The two boys were happy to play at castles with a large cardboard box which originally contained a tumble dryer. Megan left early in the afternoon, to visit, and Beryl departed just after tea. She was going to join Mary and Joan in the Rugby Club. Richard was in two minds, Beryl had invited him to go with her, or should he stay? He was going into the Army the following week. He fancied a younger crowd, so he took up Beryl's offer. The children were messing around upstairs while the remaining adults were sitting around the fire in the bar. Everyone was full to capacity, relaxed and enjoying the quiet of the evening. It was raining and windy outside and beginning to get dark with no sign of movement in the forsaken streets except for the rippling colours on the wet pavement reflecting the festive illuminations of this small Welsh town.

Mag sensed that Dowie was preparing for one of his entertaining short stories so she dragged her seat closer to him. Tom observed the move but dismissed it as inconsequential. As predicted, Dowie adopted a classical sinister pose.

"Typical Christmas evenin'," he said. "If it wasn't for the fire and a wee dram (he loved using that phrase) it would be quite cold as well. How are you two settlin' in by the way?"

Tom poked the fire to liven it up and said, "What do you mean? We like the place very much." Mag agreed silently. "But we are much busier than we expected." Mag concurred for the second time.

"No, no! I mean upstairs in the flat," his eyes lifted to the ceiling. "What do you keep in the room next to the large bedroom?"

Mag thought the request rather peculiar but replied, "Well, originally Mark was going to sleep in there, you know, but he went to live with Nana and Grandad instead."

"He loves it with us, Dowie. He's made lots of friends... But some of the stories he comes out with are incredible," Nana gave a gentle loving smile. Grandad shuffled in his chair and confirmed her statement with a grunt.

"That room, upstairs, it's haunted, Mag," said Dowie in a deep, slow, menacing tone.

"Don't be silly, I don't believe you." Mag was rarely upstairs on her own but when she thought about it, a shiver ran down her spine. She shrugged her shoulders and drew in a sharp breath and said, "My God, someone has just walked over my grave..." Before anyone else could comment, Mag spoke again. "You mean the little room with the horrible brown wallpaper where we store our spirits for the pub?"

"Exactly! Now why do you think you keep them in that room?" He paused, his eyes widened to show the flames from the fire dancing on their surfaces.

Tom could see the seasonal way the conversation was going, but he had to admire his mastery of telling a good yarn.

Mag got even closer to Dowie and Nana pricked up her ears at the mention of a haunting.

"Let me tell you," his remark was followed by a foreboding silence, then continued. "The ghost is an old crippled tinker woman who stayed one night in winter when Ty Gwyn was a real Inn and had to take in travellers... It was the time in the eighteenth century when the peasant uprisin' of Llanrheidol drove out the Englishmen from the Castle and burnt it to the ground."

Simply to perpetuate the tale, Tom said, "I have often wondered why the Castle was in ruins, when numerous others like Harlech and Cardiff are fully functional. That explains it." Dowie increased the suspense by slowly sipping his malt.

"Come on! What happened next?" said Nana who was as engrossed as Mag. Tom was equally fascinated but tried not to make it obvious that he was listening.

"It was a bitterly cold night but despite that all the residents of the pub joined the rest of the townsfolk and took to the streets to celebrate their release from the tyranny of the English. In their excitement they forgot the old woman upstairs. She was very weak from hunger and cold and couldn't move 'round very much because of her wooden leg, which she had removed for comfort." Dowie bit his lip to conceal the hairy smirk.

Tom rubbed his leg and depressingly complained. "I may be like that one day. Oh, that reminds me, Mag. I have to go for a check up after Christmas here in Llanrheidol. They've transferred my records from Bristol."

"Later, Tom... Let's hear the rest of Dowie's story first."

"It's no story, Mag. It's TRUE!" Again he paused to savour the moment. By now he knew he had his audience agog with curiosity. "She finally managed to creep down to the bar lookin' for somethin' to eat. She could only find whisky and gin since they had taken the barrels of beer out on the horse and cart to celebrate. The door was locked from the outside and the key left in so she couldn't get out. Eventually she dragged herself back to the small room next to the large bedroom where it was a little warmer and drunk the bottles of spirits. Days went by and eventually the proprietor and his family returned to find the old crone frozen stiff. Accordin' to legend, she did not rot because she was pickled in alcohol." Dowie found it difficult to contain himself. He was secretly laughing at the gullibility of Mag and her mother. The story was full of inaccuracies and complete nonsense. All was silent except for the crackling of a log recently placed on the fire. "And that's not all," shouted Dowie,

Mag and Nana were simultaneously startled, "My God! You frightened me," screamed Mag.

He dropped his voice and repeated slowly, "and that's not all." With a menacing movement of his index finger in Mag's face, he said, "Anyone who's taken over Ty Gwyn, since that do, is compelled by some strange force, to store their spirits in that room... One person apparently attempted to defy the ghost and was found dead the next day in the little room next to the large bedroom." He made a point of emphasising the location. Mag, as usual, was fascinated by his voice and his art of story telling and touched the top of his leg affectionately inquiring as to whether he would like another drink. Nana and Tom noticed but they both knew that Mag was a tactile person and was always touching people of both sexes. Dowie accepted the offer and finalised the tale by saying, "You can sometimes hear her frail voice humming a sad little song when you pass the door of the little room next to the big bedroom..." Grandad stirred in his chair, he had been listening all the time. Mag was stricken with a cold shudder and goose pimples once again.

"Mark slept in that room the first night we were here, Dowie."

"Yes, but only for a few hours, if you recall, Mag." Tom was attempting to endorse the tale.

Tom's support gave Dowie the final word. "Ah! Like most spells it doesn't work straight away, it has to develop."

Tom had to thank Dowie indirectly for the affection he received that night. Mag wouldn't pass the little room without an escort on her arm and she cuddled up to Tom in bed for fear of hearing the spectre's voice. Richard arrived home at about four but his whereabouts were never questioned, despite the lipstick on his shirt and the bruised neck.

Boxing Day was back to normal for the pubs of Llanrheidol except it was Sunday opening hours. A few dyspeptics wandered through and the regular locals gathered. Mag was on duty when Megan, as official spokesperson, told her the news. "We have decided that you have been such marvellous hosts over Christmas that we have clubbed together and decided to give you two tickets for the New Year's bash at the Royal. We'll all be there including Selwyn and Ieuan's wife... Before you find any excuses, we have worked it out that you can close up at eleven, with our help and be in the Royal within fifteen minutes."

Mag was absolutely delighted, she had tears in her eyes. "I must tell Tom." She buzzed for him to come down to share the happy news. Tom was similarly delighted but felt something of a fraud considering how much money he had taken over the holidays.

Richard was having a final fling with the boys and girls at the Rugby Club. The Royal was for the older crowd. As the poster so poignantly put it, A Function For The More Discerning Clientele. "In other words, no drunken louts," said Mag. The music was of the older Big Band type when swing was in its heyday. They sat together around two tables which had been pulled together. Selwyn was talking about things of a zoological nature to Tom. Ieuan was remarkably reserved next to his very attractive wife. She was friendly but aloof. Put it down to the fact that she is teetotal, thought Tom. He tried to engage her in conversation but seemed to get only one word answers, so he politely gave up. Babs came over and made a fuss of Tom and dragged him onto the floor. Her husband was left to close up. It was a noticeable fact that most of the publicans' wives in Llanrheidol seemed to enjoy themselves at the expense of their husbands' toil. Megan and Tom independently observed that Mag was spending an inordinate amount of time in intimate association with Dowie.

The bewitching year passed to the wail of bagpipes followed by the address to the haggis in traditional fashion. Kissing was given out in profusion, some couples distinctly more intimate than others. Tom's introduction to the New Year consisted of indulging in a little bit of slap and tickle with Babs on the verandah of the hotel. In his haste to get away before they were seen, he accidentally smashed his fragile knee against the table. He didn't realise it at the time, but next day it was excruciatingly painful.

Babs was whisked away to the confines of the White Hart while the rest went back to Ty Gwyn including Ieuan's wife who, in wild abandon, had a sweet sherry, became very talkative and started to reminisce with Megan. Mag was in a strange mood, it was difficult to know whether she was tired or drunk. She excused herself, left the party and went to bed. Soon afterwards the party dispersed. Tom found her lying on the bed partially clothed and sound asleep. He covered her with the bed clothes and got in himself.

The next few days were spent recovering from the festivities and the number of people venturing out to consume alcohol in Llanrheidol would not fill one pub let alone the numerous ones that punctuated the town. Dowie came in most nights and the girls started drifting back. Rolff and his full compliment of Bootees were back in town. The weather was changing and becoming persistently cold, so Tom thought it was time to light the fire in the top bar. Mag was not her usual impulsive self. Tom imagined it might be due to the unique combination of excessive hedonism, Richard going away, together with her recent bereavement. Tom was on top of the world, his developing interest in zoology was progressing and he was learning a lot from Selwyn. The pub was one of the most successful of the smaller establishments in town. The only drawback to his idyllic way of life was his leg which was becoming a burden. He did not complain much but some days it was extremely painful, nor did he go to the doctors because he was visiting the specialist in the hospital the following week.

Mag did not go with him to the hospital, on the grounds that the appointment was when the pub was about to open for trade. Someone had to be there to help with any meals required. Tom met Megan at the hospital and she managed, influentially, to get him to the top of the list. He was soon seen. "X-ray first and then come back to me with the plates," said the officious Mr Buxton. On returning, Tom was informed that he would have to have an operation on his knee. The patella was still damaged from his accident at work but he had also smashed and fractured it recently. Tom confessed to the verandah incident as being a solo accident.

"It will mean a new knee-cap and extensive physiotherapy. We've got a long waiting list," he snapped.

"Oh, it's all right, I still contribute to a Hospital Scheme from my previous job so I can come in privately." One of the more useful perks of being Managerial Staff, he thought.

"When can you come in?" was the immediate answer.

"As soon as possible," answered Tom. "It's very painful."

The thought of another private patient almost brought a smile to Mr Buxton's face. "Next week, then. My secretary will let you have the details by post." He shot out of the room into the next. "And who is this, nurse?" The door closed and the voice faded into an inaudible murmur.

The following week on a Monday, after a hectic weekend, he was sitting on his bed waiting for the pre-medication. Tom was satisfied in his mind that there would be no problems with the catering. It was a relatively slack time of the year and just in case, he had made extra dishes and put them in the freezer. Mag had only to look after the bar side of things. Actually, Mag persuaded Myfanwy to stay on later in the mornings to cover the lunchtime trade.

Mag visited Tom every evening for the first few days after the operation. She then volunteered her visits to other people. Dowie came once just after the operation with Selwyn and the next day with Mag. He did not come again but there was always someone there at visiting time. He was delighted at the frequency of the visits from Mary, sometimes with Carol and sometimes on her own. Babs popped in one evening with a small bottle of calvados. During the second week, they removed the plaster from his leg and he was much more mobile except for the obnoxious pain when he tried to bend his leg. Pain is often associated with some form of visual or auditory stimulus. In Tom's case, it was the characteristic clicking of the heels of the physiotherapist as she approached his bed daily at about ten o'clock. He would feel himself tighten up in anticipation of the treatment enhanced by the peculiar fetid smell of stale sweat. "We must get this knee bending again," was her daily opening gambit, while in the process of getting him out of bed and into a wheel chair. "Come on, Tom. Bend it, bend it!" She would persist for about half an hour. Tom then relaxed as the stress inducing sound faded away in the distance. Megan visited Tom every day after her term of duty. She was always curious about his visitors and relentlessly asked about Mag. If she did not turn up Tom would use the excuse that she could not get away because of the pressure of work or someone else wanted to visit.

By the end of the second week he had improved sufficiently to go home. Selwyn picked him up in his car and ferried him back to the pub. He had a lot of trouble getting up the stairs but eventually made it and flopped down in his chair. Selwyn left him to relax while Myfanwy flitted about dispensing bar meals. Between intermittent visits to the bar she talked to Tom. "I've got something to tell you, Tom."

"Oh no, you're not leaving us, are you?"

"No, nothing like that. I've got a new boyfriend." A gentle radiance came over her face.

"Who's that?" Tom didn't want an immediate answer, he was more concerned about the pain induced by his encounter with the stairs. "Could you get me a glass of water, please?" He produced a bottle of tablets from his pocket.

"Yeah, OK." She nipped away and was back in no time, eager to reveal her lover. "Remember you used to send me to Ifor's place for meat?" Before he could answer she said, "We got talking and he asked me to go out for a drink. We've had several dates since..." As if it was an evil secret, she said, "He knows about the boy, they get on well together."

"Oh, I am glad," before Tom could finish the sentence the buzzer sounded from downstairs.

Myfanwy answered, "That was Mag, she's got a big round on at the moment but she'll be up as soon as possible."

Mag eventually came up looking very glamorous and wearing her notorious blouse. She was clutching an opened letter in her hand. She kissed Tom and instantly stated, "It's a letter from Richard, you know. The postman has just delivered it in the bar. He likes the friends in his unit and they are having a great time." Mag hesitantly declared the contents of the letter more out of guilt than for information. "I'm very sorry I couldn't see you every day, you know. I've been so busy."

"That's all right, Mag. I know you came to visit whenever it was possible." He had no doubts about her sincerity.

"Selwyn picked you up. That was nice of him. Do you want a cuppa?"

"That would be nice." Tom was hoping for a chat.

"Myf will do it for you. I must get back. Beryl is on her own." She kissed Tom and disappeared.

There were only occasional requests for bar meals so Tom could not make out what was responsible for the apparent excessive activity. "Are there a lot of people in the bar, Myfanwy?"

She did not wish to appear perfidious to Mag, so she simply answered, "It's very busy for the time of year... Is there anything you want before I go, Tom?" His response was negative.

Mag closed and came upstairs. "Well, what's it like to be home again?" She did not appear excited to see him but it was not obvious to Tom. "Mark and my parents are coming to see you tonight so you'll have plenty of company."

"It's marvellous. I feel a new man and after a few weeks I should be back in form."

She made herself a cuppa, Tom declined the offer, and sat down next to him and they talked. "I see you've got that blouse on." He touched her breast.

Mag moved back slightly making out that she was not comfortable on the settee by slightly raising her backside and putting it down again. "That's better! The blouse is safe now, you know, I put a small clasp on the top." She fingered the top of her blouse, as if to reassure him that it was safe. "And, of course, I'm wearing a bra." She opened her blouse to show an expensive looking half-cup brassiere and closed it again making a shivering sound as the smell of expensive perfume spread through the air. His attempt to be intimate was again shunned.

Mag was not sure what Tom had said about his period of recovery so she repeated the question. "How long did you say it would take for you to be up and about?"

"A few weeks. Why? Did you want to take me on a holiday to recuperate?" Mag laughed uneasily.

"You know we can't go on holiday together. Someone has to look after the business."

"Why don't we get a relief manager or a retired publican to look after the place for a week or so? I'm sure someone in the LVA could give us some advice." He flicked his fingers as the obvious solution to their problem came into his head. "Let's ask Dowie to look after the pub for us." There was a pensive pause, then Mag informed Tom that Dowie had said that he was well out of it and didn't want anything to do with the licensing trade anymore. He also told her that there was a strong possibility that he may be moving to Cardiff to take up some sort of security job.

"You've asked him before then?" Mag was caught off guard. She didn't want him to know to what extent they had discussed the future so all she could do was shake her head in agreement. Moving, Tom smiled and abolished any repugnant thoughts he had about Mag and Dowie. "Bloody hell! Another party I suppose. We've just finished the last lot."

"Nobody knows at the moment and after all, it's only a possibility so don't say anything, will you, Tom?"

January went tediously onwards. Tom had plenty of visitors and by the end of the month he could negotiate the stairs of the flat once a day. Mag was going regularly to the Royal's disco with the crowd on Friday nights while Tom took his time and finished off the bar sometimes in the company of Selwyn and Megan either together or separately. Mag came home in the early hours of the morning just after the disco closed accompanied by Dowie. She would not come straight to bed but pottered around in the flat for a while. When Tom questioned her about this atypical behaviour she said that it was to unwind after the dancing.

Selwyn was not as frequent a visitor and the girls didn't come in much during the week with the exception of darts night. This was not surprising since January was the quietest month of the year. Most people had spent out over Christmas and the New Year.

Trade started to pick up again by the end of February. Late night sessions were still on, with Mag presiding but with a reduction in the number in attendance. Tom was under the notion from the subdued sound of voices, that it was only Dowie down there some nights. One thing that did puzzle him was the occasional silence between rounds of conversation. It was particularly obvious since Tom had taken to reading more than watching the television late at night. He was also becoming increasingly troubled that since his spell in hospital, Mag was less affectionate; they seemed to have lost that mutuality which made the running of the pub such fun. By the end of February Tom could hobble around using a stick but still preferred to do the catering upstairs.

One Friday evening the strange combination of Megan and Selwyn were in a lock-in with Tom. "Do you know Dowie is thinking of leaving Llanrheidol?"

"Yes, he tried to sell me his house but as far as I am concerned, one cottage is enough. I still have a spare bedroom in that. He told me not to mention it to anyone... I didn't realise you knew."

"Mag told me when I suggested he took over the pub while we went on holiday together."

Megan with her innate powers of perception was curious to find out the response. "What was her reply?"

"She said that he no longer wanted anything to do with pubs and he was going to start a new life in the security business in Cardiff.

"But..." She was about to speak but then withdrew. Selwyn recalled the gossip he had heard.

While Tom was in the toilet, he whispered to Megan, "Are the rumours true?"

"I don't know for sure, but I'm worried for Tom. It will hit him like a ton of bricks. I pray it is just rumour... you know how tales get so exaggerated in this town."

Tom returned and spoke to Megan specifically, "If he does leave I suppose we will have to have a leaving party and we've just recovered from the last run. Never mind, I'm sure you and Mag will be able to cope... What do you think we should give him for a leaving present?"

"Just a mo, Tom! We don't know for sure. Let's wait and see what happens in the next week or so." They talked about the problems of the youngsters today and how it was nice to be out of it all. Tom found it intriguing to see the problems approached by a teacher and a nurse from very different angles and the different ways they were deciphered.

Tom heard Mag and Dowie reach the outside door, quietly open it and go into the bar. There were muffled voices for a little while and then a deathly silence. A few moments later the stillness was interrupted by suppressed, intermittent moans. Tom's face drained of colour and he began to tremble. He recognised what was going on from his own experience. He grabbed his stick and thumped the floor of the flat and shouted. "What the bloody hell is going on down there?" He was too immobile to venture downstairs quickly.

There was a resounding crash and Mag shouted back, "I've just knocked a stool over. I'll be up now." The outside door opened and closed in quick succession and Mag ascended the stairs. The adulterous goings on in the bar had finally sealed the fate of Tom and Mag. Mag shamelessly walked into the flat with her hair ruffled and a tale-tale button undone on her blouse.

Tom rose from his chair and shouted at her, "What the bloody hell was going on down there and what was all that groaning about?"

Remorselessly, Mag pulled herself to her full height and said, "I was havin' a fuck. Dowie was screwin' me on the floor... I love him and I'm goin' to Cardiff with him."

Tom fell back into his chair as though devoid of any strength to keep himself standing. He experienced a horrible tightening in his stomach and a feeling like a bolt shooting through his heart. "I thought there was something going on. You have not been the same since I came out of hospital." He then began to get hysterical, laughing one minute and crying the next and rambling on. "When did all this start? Did you know he was screwing Dulcie? He's a womaniser, a two timer, a blackguard... He's not your type. What the bloody hell do you see in him?" Tom was panic stricken. He oscillated within the restricted area of the room. First near the door as if about to exit, then close to Mag almost touching her. His wretched attempts to belittle Dowie had no effect on Mag whatsoever but it was his only immediate defence. He calmed down a little, sank into his chair and put his head in his hands.

She stood coquettishly above him and announced that she knew about Dulcie and it made no difference and that she was originally going to wait until he had fully recovered but now it'd all come out, so why prolong the agony? She loved Dowie and wanted to be with him. Tom pleaded with her to stay, bringing up the good times, the length of their marriage and finally, what did she intend to do about

Mark? He would miss her terribly. All to no avail. Her mind was made up she packed a few things, including jewellery and sexy underwear and left saying that she would send for the other things later when they had settled in Cardiff. Tom was devastated. He sat in the chair all night dozing off and waking up. Each time hoping it was a nightmare. The morning came slowly but inevitably and he was eventually woken by the sound of the front door being opened. He got to the top of the stairs and shouted down. "Is that you, Mag?" To his utmost dismay the reply came back.

"No, it's Myfanwy. Why, isn't she home from the disco, yet?" She looked up the stairs and saw Tom's bedraggled condition. Her first reaction was to find out what was wrong. On reaching Tom, she could see that something very serious had happened. "What's the matter, Tom? You look terrible."

He burst out crying, then attempted to hold it back and blurted out, "She's left me, she's gone," and proceeded to cry again.

Myfanwy attempted to console him and reiterated, "What's the matter, Tom?" She was too shocked the first time for it to register on her mind.

"She's left me, Mag's gone off with Dowie to Cardiff."

Myfanwy now realised the extent of his distress and said, "When did all this happen?" It was a rhetorical question. "I had better get someone in, you're in no fit state to be by yourself." She went downstairs and phoned Megan, who was luckily not on duty that day and she came directly. Myfanwy carried on with her job. Beryl opened up a little late that morning after being told the news.

While Megan was comforting Tom, there was a buzz from the bar, Megan answered, "Can Selwyn and Rolff come upstairs to see you? They have something they want to tell you both."

Selwyn was so disturbed when he saw Tom that it made him feel queasy. "I thought you should know what Rolff has told me." Tom was in no position to reply, he was so bewildered by the whole affair so Selwyn turned to Megan for consolations. Selwyn touched Tom's shoulder affectionately, diverted his eyes from the pitiable individual and said, "Tell her Rolff."

"I was in the kitchen this morning at about two making a coffee (I work late because I'm writing up my thesis) when Mag burst in, we never lock the back door. Dowie was asleep, I think?" Rolff started to whisper as if to make it less of a torment for Tom. "She was very calm and collected and simply said that she had left Tom and was going away with Dowie to Cardiff. I simply could not believe what I was hearing... I tried to reason with her, well, as best I could, I'm not very experienced at such things," he said apologetically "Just then Dowie appeared like a big hairy thug from his room." There was a feeling of resentment in his statement, Rolff was not getting on too well with his landlord because he wanted to put the rent up. He grabbed Mag and went back into his flat and closed the door. I just stood there. I just didn't know what to do next so I made my coffee and sat in the kitchen. I could hear restrained voices and a lot of movement. Now I know he was packing. I must have sat there for what appeared to be hours, then the next thing I knew was that Dowie appeared with Mag and two large suitcases.

"We are goin' to catch the five-thirty to Cardiff," he bellowed at me but I noticed that he didn't seem to be in the same ecstatic mood as Mag was displaying, as she clung onto his arm." Rolff instantly grasped that this was not the best time to express any emotion. Fortunately Tom was not listening. "'I'll be sellin' the house so you'll have to find somewhere else to live. There's no hurry. You've paid up to the end of the month, that'll do,' and he left." Selwyn and Rolff could see how distraught Tom was so they went downstairs for a well earned pint, leaving Megan alone with Tom.

"You knew about this Megan, didn't you?" Tom was over the spontaneous lachrymation but his eyes were puffy from the severity and frequency of the attacks.

"Yes Tom, I must admit I had my suspicions and so did everyone who went to the Friday nighters. Mary wanted to tell you but I persuaded her against it. I thought it might have passed off. They were only cuddling and kissing a bit according to Ieuan. There was no hanky-panky."

Tom's eyelids welled up but he overcame the urge to give vent to his feelings, "There bloody well was last night!" Foregoing their intimacy, Tom said, "I recognised the noise she makes when we are at it."

Megan was not inclined to use expletives and especially not in blasphemous Welsh but "*Iesu Mawr*," she uttered, "it must have been a nightmare for you, poor Tom." She squeezed his hand affectionately.

Tom was beginning to get agitated again. "I couldn't get down the bloody stairs, could I? So I had to bang on the ceiling." He was pale and started to shake with the signs of a cold sweat.

Megan had seen this anxiety often in the hospital with distraught relatives and had perfected a reassuring manner to calm them down. It worked as a temporary measure on Tom. "I'll go down to the bar and phone. Who's your doctor, Tom?"

"We haven't registered yet," he accidentally used the plural personal pronoun but didn't notice.

"Never mind, I'll phone mine. I'll tell Nana as well."

"No, no," pleaded Tom.

"She has to be informed, Tom... She's her mother and she has legally abandoned her child."

"That's a bit strong," said Tom protectively.

"Perhaps you're right because you are still around but she must know the facts before she hears them from someone else, don't you agree? Also I have to go to work tomorrow and she can come to the pub and stay with you in the day."

Throughout the rest of the day, several sympathetic well-wishers had passed through the flat. Gethin was most supportive. He had recently lost Christin back to the great metropolis and could appreciate what he was going through. Tom could not associate the breakup of a homosexual relationship with the anguish he was experiencing but he could perceive that the grief Gethin was enduring was genuine. He was feeling much more relaxed. Most likely the effect of the antidepressant from Megan's doctor plus the pain killers for his leg and the innumerable free drinks that came up from the bar. Whether it was a false sense of security or not didn't matter at this stage.

"Let's take one day at a time," explained Megan to Nana.

Beryl, with the help of Mary and Carol, got through Saturday. They did not go straight home that night but with Megan and Ieuan, they all went upstairs and had a few drinks with Tom. Selwyn was too upset and made his usual visit to the Club.

"I must tell you what I heard yesterday in the hospital, Tom." She took a sip from her glass, "I popped into your old ward to see someone and do you remember that old boy who was next to you in the bed by the window?" Tom looked puzzled. "You must remember him, he kept flicking his false teeth in and out."

"Shut up Megan, you're putting me off my drink. Imagine all those bits of food including carrot," Ieuan was back in form. The girls made disapproving noises and put their hands over their mouths as if preventing themselves from vomiting.

"Oh yes?" Tom had remembered.

"He beckoned me over and he said between flicks." The present company laughed, Tom smiled. "'Remember that young man who had his knee done in that bed', and he pointed to where you were. 'Well, he died you know.'" Megan stopped and changed into her authoritative voice. "What had happened was that when I got you moved to that private room so that you could see the telly in peace, that was the end to him. He thought that it was the room where they took patients to die. In fact, the previous person in that room did die but he was terminally ill." She strongly laboured the point, "I said, don't be a dope, I was talking to him yesterday. He wouldn't have it. So as far as he is concerned you're dead."

"Amazing! I've heard of people preserved in alcoh...'" Tom stopped abruptly. He remembered where he had heard that story before.

Everybody rallied around and was so good. Mary helped out regularly in the bar. Megan and Ieuan did most of the running about and Nana came in daily to help with the catering side of things. Selwyn spent most of his time in the pub chatting to Tom who came down to the bar at night. The pub was soon running like clockwork. Dulcie phoned; she had heard from Mag and was very upset about the whole affair. She wanted to come down but Tom managed to dissuade her on the grounds that it was a bit chaotic at the moment. He really didn't want to be bothered. It was for a while a sad little pub for hapless Tom and the regular crowd.

One morning Tom realised that business must go on, the run-of-the-mill drinker is not concerned as long as the ale is there and in good condition. Like the situation with Lally, time is a great healer. He decided that it was no good feeling sorry for himself, it was time to get on with living.

He took Beryl on full-time and Mary had coaxed Carol to help out on a regular basis. Tom was going to Nana's house on his night off and staying for the evening or taking Mark out. He occasionally went to the Legion with Grandad, but he found it a bit too geriatric to go regularly. Mag was never mentioned in the household. Tom could feel Nana wanted to say something but she remained silent. He was still stunned by her rapid departure and Mark was all he had left. Subconsciously he would have loved Mag to be back, no pub and a regular family like in Bristol. It was not possible, so he progressed towards a more wayward way of life by drinking more and being less concerned about money, although his frugal nature would not let him go to excess. He did not go to the Friday disco but travelled regularly with the darts team. Ieuan had taken over as captain. They were not doing too well in the league but the girls were top of their division. When the season started again after Christmas, they were down in the dumps for a while because of the upset but they gradually reconciled themselves to the landlady's transgression. Rose proved to be the centre of attraction and more or less took over the convivial niche occupied by Mag. Some of her jokes were unrepeatable even in male company. Mostly about hospitals, doctors and nurses. The all girls' team was extremely popular with any opposing male team. This was because they were associated with the infamous Carnival win commemoration party and more recently the notorious private party held at Christmas. Both incidents had been blown up out of all sense of proportion and finished up being a befuddled sex orgy with naked bodies and fornication abounding. It was curious but none of the girls, not even Myfanwy and especially not Megan admitted anything. The air of mystery kept the busy bodies gossiping, with Ieuan refuelling the events from time to time.

* * * * *

March was predictably cold and windy but by the beginning of April it was starting to become more like spring. Tom had heard nothing from Mag and she hadn't even made any attempt to contact her mother. Nana and Grandad were very disturbed by her behaviour and complete rejection of Mark. In Tom's confused mind, it was a preconceived plan with no complications. Dowie sold his house completely furnished through a solicitor. Someone came up from Cardiff one night, according to the address on the rented van and took away all his belongings. Rolff had moved in with Gareth. Tom had not fully recovered and was reluctant to talk about his problem unless pushed.

"The same goes for Mag, she was lively and fun to be with but not unfaithful or at least I don't think so." There was some doubt in Tom's voice, "Thinking back over the years there were times that gave me some concern." He became silent and in retrospect he could now understand some of the unfamiliar inventiveness Mag practised to avoid his amorous advances and why she apparently needed to uncoil after a night out with Dulcie. "It's all in the past, let's talk about something more amusing." He dismissed it with a wave of his hand. "That son of mine, he has the most amazing imagination. He was telling me on Wednesday about how he rescued three little girls who were trapped in the classroom of his school which was on fire. He told me he went in on his own with a wet handkerchief across his mouth and..."

"I didn't hear about that," said Megan, who had been very close to Tom since his ordeal.

"No, you wouldn't, it was all in his mind. I wish I could write a story of the incident for a joke and threaten to send it to the Llanrheidol Star."

Selwyn, who fancied himself as a writer of humorous ditties and often wrote small articles for the College paper said, "I'll do something for you, Tom... Tell me the facts again, I will write something amusing. You can tell him next Wednesday that you are going to put it in the paper. Pass me a scrap of paper and a pen." Tom reached back and instantly but sadly remembered the Blaster episode and how he would like to be back there in time.

"Don't forget to let us see it as well. I could do with a good laugh," said Ieuan.

"Will you be here tomorrow?" Before anyone could reply, he answered, "I'll bring it in then."

Saturday evening was habitually the time when the Tremletts shut up shop, got a take-away and relaxed in the flat. Poor misguided Tom could not break this conditioned reflex but it sadly terminated with him eating alone. This Saturday night the after hours gathering was different and reserved for Selwyn's monologue. He characteristically cleared his throat and began to deliberate. "Who dares wins."

"That's the SAS motto."

"Shush, Ieuan. We want to hear the story... You're always interfering." Megan was quite sharp.

Selwyn cleared his throat a second time and started. "Mark Tremlett, a pupil at Llandrheidol Primary School showed that bravery is not only for adults and dogs. Yesterday the school was subjected to the fear of all Primary School Teachers, Fire! On discovering the fire the whole school was quickly and without any fuss evacuated but to the horror of the Head Teacher, Mr Emanuel Jones, it was found at role call, that three young children were not accounted for. Mark Tremlett who was one of the pupils in the school and also a prefect, overheard this. He immediately volunteered himself to go back into the blazing inferno in an effort to find the missing children. The teachers were busy trying to douse the flames with buckets of water until the fire engine arrived so they did not see him enter the school. He went in through the front door with a wet handkerchief over his mouth because of the dense smoke. Mark noticed that one of the classroom doors was jammed. He kicked it open... Later he told me that it was easy because his father, who was SAS trained, had, I quote, taught him a thing or two..."

"I don't believe this," Tom actually laughed.

"Listen now! I haven't finished. The three children were found huddled in a corner of the classroom under a desk. Mark told them not to worry, and, carrying the smallest child on his back, he led them through the smoke filled corridor to safety. On being questioned about the incident afterwards, Mark seemed very relaxed and calm and simply asked for a glass of water to soothe his sore throat."

"That's absolutely brilliant. Selwyn, you're a genius." Tom laughed again.

"I still haven't finished, this is the best bit. His father said afterwards that Mark was a very quiet child inclined towards being rather shy, but that this art of bravery was not his first time. He rescued a cat from a tree when he was only three years old and showed no fear of the height to which he had to climb." Selwyn stopped abruptly and waited for some sort of response.

"Absolutely brilliant, Selwyn. When I read that to him on Wednesday he'll have a fit. Especially if I threaten to send it to the paper."

"I liked the SAS bit. Takes me back, that does," said Ieuan without any elaboration.

Megan showed some concern. "Aren't you being a bit hard on the poor little chap, Tom?" She hesitated, "But I'd love to be there when you read it to him. How do you think he will react?"

"I'll let you know. And, don't forget, it's only for fun."

Tom dispensed some late hour drinks and received an unusual request from Ieuan. "How's your leg these days, Tom?"

"All right," he banged his knee with the palm of his hand and wiggled his leg around with ease, "In fact, I'm learning to play squash, Rolff's teaching me."

Ieuan's curiosity was satisfied. "I thought so, they were talking about it at football training."

Tom felt threatened. "Why were they talking about me? I'm allowed to play in the College courts because..."

"Don't be paranoid, Tom. It's not about the squash. One of the blokes has to have a ligament done and they wanted to know how long he would be out of the game, that's all."

"Oh!"

Megan's expertise was needed. "It depends on a lot of things. Without committing myself, I would say about two to three months. I wouldn't think he will be playing again this season."

"Sod it!" said Ieuan. "They had better get a substitute then."

The following Thursday evening, just before the darts, Megan inquired about the response he got from Mark to the fictitious story Selwyn had created.

"Oh, it was amazing. I read it to him in the presence of Nana and Grandad. It was so obvious that Mark was telling porkies because he blushed and put his head down in shame. Nana laughed about the bit where he climbed a tree to rescue a cat. Grandad was doubled over at me being in the SAS. He was actually in the Marines during the war. To make things worse, I told him I had better send it to his headmaster for approval before I sent it to the paper."

"Poor little chap," a surprising comment poached from Megan by Ieuan.

"It's all right. In the end I had to tell him it was all in fun. He was looking a bit worried in case I really did send it to his school. We finished off having one of our fights and being the best of pals."

Tom was confident enough by now to serve in the bar on his own when it was quiet. He did every third Sunday evening alternating with Beryl or Mary and Carol. Clem was still a regular visitor but the numbers varied considerably from week to week. Tom would occasionally come down to the bar and talk with the girls or Clem or go to the College Club; he had been affiliated. Some Sundays he might take Mark and his in-laws off for the day. He couldn't stay in the flat on his own for more than a few hours. It brought back memories that he was desperately trying to forget. Tom still missed her in the evenings after the pub had closed. A photograph was prominently displayed over the fireplace of Mag and Dulcie taken on the roof during last summer, suitably costumed.

Richard wrote regularly and he was aware of Tom's predicament but he was as much in the dark as to his mother's whereabouts as Tom. After his six weeks of basic training he came home for two weeks leave. Tom found the transformation remarkable. He went away a boy and came home a man. The first thing he did was to shake Tom's hand very formally but it was quickly followed by Richard putting his arms around Tom and giving him an affectionate hug. Ever since they worked together making bar meals they had been very close.

"Dad, what can I say? I feel lousy. Who would have thought my mother would have done such a thing. It's always the same, isn't it? You think it can never happen to your parents," he repeated, "your parents."

"Leave it alone, Richard. I've had it up to here." His hand touched his chin.

Richard quickly changed his questioning, "How's Beryl?" He always liked her even more so after she got him away from the old fogies on Christmas evening. A closely guarded secret known only to Beryl was that it was the night he lost his virginity.

"She's down in the bar," Tom was impressed by the tactful way he changed the conversation and livened up.

"I'll go down and see her later." Richard moved over to the window and looked out. "Are they still performing?"

"The dogs or the students?" Tom hesitated, "How did you know that?"

"We all did, all the boys. That's why we used to spend so much time up here in the evenings when the students were around."

"Bloody hell!" Tom smiled. "And I thought you were watching videos."

"That's better Dad, let's go for a drink, now." On the way down Richard informed his father that they also knew he called the lane at the back of the pub Shitters' Walk because of the dogs and their owners.

Tom laughed and said pedantically, "It's Shit Alley actually and I call the people collectively, a shit of walkers. You can change the l to an n, if you like."

"It's the same difference."

"Yes, Richard."

His presence was just what Tom needed in this time of crisis, it could not have been better timed. Although Tom was not a superstitious man, he felt that his star sign was in the right constellation for once. Tom spent a happy two weeks with his son. Richard took Beryl out once or twice but it was not serious, they were just good friends, at least, that's what Beryl told Tom. Richard was posted to Northern Ireland for a four and a half months tour of duty. His letters were quite amusing and cheered Tom up but he was restricted as to what he could say about the guerilla warfare going on there.

"We've got a problem, Tom." Ieuan was taking his job as darts captain seriously. "We are playing the Griffin next Thursday and if you can remember you banned two of their players."

"Oh yes, who could forget. What has happened to that loud mouthy lout and his equally sickening mate?"

"Mike is still not back with his girl and their language is as bad as ever." Ieuan had studied the rules of the game and he quoted almost word-for-word to Tom in his official referees voice. "If a person has been barred from licensed premises, he cannot play in a visiting darts team unless the landlord of the venue is in agreement. What do you think, Tom? Do you agree to let him and his pal in for the games?"

He caught Tom in a friendly mood. "Yes, but they had better behave themselves, no foul language. The girls won't be back because they have to travel all the way to the Red Kite for their game. But if they do start, that's it, they're out!" Ieuan wrote down something on a piece of paper and stuffed it in his shirt pocket.

Thursday came too quickly for Tom, he was a little uneasy, but adamant that if there were any bellicose, uncouth comments and the pair would be evicted.

What an anticlimax. Neither Mike the Mouth nor his partner turned up for the darts. Tom and Ieuan instantly felt the tension lifted and they had a jubilant evening winning the match five to two. After the customary refreshments they finished off with a sing-song to the silvery tones of Gareth's instrument. The traditional Counting the Goats and Men of Harlech, in Welsh, preceded the hymns.

Ty Gwyn men's team were quietly sitting around the cold fireplace. Tom would not have a fire on darts night, it was too much for the staff to handle. When the men played at home Tom worked the bar alone or if pushed, Ieuan helped out. "I enjoyed the Welsh singing," said Tom stating the obvious, "even though I don't understand it. I suppose Men of Harlech is to the Welsh what King Arthur is to the English."

There was a huge inhalation of air as Gareth sucked it through his lips with his teeth clenched.

"*Iesu*! Now you've done it, Tom," said Rolff with a big grin on his face. "Gareth is doing his thesis on King Arthur and according to him he is very much Welsh."

"How d'you make that out?" said Tom with a puzzled expression on his face. "What about Tintagel Castle in Cornwall and Camelot?"

"Actually you are closer to the truth than you think, Tom. The earliest detailed account of his life was written by a Welshman called Geoffrey of Monmouth in 1135."

"Was it half past eleven in the morning or at night?"

"Oh, shut up Ieuan. You and your bloody corny jokes." Tom was mildly indignant.

Gareth carried on as if nothing had happened. "Geoffrey later became Bishop of St. Asaph. He claimed that King Arthur was born in Tintagel Castle."

"There you are then."

"Wait! Wait a minute, don't be so impetuous." Gareth put his guitar down and started to expound on the latest theories. He responded to Tom in much the same way as any of the other Blue Bootees. When they started talking about their research topic, they always become very serious. Tom noticed that he got the same concentrated response when he asked Selwyn a technical question.

"Other authorities have claimed that Cadbury Castle in Somerset (No jokes about the chocolate, please Ieuan) and also Camelford in Cornwall are the ancient sites of Camelot. It's a romantic historical mystery." Gareth continued, "The Arthurian legend was extremely popular in the nineteenth century. It is claimed by historians that the most popular present at middle class Victorian weddings was Tennyson's The Idylls of the King. He also inspired artists such as William Bell Scott's Lamentation of King Arthur and more recently the musical, Camelot. I could go on for hours but most people get bored."

"No, no Gareth. It's fascinating - please carry on." Tom was beginning to develop an interest in subjects he had never even thought about before.

"Yes, and what a carry on," said Ieuan. Rolff shook his head disapprovingly as they moved over to the dartboard.

During a brief pause, while Gareth replenished his glass, Tom reminisced on his vain attempt to tell the history of Bass to the musical fat man and his elegant wife who were sadly no longer chording around Wales. What would they have told their friends about the little pub in Llanrheidol and the inept but talkative Bass lecturer? There again, could it not be put down to lack of experience in public speaking? He deflected his thoughts from the posthumous couple back to Gareth. Were all Welshman so eloquent as Gareth? They all seemed to be able to sing. In the case of the Arthurian scholar, Tom had heard that his natural oratory made him the envy of several of his less talented thespian student friends. Tom was becoming used to these erudite chats and found them stimulating. "Tell me, how do you reckon he was Welsh?"

"It's the latest theory in a recent book on the subject. These two authors identify King Arthur as a Welsh warlord called Owain Ddantgwyn. He lived in the late 5th century and ruled over what is now Gwynedd and Powys, in other words north and central Wales. Camelot was built on the Roman ruins of Viroconium near Shrewsbury now called Wroxeter. He died in a battle at Camlan, a desolate valley about five miles east of Dolgellau, but he was buried in Berth now Baschurch, Shropshire."

"Why did they move him and what about his sword?" Tom was utterly engrossed in Gareth's tale.

"Give it a rest, Gareth. We want to play doubles," Ieuan shouted.

"OK, we'll be there now. Baschurch was the place where they buried all the kings of Powys and conveniently there is a Berth pool to throw Excalibur in. Incidentally, this was not unusual since the Celts used to throw their weapons into lakes as offerings to the water gods."

"That's the most fascinating story I've heard for a long time. We must talk some more another time, Gareth." They joined the others at the dartboard.

"There's a letter for you, Tom," shouted Myfanwy from downstairs. "I think it's for you, it's addressed to T. Tremlett Esquire, and it's from Surrey." She gleaned all this information simply ascending the stairs.

"Surrey? I don't know anybody from Surrey."

"Yes you do, Lally's sister and daughter live there." Myfanwy's curiosity was obsessive. He acknowledged that she was right with a gesture of his index finger. Tom opened the formal looking buff envelope with a knife he was using to peel some potatoes, after wiping it on his blue and white striped apron given to him by Mag. Myfanwy did not return to the bar but lingered hoping to get a hint of its contents. It came with a shout from Tom. "Oh, bloody hell! Lally has left us two thousand quid. Apparently she did not leave a will but deposited a letter with her solicitor. Bloody hell!"

"Two thousand quid you say? That was very generous of her, wasn't it?" Tom detected a hint of resentment in her voice. "Money going to money, if you ask me," she said sarcastically.

"Myf! That's not like you."

"No, you're right, I don't know why I said that, sorry." She left to finish her work.

This created a whole new set of problems for Tom which he did not need at this stage in his life. Did he try and use the money to get Mag back, or keep it for himself and to hell with her?

In the meantime he had personal problems in the pub which were causing him some consternation. Poor cuckold Tom was not a ladies' man but it was becoming apparent that some of his heterosexual companions were becoming increasingly friendly. Babs had started visiting, especially for late night do's. One particular piece of interesting female logic was conceived by Beryl and told to Tom one evening in the flat. It was that she was the only girl in Llanrheidol who had been in close contact with Tom without panties. She excluded Mary's strip and did not know of the roof top episodes. Beryl started going up to the flat at any excuse, especially when Nana was not there. She would sit around in the most compromising positions. Tom didn't seem to notice, he took it as a normal part of Beryl's nature, like her obtuse comments. If it had been Mag instead he would certainly have taken heed of the signals.

One late evening when only Ieuan and Megan were there, Ieuan decided that he should alert Tom to certain goings on that everyone seemed to notice except him. "How are things going Tom, you know, things?" His response was immediate but not what Ieuan implied.

"I'm missing Mag a lot. It's really putting me off my stride. I can't seem to get things together. But I must admit (he was unconsciously using one of Beryl's sayings) all the crowd have been good and rallied round. Beryl is very helpful - she often comes up after hours for a chat."

"Uh ho," chuckled Ieuan.

"No, it's nothing like that. We just sit around drinking coffee and talking."

"You obviously haven't noticed her come-on signs then. They are particularly obvious in the bar."

Megan knew what Ieuan was up to because they had talked about it but even so, she had to say, "Ieuan, don't be so personal." And she nudged him, attempting to conceal her approval. "What do you mean?" Tom looked nonplussed.

"Her body language," Ieuan regarded himself as somewhat of an expert on such matters. "Haven't you noticed that when you are together in the bar she wears tight, sexy, clothes - a sure sign that she is encouraging you to be familiar?"

"Go on, she always dresses like that. Doesn't she Megan?"

"I must say, she makes a particular effort when you are working together. In fact, it's a big joke with the girls. When Beryl is dolled up they know you are working that evening even if you're not present at the time."

"Oh no!" Tom covered his reddened face.

"That's not all. Haven't you noticed that when she talks to you, her right foot points at you and she is relaxed. Unconsciously she is sending out signals that she wants to be intimate but she must keep her distance."

"That's rubbish. If she pointed her foot the other way she would be backwards."

"No, he's right, Tom." Megan could contain her comments no longer. "Another thing she does in your presence is Upper Smile."

"Does what?"

"She shows only her upper incisor teeth when she smiles. She stares straight into your eyes when she talks to you. Those responses are signs of tremendous attraction."

"You're right at the last count. I find it very disturbing and I have to look the other away."

"You have noticed some of the responses then." The authority had taken over again. "My favourite is what Megan calls... um, thingy." He flicked his wrist as though he was winding a clock.

"Passive masturbation."

"That's it!"

"Bloody hell! You two talk about the most intimate things."

"We go back a long way Tom, as I've told you before."

"I'm sure you've noticed it. She crosses her legs while she is standing and rocks gently backwards and forwards while you're talking to her." Ieuan was demonstrating the action to the annoyance of Megan.

Megan remembered his relatively unnoticed fiasco at the Christmas party and shook him, "Stop that." Ieuan stopped.

Tom disturbingly recalled Mag making a similar notion when talking to Dowie. The evening ended leaving Tom singularly pensive but more knowledgeable about feminine ways.

Mary and Carol often stayed in the flat talking to Tom after their bar work was over. Although Tom did not like talking about his wife, one night the conversation got around to adultery and inevitably Mag. They admitted that they had detected the kindling of a relationship as long ago as the Friendly darts match and they bet that Dowie would let the game go to Mag. He asked the inevitable question, but like

Megan they were not positive and hoped for Tom's sake, that it was just an infatuation.

Sometimes the girls would stay all night if the discourse went on too long. Beryl got to know about it next day from Myfanwy. But what she didn't realise was that the girls were like daughters to Tom. They had a lot of respect for Tom and *vice versa*. They slept in Richard's room which had two single beds. The other spare bedroom still contained only spirits. Despite what people thought, they were not lesbians but just very good friends and only Tom knew what Ieuan did not realise: that Carol was much less inhibited than Mary when she was in command of the conditions. She would think nothing of walking past Tom to the shower in the flat without a stitch on and sometimes she would even stop and ask for something if necessary. Carol was a big girl of about eighty kilos in weight but extremely well proportioned and sporting full C-sized firm breasts. Her action was certainly not a conscious narcissistic response like the naturists appear to do on the beaches, by standing or constantly walking up and down displaying themselves. She reminded Tom of one of those corpulent nudes which attract so much attention at Art galleries. Dulcie, last summer, adopted the same attitude. It seemed to Tom that he brought out in these girls a natural urge to be naked in front of the opposite sex, but not to be threatened in any way. He was more than just a father figure (that had unhealthy undertones of incest), he was just there allowing them to exploit their sexuality. Mag was not so uninhibited although during her short stay in Llanrheidol she was becoming less restrained. Underneath that middle class charade there was a vivacious spirit trying in get out. Unfortunately, it flew away. Tom could still not forget what she had done and question the motive. He kept thinking about her whenever he had a solitary moment so he tried to keep himself occupied. To the publicans of Llanrheidol and indeed any other middle-aged, full-blooded male, he was a man to be envied. Unattached and often in the presence of doting nymphettes. But to Tom it was a time of great indecision. His whole world had been turned on its hand. He was the type of man who could not cope with the uncertainty and the carnal temptations. Mag was always there during such periods of adversity.

He discussed the problem of Lally's bequest with Mag's parents. They had not forgiven her and were adamant that Tom should keep the money. Tom was not convinced and thought it might tempt her back into the fold. His first move was to speak to Megan who knew Dowie's solicitor, Tegwin Jones, who in turn would know the whereabouts of the absconders. He did not see Megan for a few days but she made a particular effort one night after coming off duty to visit.

"It's remarkable, Tom, but Dowie has changed his address and all his business to a lawyer in Cardiff." She stopped and requested a drink which Tom gave to her hastily and free, in the hope that it would mystically bring him extra information. She carried on using some of the vocabulary Tegwin must have used. "Tegwin said that he was aware of the counsellor's chambers in Cardiff. He had contacted them but they would not reveal the new dwellings of Dowie and his adulteress and they had passed on the message about the inheritance." Tom was intrigued at Megan's choice of noun but immediately realised that it was in fact true, she was a loose woman.

Tom waited over a week and had no response from Cardiff except a cryptic note dropped in through the door late one night. It requested that the two thousand pounds should be deposited in a numbered post office bank account. Against all odds, coming most strongly from Megan and his in-law, he almost carried out this irrational act on the grounds that it was Mag's wishes. After consultation with Tegwin, a phone call to Cardiff and words such as misappropriation of funds and embezzlement being banded around, Tegwin eventually got what Megan had suspected all the time. She was really not quite sure how to approach Tom in his present condition. To give herself time to think and get it clear in her head what she was going to say, Megan phoned and told him that she would be around after lunchtime closing with some news. As promised, Megan was in the flat just after closing. "Tom, I'm not sure whether you will be pleased or sad but we have eventually found out what is going on in Cardiff." Tom paled in anticipation of the forthcoming information and sat down in his chair. "The situation is this," she paused to swallow imaginary saliva, "Apparently, Mag only lived with Dowie for a few weeks. He then kicked her out, she was trying to chat up his boss..."

"What the bloody hell is wrong with that woman?" interrupted Tom as he jumped up from his chair. "She's becoming a bloody tart. I wished we had never come to this bastard town."

Megan exercised her expertise. "Now Tom, don't get yourself all tensed up. Sit down and listen." Her voice was soft but authoritative and he responded. She finished up by saying, "He's apparently got a young girl in tow from Llanrheidol."

"Is she..."

"No, she didn't come here." Tom was fleetingly heartened.

"Rumour has it that she may have slipped the note to you."

"I'll sue the bastard!"

"Tom, calm down, it's all speculation. You will not be able to prove it and confidences will be broken... Do you know what I mean? Tegwin has been very good to you; just let it alone."

"You know best Megan. Where do you think she is now? She must be very sad and lonely." Despite his sudden outburst, Tom was passionately worried about the survival of his spouse. He answered himself, "She is probably in Bristol or London."

Regardless of Tom's persistent calls to Dulcie with whom Mag still liaised, he could not find where she had settled. Dulcie had to act as the go-between and hated it because she was so fond of them both. Finally Dulcie had to tell Tom that Mag was too ashamed and horrified at the misery she had caused to make any form of communication with her family. Tom was overwrought and pleaded with Dulcie for her address but she could not betray a trust for fear of Mag severing all connections with her. As regards the money, keep it for the boys. Tom instinctively knew that would be Mag's decision. He hadn't been married to her for over twenty years without knowing at least some of her more obvious characteristics.

It was a cheerless time for Tom. He just couldn't conceive life without Mag. Sex was not the important factor in his equation, but it may have qualified as the prime factor in hers. He assumed that Saturday night and Sunday morning with an occasional interruption in the routine was sufficient, since there were no complaints from his partner. Obviously he was wrong and there were hidden depths boiling below the surface ready to erupt at any time. Tom falsely tried to reassure himself that Mag's misdemeanor was the result of their moving away from a steady, secure environment to one where temptation unfolded at every opportunity. He refused to consider for one minute that initially, boredom may have been the motive.

Tom was going through a stage in his life which he loathed. He hated the solitary evenings the most and was getting to a state where he was looking for comfort and companionship. To add to Tom's dilemma, Selwyn was busy with examination preparations, so they only met socially at weekends. His happy times were when the girls stayed for the evening but that was not as regular as he needed. The pub was still a good money spinner and the lock-ins carried on but most of the candid merriment had departed from these illegal drinking sessions. Occasionally Megan would narrate a funny tale of a patient or hospital situation. One of his favourite nights was the girls' darts team at home. If possible he would try and find an excuse to stay in the pub that evening and not travel with the men's team. Although Rosie did not resemble Mag in any way, she occupied the spot formally taken by her. He was also surrounded by *his girls*, as he liked to call them. One interesting move was that Gethin, since his breakup, was a regular camp follower of the girls' team. Irrespective of Tom's abhorrence of his sexual persuasion, Gethin and Tom appeared to have developed an affinity for each other. They would sit incongruously together in the bar some nights with Gethin sipping a G&T and Tom swilling Bass. When not on duty, Tom would get pie-eyed together with his homosexual ally. Mary and Carol, Megan or Beryl were usually around during these drunken sessions to ensure that Tom got upstairs safely without any impropriety. The relationship and excess drinking did not solve any problems for Tom, it simply compounded them.

Megan, who had taken on the role of mother confessor usually associated with Nana, could see the complex interweaving of fears and frustrations building up in Tom. He needed bringing out of himself. But how? She cerebrated for a split second and then shouted out, "Football, that's it!" Covering her mouth quickly with her hand the solution was not obvious to others except Ieuan.

Arrangements were made with those who cared and at the next late tripartite evening it was considered time to make a move. 'First try and humour him,' thought Megan, who had previously discussed the motivation behind her actions with Ieuan. "I had the most entertaining day today, Tom. You would think it came straight out of one of those famous British Ealing comedy films." It sounded so patronising that even Ieuan felt slightly uncomfortable. Sensing that the time was not right for telling humorous indiscretions, she instantly switched to the main purpose of her discourse. "Why don't you take a break, Tom. Go away for the day somewhere and enjoy yourself."

"But where? And who with?"

Although previously rehearsed, Ieuan could see this was the best time to act. "Why don't you come away with the football crowd? We're playing in the Mid-Wales league at Newtown on Saturday."

"Oh no! That's one of our busiest days. I couldn't get away."

"Yes you can. Megan and me have had a word with Mary and Carol and, ho ho, Beryl."

"Stop that Ieuan. Every time I work with her, I keep thinking about her body language."

"Seriously though, they are quite happy to look after the pub on Saturday. The thing is, I don't know who will be upstairs waiting for you when you get back?"

"Sorry to disappoint you but I have already made arrangements for Myfanwy to do the catering for me next Saturday and she's staying with her son."

'Not another one,' thought Megan.

Tom was up early Saturday morning, excited about his trip. He had his usual breakfast, checked the cellar and was gone before anyone had even considered Ty Gywn. Myfanwy was first to open up the pub. She had travelled down on the bus with Tom's in-laws and Mark. They were going to do some shopping, then return to the pub. Nana had been inveigled into preparing a meal for the family and Beryl, who was staying there all day. Grandad had been instructed to help boost Tom's sales.

The morning session was remarkably busy. Myfanwy and Mark must have travelled the stairs dozens of times with bar meals. The little lad was exhausted and glad to be going home in the afternoon. Grandad was equally tired but that was because of his over indulgence. Beryl closed up and escorted Grandad upstairs to join the rest for lunch. Grandad slept in the chair.

"He can have beans on toast, instead," said Nana to Mark who rocked back in his chair, gave a beautiful smile and laughed out loud. Grandad stirred but did not awaken.

They left about four o'clock leaving Beryl on her own. She walked around the flat and ventured into the master bedroom. It was tastefully decorated but much too feminine for Tom; it was obviously a woman's room. The bed was large but intimate at the same time. The periphery did not appear to be the zone occupied to any extent and there was a slight dip in the middle indicating constant use. At least, that was the fanciful conception that entered Beryl's mind. She tried it for comfort, "It's just right, I feel like Goldilocks," she mumbled to herself. Since she could not gratify herself in venereal pleasure her only aphrodisiac that afternoon was found in the bathroom. The room itself reeked of aromatic odours and was clearly a location for self-indulgence. She pampered herself in a warm bath infused with expensive perfumed oils. "I'll bet those have not been used since Mag left them." She gave no thought to the nightly excursions of Mary and Carol. "I must admit, this is luxury. Why was Mag so stupid and headstrong to clear off with Dowie like that?" Beryl was talking to herself from the sheer frustration of knowing, from bitter experience, how unreliable and insincere he was. Still talking to an illusory audience she said, "I would give anything to be living in these conditions." She fell asleep but was awakened by the coldness of the water. Her naked, shivering body was quickly ravished in the heat of a hot shower.

Suitably dressed and freshened she opened up for the Saturday night extravaganza. A crowd of stupefied girl students lumbered in, quickly guzzled their double vodkas or gins celebrating their successful win at hockey and were gone again. Beryl thought to herself Ieuan would have risen to the occasion had he seen such a magnificent display of thunderous thighs. Selwyn made an early evening appearance followed closely by Myfanwy. Her man was away with the soccer boys, so being recently emancipated, thanks to the easy going Tremletts, she felt it was justified to have a night out. Thanks to Tom's generosity, the boy was upstairs in the flat watching television. An unexpected jubilant roving band of rugby players descended on the pub. Myfanwy stepped in to help out. One of the more precocious biology students in the team bought Selwyn a pint. Not for any ulterior motive but simply because they won. It seemed that Llanrheidol College was on a winning streak that weekend.

After they had tumbled out the door Selwyn felt a little guilty about accepting the drink and thought people might misconstrue it as a bribe so he said, "After all, he's most likely to get a first, anyway." Nobody was concerned.

Mary and Carol were next to appear. "You've missed two big rounds," said Beryl from behind the bar.

"I'm sorry but we are on time," Carol looked at her watch.

"It's OK, I'm only joking." She wasn't really, any chance to get a jab at her competitors was welcomed. Frank appeared when most of the jollification had moved up town. "*Shwd mae*, Frank. You've just missed the girls. Some still had on their little skirts they played hockey in."

Joan called in briefly with her soldier friend from the Carnival days. They left early to catch Match of the Day on television. At least that's what the man of military skills thought but Joan had other manoeuvres planned. Megan and Rosie, Rolff and Yah and later Gareth and posh David all turned up throughout the course of the evening. The pub was gradually filling up with the Christmas party crowd, but without the cordial atmosphere. Gethin flamboyantly waltzed in with a brand new petite pretty looking appendage by the name of Quintin. He had picked him up in Cardiff at one of his frequent Hairdressers' Exhibitions where he was parading as a model. Megan acknowledged Beryl and sighed with relief, there was no need for any verbal exchange.

"Where's Tom, tonight?"

"He's gone away with the football crowd, they've gone to Newtown."

"How common, football crowd. I thought he would know better than that, Beryl."

"Give him a break, Gethin. The poor fella's been through a lot lately."

"So have I!" He brushed his fingers through his hair, "I'm better now, though... My usual and a Tia Maria for Quintin... with soda."

"No, not this time... I'm teaching him the tricks of the trade." He furtively glanced in Beryl's direction and gave her a wink.

When they had moved to a table and out of earshot, Beryl said to Megan, "Isn't it odd, he seems to like them all coffee flavoured," they both laughed. Gethin was impervious to anything the girls could throw at him. He put it down to jealousy. After peacocking his latest conquest, Gethin thought it was time to show him off at his favoured Royal.

"Bye, dearies."

"Cheerio both," someone shouted.

Beryl could sense that something was going on, "What's the matter Megan? All the crowd is here but there's no *hwyl.*"

Using the group as an evasion, she said, "Some of us are very concerned about Tom's welfare. He's getting himself into a state that is almost suicidal."

"Shit, you don't think it's that bad, do you?"

"Yes I do, I've seen this depression develop in people who have lost a close relative before. Ieuan and I managed to get him to go off today but we are concerned about afterwards. What about the future?"

"I must admit, he has been hitting the booze lately but there's one thing, he's certainly not the flavour of the month anymore."

Megan smiled. "You're right, there."

The music was playing quietly in the background, some of the boys and girls were playing darts and the rest just sat around, hardly moving and talking quietly. It reminded Megan of the staged Ascot scene in My Fair Lady.

* * * * *

The problem of Tom's predicament had still not been resolved.

"How about a lodger?" mentioned Rolff. "He would be good company for Tom after hours. He told me that was the time he disliked most."

"I could come and live here," said Beryl. "He would then have permanent bar staff as well as a lover, sorry! Lodger."

"I don't think he would like that," said Mary. Carol quickly enforced her declaration and mentioned that Tom would not like to mix business with pleasure.

"What pleasure?" snapped Beryl.

Carol had to think quickly. "I, I didn't mean it like that... I meant that if you are with someone all day and also when you finish work," she was desperately trying to find a way out, "you want to take off your things and relax. You couldn't do that in front of Tom, he's too shy."

"You rotten liar," lipped Mary.

Beryl knew they stayed with Tom some nights but she didn't know the precise purpose. "How do you know he would be embarrassed?"

"Come on girls," checked Megan. "Let's not talk a load of old baloney... We could suggest the possibility of a lodger and see his reaction?" It was unanimously agreed that Megan should approach Tom the next day.

Frank was none too quick on the uptake and said, "Do you really take all your clothes off after work, Carol?"

Tantalising him she said, "You must come round and see one night, mustn't you?"

"Where d'you live?"

"Now that would be telling."

The repartee animated the drinkers and the general noise level started to rise. "Let's have a game of mixed darts," suggested Gareth.

"Yeah," said Frank. "And the losers strip." He was pathetically trying to compensate for losing out last time.

There was a chorus of laughter. "Who the hell would want to see an oldie like you?" said Myfanwy.

"It would put people off their beer," an anonymous voice came from the dartboard area followed by more laughter. Megan, in her matter-of-fact way suggested the loser bought the other player a drink. The rest of the evening and well into the night was spent pleasantly drinking, talking and playing darts.

"Why don't we get Tom a dog?" said Beryl who had, by now, forgotten all about changing lodgings and Tom's hatred of the canine species.

"We could get him a Rottweiler and he could tear the arse off all those pet lovers in shit alley," said David. With his posh accent, swearing was particularly amusing and encouraged more laughter. Eventually people started to trickle away in a much happier mood than when they came. Ironically the only girl to stay in Tom's flat that night was Myfanwy chaperoned by her son.

Myfanwy was making a drink before going to bed when she heard Tom and Ieuan at the main door. They were simultaneously trying to get the key into the lock. After about ten minutes she went down and opened the door. Tom fell in and Ieuan tried to apologise for his condition. Myfanwy could not understand a word and she bade him good night. She helped Tom fall upstairs and straight into his bedroom where she plonked him on the bed and covered him with a blanket. Myfanwy sat next to him for most of the night. When she saw he was clearly over the worst she slipped out and went into the double room with her son. "He's not one of us, Welsh I mean, but *duw* he could be," Myfanwy mumbled to her sleeping son.

"Good morning, Myf." Tom was bouncing with no signs of his excessive intake of alcohol which presented such a problem earlier. "Cuppa? Two spoons and milk, isn't it?" He was perceptibly in high spirits to be poking fun of dialectal Welshness.

Myfanwy instinctively pulled the bedclothes up to cover her high-necked winceyette nightdress. 'Not one of the best images to be confronted with early in the morning,' thought Tom. 'But she is a good'un.' This diminutive phraseology was creeping into Tom's vocabulary from the young company. He did in fact appreciate her much more than he put on. But being an Englishman he retained his aloofness as much as possible.

"Thanks, Tom. No one has brought me tea in bed for as long as I can remember, thanks."

Jokingly Tom said, "Perhaps Ifor might be serving you tea one day?"

Myfanwy was cautious about replying. "Let's wait and see?" She had been smitten before but had never reached the altar.

"What do you and the little'un want for breakfast?" She moved in the bed to signal that she was about to get up, more out of embarrassment at Tom's question than reality and said that she would get something for them both later and for Tom to carry on. Tom disappeared into the kitchen. Myfanwy could not go back to sleep, she lay there absorbing the tantalising smell of bacon being fried. It was agony, she was on a perpetual diet and confined herself to fruit juice and dry toast.

Why she was so chubby defies all the rules of slimming diets. Perhaps it's glandular, someone once said to her. She thought it was probably right because he was in the College and it would justify her condition. Myfanwy was unaware that the mysterious diagnosis came from a veterinary friend of Selwyn who was studying obesity in cows.

After breakfast, Myfanwy tidied up the bedroom and Tom went down into the cellar to sort out the empties. It was a typical quiet Sunday morning and she could hear him singing something she had never heard before. Beryl came in early just in case Tom was incapacitated and she was exposed to Tom exercising his uvula. Tom's risorial behaviour amused Beryl and Myfanwy who were listening and laughing to themselves at the top of the cellar stairs.

"Shut that damned row up!" Beryl's voice echoed around the empty kegs. "Did you have a good time, Tom?"

He quickly located the source. "Just the sort of break I needed." Tom's voice started to echo back but gradually took on a normal delivery as he came to the bottom of the stairs. From his attitude Beryl could see he was in a flighty mood.

"Remember the last time I stood here and looked up?" Beryl actually blushed and chastised Tom verbally for being so flippant. To her it was a very confidential moment. Myfanwy smiled at his question but didn't understand that its inference related to that knickerless evening when Mag was still around.

Tom took Myfanwy and her son back home in his car and stayed for lunch at his in-laws. When he got back to the pub Beryl had closed up and left. She was on again that evening.

She buzzed to confirm her presence and Tom informed her that he would be down later. Clem was in early and Megan turned up with Rosie. "How's Tom?" Megan whispered.

"There's no need to whisper. He's watching his nature programme... It was remarkable this morning when I came in, Tom was singing in the cellar."

"Singing?" Megan gave out a surprisingly high pitched scream.

"Yes, something about a chain-gang."

Megan was confused, she was not familiar with jazz and its association with the emancipated blacks.

"So he's fully recovered from his depressed state?"

"I should say so. Have you ever heard him singing? He'll be down in a few minutes when his programme ends."

After the usual pleasantries, Tom replied with great enthusiasm to Megan's repeated question. "As I told Beryl this morning," he gave her an impish smile, "I had a fantastic time. The boys are so lively and Ieuan is a star when he gets with the youngsters. Oh, you would know that of course, Megan, because you are so close." Megan was listening, but subconsciously she ruminated over the acknowledgement

Tom had given Beryl. Had she got to him first and was she now the lodger?

"When we got there it was about twelve o'clock so we all went to a pub for a liquid lunch. I wasn't too keen on travelling around in a large group. It reminded me of the times here when we had to cope."

"It brings in money, though." Beryl's business-like comment reminded Tom of Mag.

"Yes. I agree in principle but I was out for a good time without too much hassle. Ieuan and I decided to go to a pub called Ty Gwyn and leave the boys to enjoy themselves on their own."

"The same name as this place?" challenged Beryl.

"Bloody hell! You're quick," said Tom. Misled, Beryl regarded it as a compliment. "When we got there Ieuan introduced me as the landlord of Ty Gwyn, Llanrheidol. He said that he had heard that his namesake in Llanrheidol was where they had sex orgies. The landlord was serious yet excited to meet someone from there. I just couldn't believe it. The middle of Wales and they knew what was going on in a small pub on the coast."

"That's nothing; you would be surprised what they know about us in the city hospital in Card..." Megan stopped and comprehended the implication then redirected the conversation. Ieuan probably told him weeks ago on one of his refereeing trips.

"No," answered Tom. "That was the first thing I asked him afterwards and he assured me that he has not been to Newtown since last year. I was just going to tell the landlord the truth about the parties when Ieuan spoke up and told him that it was not really like that but we did have a co-operative lot of girls in the pub. Ieuan was so carried away with the conversation that he was talking to the landlord as though I was not there so I thought I had better say something. I told him that our girls' darts team was very popular around town. I said that they actually have non-players travelling around with them. Do you know, he asked me if they were bodyguards?"

"What, like Gethin you mean," said Rose, who had been listening in the background.

"I told him that they just travelled with them for fun. I purposely forgot to tell him that one was gay, that would have made it even worse."

Megan thought this was an opportune moment to inform Tom about his drinking companion. "Gethin has got a new friend, Tom."

Tom paused for a second and said, "Oh good, he won't be bothering me anymore." He then started on again about his trip, which clearly had left a deep impression on his mind. "We got back to the Football Club in time for the kickoff. Ieuan got roped in to be a linesman so I was all alone on the side. I'm not dedicated to football," Tom said euphemistically. "I just went for the trip, so I wandered around the field finishing up in the Clubhouse. There were a couple of very smart looking women in there making sandwiches and I got into conversation. Apparently one of them knew you, Megan, from the hospital."

Megan shelved the elected task for now and concentrated on the unknown acquaintance. "What was her name?" Megan had a remarkable knack of associating names with treatments going back years.

"Mrs... it's a strange surname, B... oys. Warboys, that's it, Warboys. She looked a bit like Ma..." He stopped. Megan acted as though she hadn't heard the last observation.

"Mrs Warboys, I remember. Her boy had a nasty cut on the bottom of his foot from a broken bottle in the sand on the beach. It was back last summer." She physically relaxed as though she had just answered the final question in a thousand pound competition.

"What a memory," exclaimed Tom, "remarkable!"

"Come on Tom!" Beryl was at the height of her sexual frustration which distilled over into fantasy and she felt she must finish Tom's tale the way she believed it should end. "Did you get one of them across the table and make passionate love to her amid the squashed sandwiches and Scotch eggs with the other one screaming with delight as you fondl..."

"Beryl! What an imagination! You've been reading too many of those sexy books, or is it videos?" Tom was astounded yet amused and smiled while Megan and Rose laughed. Clem supped his ale. "Actually, I finished up helping them with the sandwiches, not in amongst them." Clem gave a belated laughed.

Since she had been delegated to do so, Megan made an attempt to bring up the question of a lodger. She was half expecting to find out that it had already been settled. "Tom," she said cautiously, "we were talking the other night about you being lonely at night when the pub closes. Have you ever thought of having a lodger?"

To Megan's surprise he said, "Not bloody likely. I like a bit of privacy, peace and quiet when I go upstairs." 'That's a new twist,' thought Megan. I wonder if he's got somebody lined up? He continued, "I've probably mentioned from time to time that I get bored on my own but that's when I'm depressed and all that's gone." 'Ieuan's therapeutic football excursion obviously did the trick,' thought Megan. It was apparent that Beryl had not betrayed her confidence but Megan could see from her face that she was bitterly disappointed at Tom's response.

By Monday, Ieuan had recovered sufficiently from his libatious Saturday to be his eloquent, confident self. Faced with Megan, Beryl and Tom, and anyone willing to listen it was his turn to elaborate on the proceedings of that eventful Saturday in Newtown.

"Before you start, Tom's told us about Ty Gwyn and the two girls he had in the Clubroom." Beryl could not forget her fanciful version of the events.

"What! I didn't hear about the girls?" Ieuan, for once, looked deeply wounded at the lack of intercourse between himself and Tom.

"Don't believe her, Ieuan. That's her fanciful version. As you know, I finished up making sandwiches."

Ieuan said to Beryl, "You know what you need, don't you?" Employing his peculiar sense of humour he persevered. "Have a drink, on me." Beryl accepted. "I'll bet Tom didn't tell you about what went on in the evening, though?"

"Why? What happened? Was it good?" said Beryl.

"After the game we had a meal in the Clubhouse, well, squashed sandwiches." All present laughed, Ieuan did not understand the real significance of the response and put it down to his natural wit. "Afterwards we had a game of bingo then a sort of talent competition. Some of those turns were terrible. There was a tone-deaf Tom Jones who was even worse than our Dai the Voice..."

"By the way," checked Tom, "where is Dai? I haven't seen him for months."

Megan was fully conversant of his condition and whereabouts and gave them the news that he had been in hospital for some weeks and was now in a Convalescent Hospital in Somerset.

"Oh, Weston, Weston-Super-Mare?" inquired Tom. He anticipated the answer because it was well known in Bristol that alcoholics went there to dry out.

Ieuan was getting impatient with the unwarranted interruptions and continued without any recourse to any other novel acts. "Tom was very popular."

"Tom? What did he do?" questioned Beryl. "He didn't sing?"

"Good for you, Beryl." Megan didn't like the way he belittled her about Ty Gwyn, Newtown.

"He played the piano after the concert. He sounded just like Fats Waller." Ieuan explained to Beryl that he was a famous jazz singer in the 20's. "Tom also played a lot of the usual sing-along stuff and he got everybody singing." Tom leaned on the bar motionless.

"Was that what you were singing this morning in the cellar?" Beryl made an attempt to give the impression of showing some interest.

"No, that was a Blues. Have you ever heard of Bessie Smith? Oh, never mind." Tom could not abide folk who made out they appreciated jazz but were ignoramuses when it came to the truth. Tom's philosophy was that old time traditional jazz was for the purist, the rest was entertainment for the masses. At the risk of being ridiculed he often listened to George Formby and his bawdy music hall songs and the Second World War Andrews sisters.

Megan was bewildered at this cryptic talent Tom had and wanted to know more. "Why haven't we heard you play in Llanrheidol, Tom?"

"I sold my piano before I moved to Llanrheidol. It was a large iron-framed job and very heavy." Megan noticed he was using the singular personal pronoun. "And I have never got round to buying a new one, perhaps one day?" Tom anticipated that she would be asking if Selwyn was aware of his musical ability and said, "No, Selwyn doesn't know... We have been going to jazz appreciation concerts not playing... I must thank you both for suggesting I went with Ieuan and the boys. It was a marvellous tonic and I feel so much better for it. To use a culinary saying, it was like adding a touch of cochineal to a colourless jelly."

"Yeah, he's becoming a poet and don't know it." Another one of Beryl's futile attempts at scholarship.

The following weeks in the pub were happy. Tom started to enjoy Mag's late night slot but couldn't supply the bountiful witticisms at which she was so apt. This in return allowed a wider choice of comedians. Rosie and Megan with their divers institutional ditties and Ieuan with his sporting anecdotes. Although Tom would not admit it, nights were still a displeasure to him. Mary and Carol were becoming more frequent visitors to the flat. The usual procedure was for the girls to make their beds and generally tidy up before the cleaner arrived. One morning they were late and had no time to domesticate. This was noticed by Myfanwy and shunted on to Beryl. She was now convinced that the girls were a direct threat to her. The exact function of this relationship had always been a puzzle but by now she was confident enough to ask Tom.

His answer was calm and not too convincing. "It's a peculiar relationship, I suppose they are the daughters I never had. We talk a lot about things in general and sometimes if it gets too late they stay in the spare room."

"If I stayed late one night, would you put me up?"

"Probably . But you only live round the corner."

Dulcie rang one morning when she knew Tom would be in the vicinity of the bar. "Hello Tom, long time no see." Her clichés were never very original. "How are you getting on anyway?"

Tom was still in a euphoric state. "I feel fine, I'm getting on with the work and the pub is doing well. I went away with the footballers last week." She couldn't stop him talking except by interruption.

"Tom, you're going on and on. I phoned to tell you about Mag." The phone went dead and it was then that she realised that Tom's babbling was probably a nervous reaction to her phone call.

"Sorry Dulcie, Sorry! Carry on." Tom was very nervous, she could detect it from the quiver in his voice.

"Mag called to see me. She has decided to leave Bristol..."

Tom quickly interrupted, "I knew! I knew that's where she was staying. She wouldn't go away from everyone just like that."

"Calm down, Tom, you'll have a coronary. I'm trying to tell you something," she snapped irately to get a response.

He was full of apologies once again. It was so servile for Tom that it made Dulcie cringe. His fretfulness eventually mellowed and she carried on with the conversation. "There's not a lot I can say really. She's going to Spain for the summer, working in a bar. I don't know where but she said she will send me a post card when she settles."

"What's her address in Bristol?" pleaded Tom. His benign heart-rending desire to be reunited with Mag had returned.

"There's no address. She's gone, gone to Spain." Dulcie was beginning to get upset with Tom's obsequiousness so she quickly terminated the call.

He thought he could manage by himself without the presence of Mag but it was difficult. Any slight deviation from the delicately ephemeral *status quo* could throw it all out of proportion and he would revert to wallowing in self pity. He had finally realised that Mag was a creature of the past and he had to survive without her reassurance. His reaction to the call was disturbing. He could never return to the Elysian-Grove style of living but nor could he resign himself to being a publican for the rest of his working life. He was a relatively young man with a keen interest to learn and was not unattractive to women; his future was of his own making.

The merriment at Ty Gwyn was short-lived. It was eerie but Mag still seemed to exercise her influence on whether the pub was a joyous place or not. For Tom it was time to reflect and discuss the future with his adopted mentor. Megan's fortuitous insight into sensing calamity had prepared her for Tom's relentless struggle with himself. They talked one Sunday evening upstairs in the flat. Mary and Carol were on duty. During the early part of the evening they were buzzed for a round of drinks. Carol, who had a more inquisitive nature, took them up but could detect no effective news regarding the substance of their chat. "What's going on up there, Carol?" Mary was not so impartial to the transactions of Tomos Tremlett as she made out.

"Nothing much but I did hear Tom say that Babs said, once you get past two years you're OK. He then went on to say, what she meant was two summer seasons and two Christmases. I had to leave then otherwise Tom would have accused me of snooping." Tom and

Megan ambled into the bar before closing time. Tom insisted on buying Megan a nightcap.

She then left but not before Tom had time to shout, "I'll go and see Nana in the morning." Much to the annoyance of the girls. "Don't forget, now. She should be the first to know."

Mary and Carol collectively eyed Tom who was sitting smugly composed at the bar. Carol felt bound to say, "Beryl's moving in, isn't she?"

"No, I'll tell you later." And Tom walked away from the bar to sit with Clem.

Later that night all three of them were secreted in the flat. The girls were foaming with apprehension. "You've kept your secret long enough. Is she moving in or not?" Mary sounded disappointingly reassured.

"No, I told you before. It's much more serious than that."

"Christ! She's pregnant?" they duetted.

"Oh no, how many more times? It's nothing to do with bloody Beryl," Tom teasingly growled. "If you remember in the bar just now, Megan said that I should tell Nana first."

"Tomos! Stop pissing around." Carol's formal bluntness was a sure sign that she was getting annoyed. "What the fuck is it?"

"Carol! That's not very nice, is it? I don't like it from you. You sound like a bloody tart."

"Sorry! But you drove me to it. You are irritating sometimes."

"Oh, all right but promise you won't tell a soul especially not Beryl?"

Carol flared up again. "There you are! I told you it was to do with Beryl," she addressed Mary.

"Listen, listen!" Tom bellowed out. He then calmed down and said quietly but audibly, "I'm thinking of selling the pub and getting out of the business. I've tried but don't seem to have the right personality. I can't smile all the time and listen to customers talking a load of crap."

Mary was shocked and very upset. She started to cry, "Where will you go, Tom, and what will you do?" inquired Carol.

Tom was confused at their reaction and put his arm around Mary and gave her a squeeze. "I'm not leaving Llanrheidol, just the pub. I'll find something to do, don't worry, and I will not be leaving straight away." Confirming his declaration Tom said, "I did say I'm only thinking about selling."

"Don't Tom, we've had a wonderful time here. I'll work more hours if you like and Carol can come in when she can. I've been so happy here, I don't think I have ever been so happy." It all came touchingly flooding out interspersed with some startling surprises. "Did you know that I never knew my parents and I was fostered for most of my childhood. This is the only real home I have ever had."

Tom was amazed at the stark spontaneity of her disclosure and it made him feel a little guilty about the way he teased them earlier. "How could you possibly call this place home, it's just a bloody pub?" She sobbed quietly.

"Carol was the same, we met in the Institute when we were about thirteen and we have been friends ever since. As soon as we were old enough to leave we came to Llanrheidol. As you know, I got married but it didn't work out." Carol was silent throughout Mary's emotional outburst and looked thoroughly downhearted. Tom cynically questioned the validity of their story and whether their sadness was for the potential loss of the establishment or for his departure.

"Let's all sit down and talk about the problem, shall we?" Tom was outwardly calm but his insides were churning over. They talked for most of the night and it became increasingly clear to Tom that the girls and especially Mary were more concerned about Tom's departure than, as he misguidedly suspected, Ty Gwyn. Mary was in close proximity to Tom who had placed himself on the settee instead of his favourite chair. Carol, on the other hand, had occupied Tom's chair. How on earth does she manage to get those magnificent limbs under her like that and still have room in the chair for the rest? thought Tom. It was irresistible, he had to say something to try and break the tense atmosphere.

"How d'you do that?"

"What?"

"Get your legs under there like that." He touched her gently on the knee. She did not protest.

"Double-jointed," interrupted Mary. "But she only sits like that when she is worried." The ambience was strained and uncomfortable. It reminded Tom of his predicament the night Mag left so abruptly.

"Don't look so glum, girls. It's not the end of the world." His reassurances did nothing to solve the problem.

"Why do you really want to leave? Are you fed up with us taking advantage of you?" Mary doomfully expressed her feelings.

"Not for a moment. In fact, I would love you to come and stay here permanently." He realised what he had said. The girls positively glowed but before they could say anything Tom spoke, "but I would lose Beryl if that happened and let's face it, she is a wonderful person..." he realised he had again said the wrong thing and quickly qualified it by saying, "...behind the bar."

"Why would you lose Beryl?"

"Come on, Mary. She's always lapping up to Tom. I'm sure she would move in tomorrow if Tom said."

He averted answering by saying, "She does the ordering as well, now."

They finished off a jar of instant as dawn started to break across the Bay. Fatigued but satisfied, the general feeling was that the whole problem was to be put aside for a while. They consumed their strange variety of breakfasts and went their separate ways.

Tom felt obliged to discuss the possibility of moving with Mag's parents. They were in total agreement that it was not his line of work and he should give it up as soon as possible. Nana was most persistent for purely selfish reasons. She said that her age was against her and the drag of travelling down to the pub and helping with the catering was becoming tiresome. She also mentioned that Mark should be with his father, not a couple of old fogies. She was right, of course, and it made Tom think how much he had taken them for granted.

The next few weeks passed pleasantly along with the usual lock-ins. But it did not last long and the hand of fate struck at Tom again. It was inevitable but he did not want to face the fact, but the Blue Bootees were breaking up. They were all finishing off their doctorates at the same time and would be leaving Llanrheidol for posts elsewhere. It had also been discreetly mentioned to Tom by Myfanwy that she would be announcing her engagement to Ifor Cigydd soon and after marriage, probably an end to her working life. These departures from Ty Gwyn would leave an emptiness that would be difficult to fill. 'All I need now is for Beryl to become pregnant,' he depressingly thought to himself.

Tom was feeling particularly down one Friday night. The girls had gone to a pop concert in Cardiff. Selwyn and Ieuan were away and Megan had been called out to assist in a coach accident on the Llanrheidol bypass.

"Do you fancy a take-away, Tom?" Beryl used her eyes as a signal and ceased to thank the last couple to leave. "I'll go and get it."

He averted her stare and said, "Aren't you going to the disco, it's Friday night?" Tom tried to conjure up some potted enthusiasm about the event but it didn't come out right.

"No, I thought I would go home early for a change. It gets boring doing the same thing week after week and everybody knows everybody else there."

Tom resented ever going to one in the first place. Suddenly he thought of his lonely vigil upstairs and believed he had an original thought. "Are you in a rush, Beryl?"

She hesitated, "Why?" She just couldn't believe her luck.

"Oh, why don't you get something with my order and we can eat it together upstairs. I'll walk you home later."

'Fat chance of that,' she thought to herself. "Yeah, OK, I'll be back in about half an hour, warm up some plates while I'm away." She didn't realise the hidden innuendo in her command. It took longer than she thought and Tom had got himself a glass of his apple brandy. Beryl was fickle about what she drank so he hadn't obliged. He could hear her ascending the stairs so he got up from his chair and approached the drinks cabinet. As she entered he requested her tipple. "The same as you," she replied, not wishing to be any bother.

"It's very strong, you'll be putty in my hands in no time." To Beryl, it was the first indication that Tom may have an ulterior motive.

"I'll have a double then, I knead it. Knead it," she repeated, "with a K as in bread making."

Her delivery was too prolonged and lost its impact but all the same, Tom condescendingly said, "Alright, clever," and he smiled. They had a few more drinks while the smell of the exotic spices from the meal pervaded the room. With the combination of the alcohol it gave Tom a warmed glow and reminded him of his halcyon nights in the army when he was off duty after serving the obligatory Friday curry. Beryl was sportively mellow while she plotted the next move. After the meal they finished off the wine and returned to Tom's drink.

Tom was in his chair and Beryl opposite on the settee. She did not have the ability to curl her legs under her like Carol so they were displayed directly in Tom's view and slightly apart. A stance quite familiar to Tom's but at this time of night and under the circumstances, it was an open invitation to which Beryl hoped Tom would respond. Their eyes kept meeting, encouraging Tom to think of Ieuan's observations. He felt a little excited as he got up to replenish their drinks and being less repressed than usual, he said adventurously. "Remember that day I was singing in the cellar?" She replied that she did. "Would you have lifted your skirt if Myf hadn't been there?"

"What do you mean? In the condition I was in then or at the Christmas Party?" She was beginning to simmer.

"Oh," Tom answered slowly for fear of being rejected. "At the Christmas Party, that would be best."

"Like this you mean." She stood up to repeat the performance and accidentally knocked over her drink into her lap. "Shit! I'll have to go and sponge this otherwise, it will stain." She left the room with her skirt at waist level revealing that she was not ready to faithfully re-enact the Christmas display. Semi-inebriate Tom poured himself another glass and contoured into his chair.

"Look what I've got?" Beryl re-entered the room wearing just a basque. "I found it in the bedroom."

"Oh, that's Mary's," exclaimed Tom nonchalantly. "She left it after the party."

Beryl did not question the reply since she thought she understood their relationship. "It's a bit tight. Can you release the top for me?" She came closer to Tom then turned around. He had finally got the message and he proceeded to unzip the back. It fell to the floor and she stood naked.

"Turn around Beryl, I want to do something. He placed his hands with outspread fingers on her buttocks and pulled her close to himself, "Oh boy!" Still holding her close he spluttered, "D'you know I was nearly going mad at the party when we were behind the bar. Do you remember you kept teasing me with that short tennis skirt, I wanted so much to do this." He stroked her firm, rounded bottom and wiggled his fingers. She repaid by writhing her warm naked body and giggling sensually. Tom's arousal expressed itself physically for the first time since Mag left. This turned Beryl into a ravenous animal as she unloaded all her pent up emotion.

Next morning when Tom woke up he found himself lying next to a beautiful young girl separated only by age. His infatuation with Beryl was no longer a fancy from afar since their relationship was truly consummated. He untangled himself from the warm limp body and gently rolled back the clothes to expose two naked bodies and a plea by his sleepy accomplice to remain. The temptation was almost too great but he overcame his lust and threw the bedclothes back over her. She grabbed them and pulled them close to her as if taking up her reluctant lover. As he left the room a thought entered his mind, I wonder where she sunbathes topless? At the last exposure they were milky white.

'Oh, I'm an adulterer like Mag now. Bloody hell!' He felt grubby.

Throughout the day irascible Tom was not a kindly person. He was under the impression that he had let everyone down and particularly Beryl. Tom was not yet totally emancipated and to him the sexual act was to be treated with reverence. Religion played no part in his disapproval but he detested the indiscriminate sex that was commonplace with the youth of today. It was an act that was beautiful when performed with ecstasy between two lovers but not as simple animal lust. Perhaps this prudent attitude was the reason for Mag leaving and the girls staying, he surmised. Babs and the verandah on New Year's Eve was simply horseplay. Beryl's world belonged with the youngsters and with no pangs of conscience she was thoroughly smitten by her recent conquest. That evening they worked together behind the bar and during rest periods she kept touching him in a very tender way when they talked. It reminded observant Megan of a doting mother checking her son's attire just before going on stage at the Eisteddfod. The association was so blatantly obvious that Megan and Ieuan had to make a comment at that evening's lock-in. Beryl left early, she was tired.

Ieuan was the first to speak. "What's going on with you and Beryl? Me and Megan have been watching the way she sidles up to you at every opportunity. You didn't score last night, did you?"

"Ieuan, don't be so crude." It was Megan's usual ploy to get an answer without giving the impression that she was the instigator.

Tom felt so distressed about the whole affair that it was healing to talk about it.

"To tell you the truth, yes."

Before he could explain, Ieuan replied with his usual juvenile comments. "You lucky bugger! I've been trying for years. I'll bet she goes like a bomb."

Megan's face exposed her amusement. "I thought you had more willpower than that, Tom?"

"Please, please don't poke fun about it," Tom was almost in tears. The comment was open to ridicule but Ieuan could see Tom was serious. "I feel so terrible about the whole thing. I feel I had defiled our relationship and it will never be the same again. I tried to put on a brave face today but I felt vile."

"Tom, you don't think you're the first do you? Beryl has been around. I can name at least six blokes she has been with in Llanrheidol and that includes Dow..." Ieuan stopped.

"She's a lovely girl, Tom, don't get me wrong," Megan was attempting to erase his guilt, "but she's a modern girl and one night stands are commonplace."

"But how do you explain this devotion she is showing me in public?" Tom was genuinely bothered.

"Don't worry Tom, it's infatuation, it will wear off. It was the same with the others."

"Give her another one," Ieuan thrust his forearm forwards and upwards.

"Stop it, Ieuan. You can see Tom's upset. Don't worry Tom, it'll be all right, believe me." Tom had a lot of respect for Megan.

Tom was about to be confronted by the self appointed custodians of his morals. He could hear them coming up the stairs before their Sunday morning bar session. Why should he have such a guilty conscience? He felt like a naughty little boy about to be chastised by his mother. To soften the blow he convinced himself that it was their fault, they went to their bloody concert and left him alone. Even that did not lessen the fact that he was still a scoundrel in his eyes. They crashed in, banging the door against the wall. "What the hell have you been up to?" Carol shouted at Tom.

"I, I don't know what you're talking about?"

"Yes you do! We saw Megan in the paper shop this morning." She knew about their relationship with Tom and told them to be diplomatic in their approach. Carol thought it was an ideal opportunity to return the badgering he gave them. "We were only away for two nights. Mary is very upset, you scallywag."

He thought the best defence was attack and said, "It's your bloody fault. You left me on my own. I'm fed up of being on my own."

"If you were that frustrated why didn't you tell us." Carol's attitude changed from aggression to sultry seduction. "I could have given you a good time."

Tom was appalled and expressed it physically and verbally. "Bloody hell! Is there nothing left in this bastard world to cherish." He stared at Carol. She stared back and subsequently burst out laughing. Tom felt a tremendous feeling of relief.

"I could have done the same," said Mary innocently and she started to laugh as well.

"Don't be stupid," said Tom protectively.

"You are a bloody fool, Tom. When the cat's away... What if she's pregnant?"

"Everybody seems to be obsessed with Beryl and pregnancy. I hope she's on the pill. There won't be anyone left in the pub, otherwise."

"She's not that good a barmaid?" said Mary. The girls were unaware of the Blue Bootees imminent departure.

Tom felt so relieved about their attitude that he had to try and justify his actions. "To be quite frank, I can't remember doing it. I just remember waking up the following morning next to her..."

"You've never done that with me," tormented Carol.

"No, but I know what I've been missing." Carol flushed. He rang Nana and cancelled lunch and took them to the Royal. Tom went to visit Mark that evening but came back early. They stayed that night but all in separate beds. It was less provocative but very affable. Tom was essentially a family man.

* * * * *

The stark reality of running a public house always erupted on Mondays. It seemed to come around with great frequency and last only a short space of time. Most of it was spent moving barrels and stacking crates. On this particular Monday facing Beryl was another reason for Tom's anxiety. On the advice of his brace of females he was chatty and friendly to his succubus but kept himself detached. He had no flights of fancy about a young girl falling for an older man. There were no ringing bells and rose covered porches. To his delight Beryl was extremely happy and contented with life. They joked and larked about like they usually did, but the body language was reduced to a barely perceptible rumour.

From now on there will be no more Friday night take-outs or take-offs without his girls, a fanciful negative promise Tom had often used after a heavy drinking session. It wasn't that he did not enjoy his physical juxtaposition with Beryl, in fact, what he could remember, he liked. It went much deeper than that. Although Megan and Ieuan had almost convinced Tom that Beryl didn't care about their relationship she was a beautiful young girl with a sparkling personality but she also had feelings. He had to be satisfied in his mind that he was doing the honourable thing. He knew, at close hand, the ordeal of rejection.

Late that evening, with the support of his two devoted confidants he approached Beryl. He affectionately put his arm around her shoulders and said, "They know about Friday night."

"Who told them? I thought only you and me knew that." She sounded disappointed.

"I only told Megan and Ieuan, I was worried about how you would take it and they have known you much longer than me. I'm still married and I did take advantage of you. I feel such a swine about the whole thing. I feel I have let you down, you trusted me." He went on and on in a touching string of apologies.

"Tom, I'm not worried about anything. At the time it was great and I feel over the moon, I must admit, I've always fancied you and even more so when Mag..." she hesitated briefly. "It's done and that's that. I won't demand that you marry me or anything silly like that and I'm not likely to be pregnant since I'm on the pill."

Tom visually sighed with relief.

"It's OK, don't feel sad, I loved it and I would do it again if I had a chance." She grabbed Tom around the waist from behind. He smiled nervously as she playfully uncoupled her hands.

"I told you Beryl wouldn't be awkward, didn't I?" Ieuan turned towards Beryl who shrugged her shoulders in approval.

"It just happened, Tom. If I hadn't spilt that drink who knows what would have happened?"

It was ripe for a gibe. "Hey! And then what happened?"

"Shut up, Ieuan, leave them in peace, it's a sore point. Don't you dare!" Megan threateningly raised her index finger in the air and waved it at Ieuan; Tom smiled approvingly. The rest of the night was dominated by Tom relinquishing all signs of his miserly nature and giving away numerous rounds. Beryl left with Ieuan on her arm but Megan stayed.

"I told you it would be all right. She's a lovely girl, she likes the men but only one at a time... Who else knows?"

"The girls, you told them," said Tom

"That's different, they're like family to you, aren't they? Like the daughters you didn't have." He looked guilty and dropped his gaze. "Come on Tom, I wasn't born yesterday. I simply told them to be concerned because you were feeling guilty."

"I s'pose you're right, although we tease each other, I think the world of those two girls but in some ways it's deeper than family."

"Watch it, Tom. I'd be careful who you say that to." Megan was strengthening the relationship. "They are devoted to you as well but I'm sure you know that."

Tom was feeling a little ashamed about his lewd comment and said. "Ieuan is quite a character, isn't he? He never seems to stop playing the fool and chatting up the girls."

"It's all a front, Tom. I know him so well. We were sweethearts at Primary School for a long time although I was several years older..."

"That's a lovely word, sweethearts. I haven't heard anyone say that for a long time. Some of the old biddies used to use it in the factory where I worked in Bristol."

Megan progressed with her shortened biography of Ieuan. "He was always the joker and very popular with the girls but strangely he never seemed to get involved. He's devoted to his wife and the thought of an affair is out of the question. All his bravado is a sham and I think if he was compromised he would freeze to the spot. He wouldn't say it to your face but he's a bit of a romancer and his opinion of you has gone up a hundred fold. Remember that incident when the darters took his trousers? He was so embarrassed about the whole episode you just wouldn't believe. He told his wife and she gave him hell for being so gullible."

"Didn't you make a comment at the time about his underpants and that you expected him to have his best on?"

"Did I? That was probably part of our party piece for the sake of the spectators. I usually try and elaborate on any of his stories, if I can."

"Do you know his wife?"

"Gosh, yes! We are great pals. She nursed with me in London. She started her training just before I came back to Llanrheidol. She has packed it up and doesn't do anything now except WVS work. I see her everyday in work."

Being reminded of Megan's time in London, Tom immediately recalled an unanswered question that had been nagging away at him for a long time. Although they were the only two in the bar he surmised that it had to be asked in a whisper out of respect. "Tell me, what's all the scandal and mystery about Lally and her family and why didn't they come to her funeral?"

Megan didn't have to censor her reply for she knew it would go no further but as assurance she said, "This is between you and me." Tom accepted without question. "Give me another drink Tom, please. This may take a while."

"Oh, it's on the house."

She thanked him.

"I was not with Lally that particular evening. She had gone to the party with her boyfriend who later became her husband. It was one of those arty rave ups with plenty of booze and cannabis rolled in a cigarette, they used to be called reefers."

"That's right, Megan." Tom recalled the jazz club scene in Bristol but he never indulged.

"In those days possessing cannabis was a serious offence, not like today with all these other weird and wonderful killers. (Megan was a fanatical anti-drug campaigner.) The party was swinging when one of Lally's ex-boyfriends came up to her. He was obviously high on drugs and drink and he stabbed himself in front of her, right in the chest." Megan put her hand against her matronly bosom to emphasise the point.

"Bloody hell!" Tom roared. "Did he die?"

"Yes, eventually."

"I don't believe it, Lally! She was such a quiet, lonely person."

"Not in those days, she was a real hell-raiser, an eccentric... The point was that there was blood all over Lally and her boyfriend and to cap it all, she grabbed the knife as he went down and it appeared that she had done it. Naturally someone called the police. There were several arrests for drug offenses and Lally was taken in with her boyfriend as an accomplice for attempted murder or some other jumped up charge. It was in all the papers because he was from a well-to-do family, a stockbroker in the city. You must have seen it at the time."

"Probably? But I can't remember," Tom was mesmerised.

"To cut a long story short, she was finally let off but the stigma remained. Her boyfriend came from the county set and his parents forbade him to have anything to do with Lally otherwise he would lose his allowance. Drugs, booze and debauchery were certainly not on their social list. He was a student as well but studying economics at the LSE. That's how he eventually became a successful businessman. Dabbling with Daddy's money on the stock market," she said venomously. "Despite the ban they carried on seeing each other and secretly got married. Lally was six months gone when her husband finished his degree. She did not finish her course at Art College, which she bitterly resented for the rest of her life. Eventually all was forgiven and Daddy set them up in a little cottage in Sussex somewhere and they went on from there, having a second daughter. Like so many marriages these days," Megan sounded disappointed, "they drifted apart. By the way," Megan whispered, "I don't think the daughter who came here was his and that's when the hatred started to creep in... You know the rest."

Tom could see the hint of a tear in the corner of Megan's eye which she wiped quickly with her handkerchief. "That's very sad, Megan." Still harping back to the past he said, "Did Mag know about it?"

"I doubt it very much, Lally was a very private person. Ieuan was at the party. He was studying to be a surveyor."

After a brief contemplative silence she said, "Gosh, is that the time? I must go, I'm on earlies tomorrow."

Beryl arrived at her door with her escort. She gave him a friendly kiss. He made no comment, there was no audience and she went inside. Safely in the privacy of her flat she shed a few tears of unfulfilment but later convinced herself that Tom was too old and set in his ways for her.

Now he had settled in his mind the distress of his encounter with Beryl, it was time to finally deliberate on his destiny. To sell or not to sell? His postgraduate friends were going, Myfanwy, most likely and Clem was in hospital with a stroke; no more Sunday nights for him for a while. In the course of about a year a cornucopia of delights had quickly been displaced by a plethora of pessimisms. It was time to get out. The first thing he had to do was inform the girls like he promised. They were naturally disturbed but displayed less emotion than last time. Their main worry was where Tom was going to live, their one room was too small. He baited them by suggesting Nana's but they thought a flat of his own might be more applicable for obvious reasons.

On Monday morning the pub went up for sale. Descriptions of the property were sent to the local paper and the Brewers' Gazette, a monthly publication for the licensing trade. Mag's parents were informed and they were overjoyed with the move. Nana's natural response was to offer Tom accommodation. It was a genuine gesture but they all recognised that even their flat was too small. In the meantime, Selwyn had offered him the spare room in his house with the use of all facilities. He provisionally accepted much to the relief of his in-laws. The question of Mark's future was to be discussed at a later stage in the transactions.

Tom was baffled at the lack of response, no phone calls or letters, nothing, not even an inquiry. He was becoming impatient now that he had made up his mind to vacate the premises.

Wednesday evening, when Tom was entertaining his son, a couple strode into Ty Gwyn. They acknowledged Beryl in Welsh and she replied in her mother tongue then switched to English for the customary request. They took their drinks and sat down near the fireplace at the top room. There was a genial crowd of girls and their boyfriends. They included some of the opposing darts team practicing for the next game. Few of the locals were in, except for Frank, they were accustomed to Tom's habits on Wednesdays and no lock-in. To any stranger it looked a warm, jovial establishment with plenty of atmosphere. The masculine stranger came back to the bar with two empty glasses.

"Two more whiskeys please, Irish. Are you the landlady?" he requested.

"Almost," muttered Beryl inaudibly.

"Pardon?"

"No, I just work here. It's the landlord's night off. He's out. Can I help you?"

"No, could you tell him that we will call tomorrow morning. We would like to discuss some business with him." They finished their drinks, stayed a little while longer, then left, acknowledging Beryl in Welsh.

"*Nos da*," she replied.

Beryl instantly contacted Tom about the incident. Although she was worried about her job she was still loyal and concerned about Tom's future. He was back in the pub in about thirty minutes.

"I don't know why I've come back. You said they had left, didn't you?"

Beryl nodded and sat down on the server's bar stool. "I feel all at sixes and sevens, I'm lost." He was getting excited. "Pass me one of my specials and one for yourself." Tom passed over the money. It was always the policy of the Tremletts to let the customers see the proprietors pay cash; it could be retrieved later. Tom was exultant. "I'm sure these are the people, Beryl." It was then that he noticed she was astutely unveiling her physical attributes to him as the only person at the bar. *Déjà vu* thought Tom as she repeated a move for which Mag had been verbally chastised one Sunday evening last summer. He felt inflamed with the fusion of stimuli.

"They appeared to be quite taken with the place. They spoke to me in Welsh." She crossed her legs over very slowly.

"Did you reply in Welsh? Who was here?"

"Don't get so excited, Tom, watch your blood pressure... Yeah, and the crowd that's here now." The answers didn't matter. He was chatting to Beryl who was unmistakably responsive in a way that he remembered from the not too distant past. A large crowd of pre-nuptial drunks stumbled in so Tom helped behind the bar. After the rush he returned to the other side while she seated herself in a negotiating position back on the notorious stool. Tom was happy, relaxed and unfettered; he could foresee the possible end to all his problems and with uncalculated spontaneity squared up and said, "Fancy a take-away afterwards?"

"OK, yeah!" she loved Tom when he was in a flippant mood. "Will you want afters?" This banter was out of reach of the other clients but of major importance as literal foreplay.

'Not half! It's a good job I didn't pledge total abstinence after the last session,' Tom thought.

Next morning, Myfanwy found both of them suitably dressed at the breakfast table.

"You're early Beryl," pryingly challenged Myfanwy.

"Yeah, Tom's got someone coming to look at the place this morning and he wanted me to come in early to help out."

Myfanwy accepted the account without question. No one ever knew of their repeated Beryl-garnished, curry take-away.

As Tom correctly predicted, once a sale was pending it would be quick. The new owners had sold their house in North Wales and were looking for a little pub in this area.

Tom decided that he would forfeit another of his highly acclaimed Ty Gwyn ribald parties and go out with dignity. So many participants were missing or were unable to attend. He invited the pub staff, together with Ieuan and Megan, to a farewell dinner at the Royal. They met Gethin and his partner in the bar. He was very sorry to hear Tom was leaving, but more preoccupied with his latest conquest. The meal looked good, almost as presentable as Richard and Tom's buffet at Ty Gwyn, but as Tom pointed out, much more expensive.

Without thinking and of course not knowing what Tom intended, Carol said with her usual openness, "Mean to the end, Tom."

"That's right, must keep an eye on it, nobody else will." He winked at Megan. There were the usual speeches about leaving and how they (Tom) had transformed the pub into a jolly, friendly local which they hoped the new people would maintain. The previous owner's contribution was not mentioned. They pecked at the buffet and drank copious amounts of wine. Towards the end of the evening in the company of numerous empty bottles, Megan presented Tom with the old faithful, a carriage clock, suitably inscribed.

Tom responded by offering an envelope to all the girls on his staff which was not to be opened until at home. Each contained a cheque for one hundred pounds and a card thanking them for their invaluable help throughout his numerous crises. Beryl received extra: she was an honest, faithful and thoroughly good bar person as well. The wine was replenished in the bar by Tom and drinking went on until dawn. Megan and Ieuan crawled away, mainly because of the weight of Ieuan more than alcohol. Mary gave Tom a huge cuddle; she had opened her envelope. Carol and Beryl were slumped at a corner table with their arms around each other. Tom ensured that everyone got to their dwellings including Beryl who insisted that Tom should see her dog... He eventually returned to the pub expended and happy, ready to finalise the last day. The new tenants ran the pub that evening for practice.

The following morning Beryl and Myfanwy came in together. Tom was unsuccessfully trying to tackle a piece of burnt toast. Black coffee was the beverage that morning. In the evening, after a hectic day at the solicitors, Tom settled down in the bar with Beryl serving. All the gang were there including the Blue Bootees and the nurses. Tom disappeared upstairs and produced a huge box. "Mag never called for a lot of her clothes and I certainly don't want them, help yourself." He handed the box to Beryl at the bar. She rummaged through and produced the infamous blouse. She instantly removed the added fastener Mag had applied for modesty and proclaimed that she would wear that in the bar. Tom shuddered momentarily. "Here you are girls." He threw the box into the middle of the room.

"Any basques left, Tom?" Rolff was joking. Yah pulled him away and said something in his ear. He laughed out boisterously.

"Carol's got yours, isn't that right Carol?"

"I've got mine, if you remember, Rolff borrowed it," she snapped at Tom.

"Oh, bloody hell! I've said the wrong thing again." Still elated and suffering from the previous night, he rushed over to Carol and said uncharacteristically, "Let's have a look, then."

"Don't be daft, Tom. I don't wear it all the time. She was not amused and looked sad but affectionately kissed him. Mary who was sitting next to her, gave a weak smile. Megan with her usual authoritative skill stated that anything left would go to OXFAM. Mary was very tearful and Tom had to reassure her that he was not leaving Llanrheidol, just the pub. Tom thought this was the ideal time to inform his friends of his intentions.

He stood up and said, "Quiet everyone, I have a surprise to tell you about what I intend to do next."

"Which one are you going to marry?" Rolff was convinced that was the answer. Beryl and the girls gawked at each other in alarm.

"No, that's not it."

One of Ieuan's witless remarks followed, "Who's pregnant then?" To his delight everybody started to laugh.

Selwyn knew the answer and was getting frustrated. "Come on Tom, tell them."

"I'm going to be a student and study for a degree in Zoology in Selwyn's Department. It's all been cleared by the College authorities; I will be a mature student."

"You can say that again!" Beryl glimpsed at Tom with a glint in her eye. Megan spotted it, Tom turned his head away nervously.

"Best of luck, Tom!" shouted out Gareth.

"Yes, best of luck my dear chap." David walked over and shook his hand. "You'll get some stick from the babies but don't you take any notice."

The rest of the residents congratulated him in turn. Megan was impressed but disgruntled that she hadn't been consulted since she was thinking of studying for an Open Degree and realised the hard work involved.

"Can I just say one more thing before I stop being landlord? I saw a large poster in the Card Shop this morning and I just had to buy it for Beryl." He disappeared upstairs.

Murmurs circumvented the establishment about various posters currently in vogue. Selwyn in one of his philosophical moods suggested it might be the farewell scene in the film Casablanca.

"No," said high-brow David. "It's got to be something by Rubens showing a voluptuous virgin, like say, Venus's Toilet."

"Do you mind, I've got a nice figure," said Beryl who assumed he was referring to her volume and not her sensuality. Too many strangers were present, including what she hoped would be her future employees, to repeat a previous Sunday exposition.

Tom produced a long cardboard tube and pulled out a tightly rolled large piece of paper and exposed it to Beryl and then the assembly. The whole pub burst into laughter. It was a photograph of a beautiful model scratching her knickerless bottom dressed in tennis gear and facing away from the camera. It was Tom's way of saying thank you for all those extras that were unobtrusively executed. The poster remained pinned up on the wall of the bar until removed and suitably replaced in its tube by Beryl at the end of the night. No one noticed, except Beryl, that on the back was written. 'Thank you, love, old Tom,' followed by three symbolic kisses.

Everyone was sad yet fleetingly happy. Tom made a point of associating with Mary for the rest of the night, Carol had gone over to the Bootees' for darts. "It will be a tremendous drop in earnings but what the hell. Life's too short and I want to do what I want to do in future. Please say you approve, Mary. It would make me feel so much better." He held her hand gently and said, "I love you so much, you're the daughter I never had." His eyes started to water and he wiped them quickly with the back of his hand.

"You sentimental old soak, of course I approve." He received the second kiss that night from his second filial love.

It was decided not to close the pub during the take over, for it would disrupt the continuity of the lunchtime trade. Tom moved out at eleven, just before opening, with his old chair and some photos; the rest he sold to the new owners who moved in at eleven five. The moment he stepped over the threshold Tom promised himself that he would never put his foot inside Ty Gwyn again. The emotional upset of living there was too traumatic... The students were preparing for their exams in May and June and the summer season was about to start. Tom selfishly hoped the new publican would carry on as before, at least, for a while. His temporary job was supplying the bar meals he had established until they decided on their own preferences. Mary helped Tom prepare the meals in Selwyn's kitchen and with Carol's help had the task of taking them to the pub. Beryl and Myfanwy who had been highly recommended by Tom carried on working at the pub. According to Mary they were very happy with their Welsh speaking landlord.

It was a strange time for Tom and such a let down. All the things he thought he would do during his temporary retirement did not materialise. Both his girls were working and Mark was at school for most of the day. It made him realise why the old Bass drinkers spent so much time shopping and in the pub. He was beginning to get like them even after only a few weeks. The highlight of his morning was to get the paper and something from Ifor who was still giving him good value for cash... With Selwyn's help, on one afternoon a week he would sit in a hide in the mountains behind Llanrheidol and guard the nests of the rare red kites from egg poachers. The weather was clement and it was so peaceful he had time to recapitulate on his financial position. With the proceeds from the sale of Ty Gwyn and Lally's bequest, he was a relatively rich man. But it was still on his conscience that half of it legally belonged to Mag, despite the fact that the encumbrance of trying to find her was becoming more and more difficult. Did she know about the sale of the pub, or care? She had in fact severed all her ties with acquaintances and friends. She no longer phoned Dulcie but sent her the occasional postcard to establish that she was still alive. The latest one was from Fuerteventura, one of the lesser known islands of the Canary group. According to Dulcie she was working there in a bar. She was obviously not on the mainland of Spain as everyone thought. Dulcie always informed Tom of her whereabouts when possible. Mag was beginning to become something from the past with her self-imposed ostracism, like Lally and Dowie who were never mentioned, at least, in Tom's company. Irrespective of his waning feelings for Mag, he felt he was compelled to make a final search for her, albeit a tenuous one.

In Selwyn's kitchen one morning, between boiling the mince and slicing the onions, Tom made a decision. "Time to have a holiday." Since leaving the pub Tom was prone to sudden audible outbursts. "But I don't want to spend it on my own." 'Shut up Tom, you're talking to yourself again.' He thought that this was an ideal opportunity to make amends. Dulcie had been overlooked, despite her considerable loyalty to the Tremletts and it was time he made it up to her. After all, he did reject her consolation at the time of the breakup. He would invite her to go with him to Fuerteventura. No monkey business, besides he would also invite his in-laws who had not had a holiday for years and naturally Mark. Tom budgeted for five, four adults and a child. He rang Dulcie, showered her with a glut of excuses for not ringing and informed her of the sale of the pub. She was aware that Tom was thinking about it, but didn't realise it had happened. He explained the idea of the vacation to Fuerteventura with the intention of trying to find Mag. Tom spoke to Dan at the specific request of Dulcie to explain the why's and wherefore's. Dan was particularly talkative for Dan, but sartorially liberated Tom could not help smiling to himself. He imagined Dan standing next to the phone in his carpet slippers and old cardigan with a smouldering pipe in the other hand from which he would take a well earned inhalation during Tom's turn in the conversation. There was no problem about Dulcie. Tom could sense that Dan was happy to be rid of her for a little while. The idea was not completely original, since Dulcie had been on holiday with the Tremletts to Florida a few years previous. The only difference this time was it was the in-laws. He handed the phone back to Dulcie who was overjoyed with the holiday news. To give the impression to Dan that this adventure was solely for locating Mag, she said on the phone sufficiently loudly for him to hear, "I've just had another look at the postcard Mag sent me and the postmark is somewhere called Corraljo so that should narrow the field down a bit, Tom."

"Oh, good," came an unconvincing reply. "I'll do everything from my end. If we can fly from Cardiff you can travel from Bristol. It will save you a wasted journey here. Let you know anyway, all right?" The phone went dead. Dulcie paused waiting for a sound then slammed the phone down in anger. Tom did not realise that she had been deprived of the latest goings on in Llanrheidol.

Tom did not mention the holiday to his in-laws; he wanted to surprise them. He no longer had to wait until Wednesday to visit. Leaving the licensing trade was such a relief but the cooking of bar meals for the pub was fun and kept him occupied and close to the girls.

The following day he booked the trip to the Canaries, four adults and a child, flying from Cardiff on the fourteenth at noon. The monotonous, well rehearsed, emotionless voice from Mavis the Travel confirmed what Tom had written down.

"Yep!" said Tom. He gathered up all the bits of paper that sealed the contract and went back to his accommodation at Selwyn's place. He was so excited at the thought of getting away for a while that he had to go to visit Nana that afternoon. When he arrived Grandad had gone to get Mark from school. The first thing she wanted to know was the temperature at that time of year.

"Oh, up in the 80s," Tom boasted, he had made a point of noticing it in the brochure. "Just right for you to laze around."

There was a meaningful pause and Nana replied, "We couldn't possibly stand that heat, Tom. It would kill us off." She observed the look of excitement on Tom's face drain away and felt wretched. She tried to compensate for her ungrateful reply and made it less displeasing by confirming that Mark would love it. Still worried at the inconvenience she had inflicted on Tom she pleaded, "Why don't you get Selwyn and Megan to go with you? They are good friends."

"Selwyn's going to a Conference and Megan couldn't stand the heat." Relentlessly Tom endeavoured to rekindle her interest by alluding to Mag. "Fuerteventura is where Dulcie got her last card from Mag, did you realise that?" Even the thought of being reunited with her daughter was not incentive enough. Mag was still regarded with contempt as a child deserter even more than abandoning the marriage. Tom could see her point of view and unintentionally forgot how old they were and the responsibility he had thrust upon them in their declining years. Should they really have to bring up a young child? Strictly speaking, it was his duty. He couldn't be angry, if he had been less impetuous in the first place his frustration could have been avoided. Mark came rushing in. He recognised the car outside and gave Tom an endearing hug. After consultation, Grandad was of the same voice as Nana, even to the extent of reiterating that Mark would thoroughly enjoy the holiday. Mark quite naturally was overjoyed. He had a glass of milk and left as quickly as he came to inform his pal across the road about his impending trip to Canary.

"Ha ha Canary, what a funny name, Daddy?"

Tom could see the futility of his request, so he changed the question. "The house next to Selwyn is coming up for sale and I've got first refusal. What do you think I should do? It's quite big, it's got three bedrooms."

Nana could see that this was a way of turning the conversation and getting Tom's approval. "Buy it Tom. You can put a couple of students in the spare room and that will help with your grant." His mother-in-law knew of Tom's academic intentions before anyone else, except Selwyn.

"That's a good idea. I'll put in a bid tomorrow and see what happens." He was still not sold on their refusal to go on holiday and needed final confirmation. "So you definitely will not be coming to Fuerteventura with us?" In a conclusive attempt to get them to come, he said foolishly, "I've asked Dulcie to come with us and you were to be her chaperone" He smiled, so did Grandad.

"Don't be silly Tom, Mark's there and..." she delayed her reply as a germ of an idea popped into that old but agile brain, "Why don't you go the whole hog...?"

'Strange expression for Nana,' thought Tom.

"Invite the two girls in your life, Mary and Carol." She had observed their platonic friendship developing for some time.

"Bloody hell! That's it." He apologised for his outburst and responded as though it was his idea. "They can be the chaperons." Tom stayed and talked ceaselessly about his future until Mark returned for bed.

He did not see the girls that evening, it was too late. He gave Selwyn a message the following morning to give to Carol who worked on the College farm. Mary had found employment in the fashion shop Mag used to frequent but it was an area treated with contempt by Tom. They met at lunchtime in Selwyn's house which was halfway between the College and town.

Mary looked worried, she didn't seem to have settled since Tom left the pub. "There's something wrong, isn't there Tom? You wouldn't have called us so quickly otherwise."

"On the contrary, I think you will be delighted at what I have to say." He put the proposal to them. "It's already booked so you'll travel free. There will, of course, be Dulcie and Mark as well." They were so overjoyed that Mary was late back at work. She kept on about summer bargains in the shop. To them it was the holiday of a lifetime; neither had been abroad or travelled by air before.

The next day, Tom contacted Dulcie to explain the change of plan. She did not feel obliged to acquaint Dan with unnecessary details. Dulcie liked to be in the company of the girls, it made her feel young. Having them about on holiday would give her a matriarchal status that would impress the most critical holiday makers.

The girls came to Tom's place that evening but they stayed in the kitchen, there was more room. Selwyn was in his rooms working on a scientific paper. They talked for hours thumbing through the brochure showing all the best parts of the island and the exact locality of their chalet complex. Passports and clothes were discussed.

"You won't need many clothes, girls." Tom meant good, expensive, tailored clothes.

"You're not taking us to a nudist camp are you?" said Mary who was not affected either way.

"No, of course not. You've seen the location in the brochure." He pointed to a glossy periodical on the kitchen table. Tom was taken off guard and felt slightly embarrassed. "What I meant was, we are self-catering so we don't have to dress for dinner, like in a hotel. Just a swimming costume, a bikini or shorts. Incidentally, they all go topless out there."

Mary looked disturbed, "Won't that upset Dulcie?"

"Bloody hell, no! Do you recall last summer when she stayed here," he consciously did not include a personal pronoun. "She was sunbathing in the nude on the roof. Naturally, I didn't publicise the fact. Can you imagine Ieuan's reaction?" He made no mention of Mag's part in her display.

"You're going to be titillated this holiday, aren't you Tom?" Carol incited laughter in all three.

"Oh, I think I've seen quite enough of that bit of anatomy in Llanrheidol to keep me going for quite a while. Did you..." he was about to mention Beryl's change of colour when he realised. "It's not important, never mind." The hour was late but the situation was not like in the pub so they had to graciously bow out and go back to their one room.

* * * * *

As arranged, they met Dulcie at the airport. She was looking like a teenager with her mini-skirt, cheap plastic baubles and high heels. The embellishments were not displayed until well into her rail journey and far away from her other life-style. Everyone was in high spirits; Dulcie had to have a G&T before the plane and Tom had his last Bass.

"They don't keep it right," said Tom lifting the glass and looking at it against the light. Nobody took any notice and especially not the bar staff. The two girls were at the observation window with Mark trying to decide which plane was theirs.

The flight was relatively uneventful. Mary was disappointed at seeing mostly cotton-wool clouds through her haze of a window.

"Don't they ever clean them?" grumbled Mary. Mark messed around with his Kiddy Pack after the initial excitement of taking off. Carol read while Tom and Dulcie absorbed the ambience with in-flight beverages. With his own harem Tom didn't seem to find the air hostesses so pretty as on previous trips.

The still hot, late afternoon air embraced them as they descended the steps of the plane. Mark was holding on tightly to Tom's hand as if his peace of mind might be violated at any moment. Tom recalled that terrifying first night in the pub and gave his hand an affectionate squeeze. The little face looked up at Tom and beamed. They trundled their cases into Reception after a remarkably smooth ride in an air-conditioned coach. Normally the roads were absolute hell and the transport hot and smelly. Tom was exaggerating his continental experiences of ten years previous.

"Tremletts!" The courier put his hand in the air brandishing a key. Tom approached him, four adults and a child, and officiously talked slowly and loudly at the courier.

"Why are you shouting, Tom?"

"I don't know Mary, but everyone seems to shout at foreigners."

The very English, Spanish-speaking receptionist said abruptly, "Number sixty-three, over there!" He pointed to a relatively large chalet with a beautiful purple creeper growing up one side of the building. He droned on, "We meet tomorrow at ten-thirty in the bar over there," sluggishly pointing to a noisy, bustling offshoot of the swimming pool. "I'll tell you about the various trips you can go on and you can try some of our famous Sangria." The smile after Sangria displayed a touch of queasiness. It must be difficult to muster up enthusiasm for such a nauseous libation, together with twice a week for six months of the same prattle, thought Tom. I wonder how actors can carry on a performance daily month after month? Tom cynically answered himself by supposing that money was the incentive.

Tom turned the lock and entered first. "Bloody hell! Open some windows." The heat hit him like opening a blast furnace doors for inspection. There was a scurry of helpers taking latches off windows and opening doors.

Mark spotted the swimming pool at Reception and the chalet was even closer. He was costumed and out before the rest had finished bringing in the cases. Tom let him go without unduly worrying about his safety: he could see him from the chalet.

Inside the chalet, hot, weary, sticky adults were jostling in competition for a refreshing shower. Clothes were being peeled quicker than a stripper forced by time. Carol exploited her gross proportions and scrummaged her way in first. Soon the cooled company were sitting at an elongated bar, aptly towelled. The Welcome Pack was opened and a well earned cuppa dispensed. Mark remained in the pool, oblivious of his amiable companions. Dulcie and Tom, dressed in their shorts and thin tops, went on a reconnoitre to find the nearest *supermercado* and stocked up. When they returned, the girls wandered off looking for anything of interest, discos, bars, boys. Tom heard Mark from the chalet, but despite Tom's calls he insisted on continuing his aquatic displays with a befriended boy from the North Country.

"If he stays in there much longer, he'll sprout gills and he'll be all wrinkled," remarked Dulcie. "What are you grinning at, Tom?" she said indignantly.

He concealed his reason while leisurely breaking the seal on a bottle of Pastis. "I'll get him later and give him an iron."

A joke from Tom was so unexpected that it was not fully appreciated. "I use wrinkle cream myself, look." Dulcie flashed a pair of beautiful, smooth, shapely legs.

"You like the flavour of aniseed, don't you Dulcie?"

"Yes, but Pernod is too expensive to buy regularly."

"This is a drink very much like it. Have a glass." He poured some and diluted it with a large volume of water. "Try that, it's strong so I diluted it." Tom compounded his drink with a paltry amount of water.

"Umm! That's nice... You're looking very contented, Tom."

"I haven't felt like this for ages. No problems, it's nice and warm and I'm in the presence of my lovely people."

"You'll be talking about flower power next. I'm in with a chance then." She moved forward and touched his scarred bare knee affectionately. "How is it these days?"

"The knee you mean, is it?" He didn't realise the Welshism.

"Well, what else is there to bother about?"

The connotation went unnoticed by Tom. "It's perfect, just think I had to go all the way to Wales to get my knee fixed. They just messed me around in Bristol. Too many chiefs and not enough Indians."

Dulcie removed her tawdry earrings and necklace and alluringly moulded herself into a chair. Beryl's precoital behaviour immediately sprung to Tom's mind and his indifference to it. Tom felt so family orientated, a sensation he had not experienced throughout the whole of his stay in Llanrheidol. Although they were essentially a surrogate family, they were what Tom always wanted; two girls and a boy. He could have sat there forever sublimely happy and at peace with the world. Dulcie was beginning to show signs of the trip and the aromatic drink and kept dozing off. "Why don't you go to bed, Dulcie?" As if in a trance, she slowly rose from her chair, wandered into her prearranged bedroom, and closed the door. Throughout the rest of the holiday this was the only time a bedroom door was closed.

Tom wandered over to witness the exaggerated springboard antics of his son showing off to his English pal. He was reliving his diving fantasy from school, recollected Tom. Mark eventually bade farewell to his fellow aquanaut and Tom carried him on his shoulders back to the chalet. After being showered and fed he was soon asleep in the same room as Dulcie. She was lying naked and face down on the bed, a position Tom vividly remembered from the summer. Tom covered her with a thin sheet and left the door open. Like a dutiful father, he waited up for the girls. They were not very long.

"Tom, it's beautiful, you are a darling. Will you marry me?" Mary was in a state of enamoured insobriety.

"Carol, look at the state of her." He spoke softly so as not to break the spell.

"We only had a couple of Bacardi and Cokes."

"But out here they give you a treble as one drink."

"Sorry Tom, I didn't realise, I feel awful," and she pouted.

"Don't be silly, Carol. I love you both and I don't want you to come to any harm." He gave her a fatherly kiss on the cheek and all was well. Both girls shuffled off to their bedroom.

In a jiffy, Carol emerged ready for a shower, as he slid naked into his bed settee. She was responsive to Tom's bashfulness and said, "You just made it that time." She coursed slowly but unsteadily, past him. On her return he was presented with a clumsy shower-wet kiss during which time he accidentally touched her damp firm breast but immediately withdrew his hand. "Now, now, Tom." She noticed his anguish and said defensively, "Sorry Tom, only joking." Tom covered his head with his pillow.

He woke to the coolness of early morning and started the day like he intended to finish most days throughout the vacation, with a walk around the complex and the wooded area behind. It was already starting to get warm. Tom opened the back window and the front door to get some air circulating. So as not to expose too much flesh to an unsuspecting public he considerately pulled the curtains over the front porch. Carol was up next, she intentionally stopped at Tom's bed and noticeably displayed disappointment at his absence. Abluted and in her swimwear she sat at the breakfast table opposite Tom. She said nothing about the previous night's encounter as she nibbled at a piece of toast and drank profuse cups of coffee. Although she was of ample proportions it certainly was not due to an unwholesome diet. The rest of the inhabitants gradually emerged like zombies. They crawled out of their cocoons until finally Mark appeared aptly attired for the most important event of his day. He gobbled down a mish-mash meal and was last seen heading in the direction of the pool. The adults nattered over breakfast waiting for Tom to organise them: "We'll just laze around for today and explore the area." All agreed without any hesitation. "I'll make arrangements to hire a car so that we can see some of the island while we're here."

The girls joined Mark at the pool determined to go back as bronzed as possible. Tom watched them through the window where he was washing up and couldn't help feeling proud. Two beautiful young girls and a happy little boy. There were a few couples about Tom's age and some younger families with children. They were all British in this particular complex. Some of the females, including the girls, did make an effort at trying to be Continental but it was betrayed by the whiteness of their female form. Dulcie sat outside the chalet in her bikini bottom painting her nails which had been chipped during the voyage. The day drifted aimlessly by; Tom was relaxed and occupied himself by preparing something for the evening meal. Dulcie spent most of the morning listlessly in Tom's company but later joined the rest at the pool. It was the perfect occasion to display her already chestnut-coloured torso. The supposedly main purpose of the visit was beginning to become of less consequence.

Following the evening meal while the girls assaulted their tormented areas with lashings of Aftersun, Tom took one of his many solitary contemplative walks. For zoological reasons it was decided that these strolls should be later in the evening from now on. During this particular walk he discovered a kitten stuck up a tree in close proximity to a lively Taverna. Mark would have had no trouble. He appreciated Selwyn's tale and laughed out loud. After some minor problems he rescued it and was gently smoothing it when a beautiful young Spanish girl appeared from the Inn. She was obviously delighted to see the cat. Tom was wined until the early hours of the morning. She could speak English and Tom a little Spanish and they both had an interest in Dali. On his arrival at the chalet, he was surprised to be welcomed by three wide awake females. They expressed some concern for his whereabouts in no uncertain terms and questioned the reason for his badly scratched legs. Eventually, all was amicably settled and they retired. Carol did not disturb Tom that night.

Next day, they decided to pay a visit to Mag's stamping ground, Corraljo, which was about twenty minutes in the car. It was a busy fishing town about the same size as Llanrheidol but the tourists were much more cosmopolitan, including Spanish from the mainland. The group split into three but arranged to meet later by the car. Tom wandered into a bar; he was uneasy about what might be awaiting him but the pressure to satisfy his thirst was paramount. Gaining boldness with each glass, he visited several bars but found no signs of Mag. Dulcie in her tight white shorts and clinging blouse paraded herself along the harbour wall using the excuse that Mark wanted to see the boats. She certainly turned a few heads. The girls had gone off to locate any discos or bars which were lively at night. Their holiday complex only had two small family orientated bars. After a pleasant morning they met as arranged. Tom arrived a little later than the rest. He got talking to the cat loving señorita from the disco bar.

"On the way up we passed those enormous sand dunes. I thought we might stop there for a while and have a swim?" All concurred. They parked the car on the roadside and bared themselves to their swimwear. The dunes were immense and a fair distance from the sea but with true British spirit they tackled the obstacle, pausing occasionally to dislodge small stones and bits of shell from between their toes; the sand was too hot to go barefooted.

Tom was carrying Mark on his shoulders so he had a much better view of the surroundings than the rest. "Daddy, Daddy, look over there." He pointed in the direction of a sand dune which was obstructing their view.

"What is it, son?"

At the same time, Dulcie stopped Tom walking with a tug of his arm. "Slow down, for God's sake, I'm worn out."

"It's people with no clothes on. They're coming this way."

"That boy of yours has got the most amazing imagination," said Dulcie as she wiped her brow with the end of Tom's shirt.

Shortly after Mark's reply a couple appeared completely naked and walked slowly past them hand in hand. No one spoke, they were so bewildered. The nudists were not teenagers, more in the twilight of their years, but they looked very fit and composed.

After they had disappeared over the next dune, Tom spoke. "Probably Germans, they are very keen nudists. You often see the odd one or two on a secluded beach." Contrary to Tom's comment, the closer they got to the beach the more prolific were the naked bodies. By the time they got to the waters edge the three girls wearing only the bottom part of their bikinis were overdressed. Tom, who had kept a shirt on to protect his tender skin from Mark's fidgeting looked unmistakably foolish to the extent that he was the centre of attraction.

Mary was the first to strip but unlike the pub it was a bikini bottom and not a basque. After a short space of time only Tom and Mark were left. Eventually Tom waived his abashment but no amount of persuading would convince Mark to surrender to this ritual.

"It's like this, Daddy," his small frame dominating the horizontal bodies, "if I'm in the shower after gym at school everyone will notice that I'm brown all over and they will laugh at me." He was the sort of child who didn't want to be the odd one out. Perhaps his highly developed imagination was a safety valve for his individuality, concluded Tom confidently.

"Oh, fair enough, but don't tell Nana, will you."

"You daft bugger," whispered Dulcie, who was lying next to Tom. "That's an open invitation."

It was unmistakably obvious that Tom was lying in the prone position while the girls were freely displaying themselves lying on their backs. Dulcie glanced at Tom and said, "Ostriches bury their heads in the sand and assume they will not be noticed." She could see Tom's neck reddening.

"Let's go for a swim," came a voice from amid the tarnished, oily, sweating, overheated bulk. There was a hurried surge to the sea by the females followed by a coy Tom. Mark who was already playing indefatigably at the waters edge was completely oblivious to their antics. The water was blue and transparent but it was not as warm as expected. It was the Atlantic and not the Mediterranean, pointed out Tom. They were soon back in the cuddling warmth of the sand dunes, leaving Mark rapidly excavating holes in the sand before the next flooding by the waves. Dulcie, who seemed on this occasion to be the leader of this jubilant birthday suited band, tormented Tom about his contracted masculinity particularly straight after the swim.

He heightened the frivolity of the remark by saying, "There's a lot of dormant muscle there. You ask Megan."

"Megan?" came an astonished general reply.

"She nursed me, didn't she?" No one made any reference to Beryl. He stammered, "And if you want to be personal, it's amazing how that inverted triangle, shows the true natural blondes."

"That's naughty," gestured Dulcie. Mary and Carol seemed so unconcerned as they applied more lotion to their accessible tender parts. As Dulcie mentioned to them, Tom was very good at the other regions.

The scathing heat of the sun was weakened but a gentle breeze blowing off the sea which caressed Tom's exposed skin as he stood, lordly, observing Mark. Together with an overall feeling of freedom it evoked a tingling sensation throughout his whole body. He had never endured such a sublime response before. Perhaps it was the feeling the girls got during THEIR nakedness? The emotion was hypnotic and, he imagined, addictive as heroin. He now understood why most sun worshippers spent so much time on their feet and not lying down. Tom made up his mind there and then that any future holidays would have to include access to such a habitat.

The intoxicating vacation drifted gently along. They visited the dunes nearly every day; four adults and a costumed child. One day the breeze was more inclined to a wind and it was blowing off the dunes. The girls were lying down and sleeping or dozing. Routinely lotioned they slowly but inextricably became encrusted with fine sand. Tom who by now had become a devotee of naturism portrayed himself like most of the other males on the beach, erect and, to the uninitiated, an exhibitionist. Since such a stance confines activity to observation or contemplation, Tom's thoughts turned to the sand storm story so humorously narrated by the now inaccessible Rhodes holiday makers. The more he thought about it, the more he found the present situation funny. It finally got to the stage where he rashly laughed out loud. It animated the girls who quickly learned that they were coated in fine sand. They frantically tried to brush it off with their towels but eventually had to resort to the sea, like Lally did. By now Tom was on his knees laughing as a consequence of both the past and present sandings.

Mary bent down to Mark who was in his usual play area and said, "Shall we get him for laughing at us?"

"Yeah," remarked Mark, who was excited at the thought of throwing his father in the sea.

Before Tom could rebuff the salty assault, he was woman-handled into the withering briny. To Tom, the encounter was inexplicably sensuous, yet terrifying at the same time. Their hands invaded the privacy of his body so much so that he was restrained and entirely dependent on their wishes. It enhanced his revulsion of the ever increasing incidents involving gang rapes.

The girls either together, or with Dulcie, visited numerous bars in Corraljo throughout the holiday in a vain attempt to locate Mag. It was not surprising since there must have been at least fifty bars not including discos and clubs in the town. Tom agreeably squandered most of his evenings in the chalet with Mark unremittingly swimming and diving in the pool, and Dulcie occasionally on the porch, but more often gallivanting with the girls. The evening isolation during the early part of the holiday was self-inflicted. When Tom was preparing to come away he packed a small portable cassette player but in the heat of the moment neglected to pack any tapes or earphones. The only tape available was in the machine. It was one of Tom's favourite recordings of the ukulele played by George Formby. Such mundane things as tapes did not occur to the girls in their pre-vacation excitement. During Tom's Happy Hour which lasted from four to seven in the evening, he would play this tape *ad nauseum*. For the first few days the girls found it comical but after a while it began to abrade their sanity and they usually slipped away to one of the site bars until seven. Dulcie, who was used to the monotonous stability of Dan, was the last to break. The girls had a great time at the bars and were very popular with the boys. Mary was the attraction for the few British boys around but Carol appeared to charm the Spanish boys who were more in favour of larger, well-proportioned girls. Dulcie was not left out and was propositioned several times. It was decided that these flirtatious early drinks sessions were all very well but it was really the time to relax and shower before the nights festivities. One evening they were in the bar near the swimming pool and it was unanimously decided that Dulcie was to relieve the area of George which was transmitted as far as the pool bar when they were relatively quiet. She explained her motivation to Mark who excitedly informed his friend.

"Right!" Dulcie had been suitably Pastis-ed. The bar became hushed and even some of the people swimming slowed down. Mark had seated himself on the side of the pool with his friend. Dulcie stamped off towards the chalet. She crashed through the curtained door and screamed, "Tom! If I hear what Nelson did with his bloody one arm and one eye once more, I swear, I'll go raving bonkers. And isn't it about time that chap leaning on the sodding lamp-post got a proper job?"

The girls and most of the bar inhabitants screamed with laughter. There were also some chuckles emanating from the pool.

"Don't swear, Dulcie," said Tom softly and slowly but without moving from his chair.

"Turn it off!" She shouted in his ear. He jumped out of his somnolence and obeyed instantly. Before Tom could fully recover she had left. Dulcie could hear the infectious laugh from the audience and had to respond. She laughed all the way to the bar were she was congratulated on her boldness.

The silent chalet was like a purple mausoleum. Tom eventually appeared at the open door blurry eyed from the drink and the bright sun. A second ripple of hilarity flooded across the pool. He smiled back and waved at Mark but didn't know why. It was all amicably explained to him later that evening and as a result, the single recording only came on once a day and Happy Hour was confined to one hour. To ensure no repetition, the girls bought some Spanish pop tapes. As a result of Dulcie's boldness, they all saw much more of each other in the evenings. Even Mark called in from time to time.

Dulcie was feeling a little guilty about the joke she had played on Tom and how he regularly baby-sat while they enjoyed themselves. "Why don't you go out with the girls and enjoy yourself, Tom. I'll look after Mark."

"Oh, no thanks. I don't think I could stand a disco. (They were too closely associated with distress for Tom.) I'm quite happy here."

"I know what we can do," said Mary, who was missing Tom's company in the evenings. "Why don't you come with us to the bar next to the disco and then you can drift back here when we go in?"

"I haven't showered or anything. I usually leave it 'til later on."

"That's OK, just splash on some after shave." Tom conceded.

The girls didn't realise Tom had been there on his own. He silently but sincerely resented the familiarity made by some of the boys towards his equally responsive girls. In reply and to their astonishment, he amused the cat loving Spanish girl at the bar with a few anecdotes about the sand dunes. She was in stitches.

"What was ze word, Tom?" She touched his unclothed thigh gently. He whispered something in her ear. She screamed with laughter.

The girls had to admit, they were outclassed and decided it was time to go. They left with Tom but went their separate ways. Dulcie was sitting on the porch sipping Pastis, for which she had taken a liking, and felt desperate for company. On spotting Tom, she gratefully filled another glass.

"I didn't realise how lonely it gets sitting on your own. I'm glad you've come back." She affectionately moistened his lips with an aniseed flavoured tongue.

"That's a nice dress you've got on," said Tom, a little tiddly from his caper.

"It's a wrap-around, I bought it in Corraljo." Tom could smell the expensive duty free perfume wafting towards him. "It's pure silk." Tom touched it gently and realised it was the only garment she was wearing.

"That's a bit daring isn't it?"

"You're supposed to wear something underneath but it's too hot and I'm sitting down so no one can see anything anyway."

Dulcie's fragrance reminded Tom of the soporific nature of the day and that he gravely needed a shower so he excused himself. The warm caressing water and the few beers made Tom fidgety. He thought of the pub roof, the sand dunes and Ieuan's unintentional proudness at the Christmas Party. The curtain moved and parted slightly allowing a hand to enter. "Here's your drink, Tom. You left it on the table." In his haste to retrieve the glass the curtain slid open sufficiently to divulge Tom's ample proportions. "Your comments on the sand dunes were right, after all." Dulcie slipped out of her silk as she joined him in the shower. He never did finish the drink. Dulcie had been totally enamoured with Tom for years and the time was ripe to release it in a frenzied outburst. She was remarkably light and agile. Her bronzed thighs belted around his waist as he pinned her against the slippery wall.

"They did a good job on my knee it's holding well, Oh!" Tom expressed with each of his slow, forced expirations.

When the girls returned, Tom had weakened to a chair on the porch sipping replenished Pastis. Dulcie and Mark had retired for the night. He now accepted her passion for the claustrophobic confines of her Mini.

One disco evening, when the girls were occupied on the floor, Dulcie, who spent most of her time at the bar, was handed a slip of paper by one of the barmen. It contained a telephone number and was signed, *Mag*. The following evening, using the guise of ringing Dan, Dulcie engaged the number and arranged a meeting.

On that particular evening Dulcie accompanied the girls to Corraljo but did not stay with them. Her excuse was that she fancied a walk on her own to absorb the Spanish atmosphere and she would meet them later.

Carol had taken a little too much in the Taverna that night. "That's rubbish! She's meeting that Manuel, the one who keeps looking at her tits and is always making a lot of fuss of her." Mary was used to Carol's tipsy sarcasm. "I'll bet you he's not there tonight." By a strange coincidence, she was right.

They met in a small bar near the harbour. Mag seemed very introverted and had lost her sparkle but still retained her good figure.

"I saw you first waiting in the car park, you know. I was about to come over when I saw Tom running towards you. He looked so happy and carefree I felt I had to pull back." She hesitated, "Were those two girls Carol and Mary?" She declined to mention Mark.

"Yes, they've come on holiday with us. It was originally going to be Nana and Grandad. They miss you terribly, Mag." She hung her head and declined to answer.

"Is he bedding them?"

"Come on Mag, you know Tom better than that. (She was lying and often wondered to herself exactly what their relationship was.) He treats them like daughters and they're great fun be with."

"He always wanted a daughter but it was not to be. Perhaps the one we lost might have been?"

Mag had changed from the girl Dulcie saw off to Spain and she was beginning to get depressed at Mag's guilt. She declined to ask her about herself for fear of other misfortunes. They had another drink brought over by an aristocratic looking waiter who obviously knew Mag well. Soon after, Dulcie excused herself, on the grounds that she had arranged to share a taxi with the girls. Mag showed some signs of emotion as she kissed Dulcie and promised to write at the end of the season. Dulcie glanced back as she left and the handsome waiter was sitting next to Mag who looked tearful.

Dulcie was very depressed when she met the girls in the disco. She gave vent to her feelings by getting drunk and passing out. No one informed Tom or mentioned Manuel.

"The holiday's coming to an end and still no sign of Mag. She's probably shacked up with some rich Spaniard." Tom's conviction was changing and he was beginning to resent the fact that she might be found. Why should she desecrate his balmy days on Fuerteventura. Dulcie, once again, was in an awkward situation. Should she tell Tom about her private meeting with Mag? If she did, what would be the outcome? She decided to be discreet and keep the holiday exciting.

Tom realised he had to face up to the fact that his parody of a family would soon be dissipated, leaving Dulcie reluctantly back to Dan. The subtley perceptible hint of an amorous liaison was detected by the girls but the two adulterers kept it well under control. If Dulcie had been given a free hand it would have triggered off a chain reaction that would have got hopelessly out of control. Was this the reason the girls invited her out with them as often as possible? After all, Beryl managed it once(?). Mark would be back with Tom's in-laws. But that was not a departure just a different address and perhaps one day soon they would be back under the same roof. The girls had to go back to their one-roomed flat. But was that necessary? His affection for them had blossomed during the holiday almost to the height of his love for Mark. His fatherly possessiveness had become reality. Tom's shortened early evening entertainment brought them back into the household and away from amorous youths. Tom was not perceptive enough, but their response was voluntary.

One evening when the girls were out at a disco with Dulcie and Mark was asleep after an exhausting day, Tom strode across the road to a telephone box and got in touch with Selwyn. During the course of the conversation, Tom inquired about the house and to his delight they had accepted his offer. "Can you get things moving at your end for me, Selwyn? See John Jones who is my solicitor as well as Megan's and get him to carry out the search, I'll be back at the end of the week. If he's a bit cagey, get in touch with Megan, she'll make him spring into action." Tom was most excited but he faithfully reported back to Selwyn about the lack of small animals on the island despite his late evening excursions.

The following day, on the morning dunes, it was decided unanimously to have a special leaving party in the chalet that evening on the assumption that Tom provided the meal and the rest baked by the pool. Tom had to have his sand dune fix but too much exposure made him restless. That was the reason he agreed and not, as the girls thought, their persuasive powers.

They were all sitting early evening wrapped in an assortment of garments from a towelling gown to the transparent silk that decorated the shower floor recently. The conversation was irrelevant nonsense which Tom arrested.

"Listen everybody, I was on the phone to Selwyn last night and he said that my offer for the house has been accepted."

"Wow!" said Mary. "We can now come and stay." She put her hand over her mouth as if to stop the sound being emitted.

"Oh, that's all right, Mary. Dulcie knows all about you two staying in the pub," he said proudly. "Like Megan and Ieuan we have no secrets. You'll be surprised what we get up to when you are out at your discos," he said teasingly.

Mary glowed and Carol said, "No we wouldn't. I pointed out to Mary a few days ago the mess in the shower." There was a particularly long pause. Tom glanced across at Dulcie who lowered her eyes and nervously brushed an object from her silkened bosom.

"How did you get soap suds on the ceiling?"

Alleviated of guilt, Tom said, "I'll ignore that. I have something more important to say." He savoured his drink and put on his sober voice. "It's been weighing on my mind for some time now and since our holiday is drawing to a close I thought it might be an ideal time to mention it... If you agree, I want you to come and live with me in my new house."

Dulcie melted into heavenly fantasy but knew in her heart the remark was not for her and replied, "Tom, what would Dan say?"

"Not you, bloody hell!" and he laughed nervously. His feelings for Dulcie were like his attraction to Beryl but he daren't take the risk of pressing for a return episode. Tom sensed that her feelings towards him could become a serious problem and secondly, she was married, two good reasons for restraint. His unpleasant first-hand knowledge of how humiliating it can be once caught up in that destructive triangle was still on his mind. "No, the girls." The immediate response was silence, they concurrently sipped their drinks and sandwiched Mark on

Tom's makeshift bed. "You can pay my rent and that will help with my grant."

They then realised the implications. "Wow!" Mary repeated. "That's a fantastic idea. What have we done to deserve you?" Mary was ecstatic and hugged Mark. Carol who was highly delighted at the idea and kissed Tom rather affectionately on the lips. That was the first time Carol has ever shown any physical signs of emotion towards Tom in company. Dulcie would have preferred a less demonstrative answer to his question but agreed that the move was a good business venture.

"Daddy, can I come to?"

The utterance Tom had deeply feared for a long time had come to fruition. What was he going to tell the lad and what was he going to do? "Oh, poor Nana, don't you think she will be lonely and Grandad will miss picking you up from school?" Tom made an unconvincing attempt to deviate from reality.

"He can still pick me up from school and I can go to Nana's house and wait for you."

"He is right, of course." Tom lifted his shoulders and exposed the palms of his hands as a motion of frustration.

"I had better give this some serious thought, son. In the meantime, let's wait 'til we get home and see what happens then, shall we?"

Mary, to whom Mark had become intensely attached during the holiday, saw the pickle Tom was in and purposely redirected his attention. "Let's go for a swim Mark, last in is a sissy." They were costumed and rushed out through the door.

"Don't run, you might slip," shouted Tom, who was concerned for their safety.

"Boy! That was a sticky moment. What are you going to do?" Dulcie was unquestionably worried. "If he comes to live with you, you'll need a baby minder."

"Can we forget it for now? It's my problem and I'll sort it out when we get back to Llanrheidol. Let's all go for a swim." Tom was in a frivolous mood. Towelled Carol shot off to the shower so he turned to Dulcie.

"Don't you dare." She held the top of her garment lightly and simply as a gesture. Tom grabbed her hand and pulled, once again he had taken the bait.

Thinking of the outcome, he said, "Get something on quick and join us." She stood by Tom's makeshift bed naked and displeased.

Tom was first back to the chalet to finalise the meal. He had also bought some bottles of Cava to celebrate being a householder once again and the saddening end of their happy two weeks in the sun. The fact that the whereabouts of Mag had not been discovered was of secondary importance to him.

Back in Llanrheidol, there was an abundance of matters to consider. The purchase of the house, the final preparations for his three years as an undergraduate and Mark's living accommodation. The new dwelling would be paid for with the compliments of Lally and the sale of Ty Gwyn. Rent from the girls, a student grant and a small grant from the DHSS as a one parent family allowed him room to employ an *au pair*.

Mark wanted to stay at his old school, so as he predicted, he would still be seeing his grandparents everyday. The unsettled doubt was the *au pair*. A message was sent to the girls through the usual channels for a meeting.

Mary was apprehensive, everything was going too well of late, something had to go wrong.

"Don't say you have changed your mind about us coming here, Tom?"

"No Mary, you worry too much. It's just an idea I've had about Mark. He is coming here to live with us, that is certain, but I have to get someone to look after him and the house, a sort of wife," he smiled nervously and indicated quotation marks by flexing the same two closed fingers on either hand.

"Why don't you get Mary to do it," said Carol. "She was telling me how fed up she was at the shop and wanted to leave." Carol was talking to Tom as if Mary was not present.

"Hey! Don't I get a say in this?" said Mary indignantly.

"Sorry Mary, I just thought of it on the spur of the moment."

"I'm always in the background, you're talking about ME, you know." Tom recognised the corollary from another wife. Strange it should be repeated under the present circumstances. "If you're talking about me, talk to me!"

"What's got into you? I don't think I've ever heard you speak up for yourself like that before." Tom had this move in mind ever since they returned to Llanrheidol but he was not sure how to tackle Mary. Nana and Megan both agreed that the best approach was simply to ask her. Tom was more aware of her sensitivity and he was hesitant for fear of her feeling duty bound. To Tom, Carol's proposal was perfectly timed (and well rehearsed among the four females) and it gave him the freedom to explain the duties in more detail. "What you would do," Tom thought he might be taking her for granted so he said, "if you took the job, is to look after us all. Naturally, you wouldn't pay rent. In fact, I would pay you... You would be a sort of housekeeper. Sounds posh, doesn't it?"

"You said wife, just now, which one is it going to be?" Tom evaded replying by pretending to hear something in his bedroom. While he was away, Carol quickly told her that she was going too far. She instantly became less aggressive and did not press for an answer and shouted to him in the other room. "Can I think it over? I love Mark and I think he likes me."

Tom reappeared, "Oh, for sure."

"It would be like our holidays without Dulcie."

"Yes, I suppose... I hadn't thought of it that way, Mary."

"Perfect!" Mary gave Carol an enigmatic smile.

* * * * *